Discovering America

D1457029

DISCOVERING AMERICA

Bicycle Adventures in All 50 States

Martha J. Retallick

Lone Rider Productions

Tucson, Arizona

Copyright © 1993 by Martha J. Retallick
Cover design by Jeff Neff/Neff Design
Typesetting by Wendy Voorhees/Painted Pony Desk-Top
   Typography Service

Published by Lone Rider Productions
Post Office Box 43161
Tucson, Arizona USA 85733-3161

Set in Palatino.
Printed and bound in the United States of America.

Cataloging-in-Publication Data

Retallick, Martha J., 1957-
   Discovering America : bicycle adventures in all 50 states
      p.   cm.
   Includes bibliographical references and index.
   ISBN 0-9637803-0-1
   1. Bicycle Touring—United States.
2. Bicycle Touring—Equipment and supplies.
3. Cyclists—United States—Biography. I. Title.
GV1044R47   1993
796'.64
                        93-79530
                          CIP

This one's for everyone who
helped me along the way

Contents

Acknowledgements

Bicycling in all 50 states, then writing a book about it, would seem like two of the most solitary pursuits imaginable. True, I did pedal that bike all by myself, and I also had to sit down at the computer all by myself. But not only has this project that has consumed much of the past thirteen years of my life been a solo venture, it has also been a group effort. Since that afternoon in July 1980 when another cycletourist told me of his goal to pedal all 50 states—a challenge I found too tantalizing to ignore—I have received the support and backing of countless individuals. Let me say now that I could not have completed my riding or my book without you. Some special "thank you's" are definitely in order.

First, I would like to thank my parents, William and Kathryn Retallick, who first introduced me to the fascinating world of cycletouring when I was 22 months old. Our first family ride was a day trip around Nantucket, an island off the coast of Massachusetts. My father piloted the rented English 3-speed while I took a nap in the kiddie seat.

I owe much more than I could ever repay to all the people who invited me into their homes during my travels. Some of you were family, others were friends, and still others were complete strangers who decided to take a chance on this tired, sweaty, grubby cyclist and put me up for the night. I would especially like to thank the Spalding family of Phoenix, Arizona, who offered their home and friendship to someone they'd never seen before. I'll always treasure the four months I spent with you as one of the high points of my life.

Thank you also to the members of the Muriel Lester Cooperative House at the University of Michigan in Ann Arbor. Back in 1978, you believed that I could succeed athletically before I believed it myself. It was with your encouragement that I was able to swim a whole mile without stopping, and later, to mount that most fearsome of steeds, the ten-speed bicycle. And of course I would also like to recognize the members of the Ann Arbor Bicycle Touring Society, especially Effective Cycling instructor Reuben Chapman, for teaching me the craft of cycling.

An earlier version of a portion of this book was published in 1985 as *Ride Over The Mountain*. I would like to thank everyone who supported that effort, especially my good western Pennsylvania friends the Heinrichses, the Naesers, the Staleys and Jane Twomey. Thanks also to the Western Pennsylvania Wheelmen bicycle club for your unending encouragement.

During the past six years, it has been my privilege to live, work and ride in one of America's most bike-able cities: Tucson, Arizona. Special thanks to my coworkers at The University of Arizona Foundation for supporting the author in their midst. Thanks also to the Tucson chapter of the International Association of Business Communicators for always being excited about this project—it was a great motivator! And hats off to the Greater Arizona Bicycling Association, a class act from start to finish.

I also would like to recognize those who have helped me produce this book: cover designer Jeff Neff, typographer Wendy Voorhees of Painted Pony Desk-Top Typography Service, indexer Michelle Graye, proofreader Carl Gradolph, and manuscript reviewers Jay Rochlin and Jill Hansen Smith.

Last, but certainly not least, I would like to thank the others who have helped me on and off the road during the past thirteen years. Listed by state and province, they are:

UNITED STATES
Alabama: The Selfs, the Griffins, the Kellys
Alaska: The Devoes

Arizona: The Spaldings, Chuck Malenfant, Yvonne and Mary, Monica, Susan Benitez, Donald and Barbara, American Cancer Society Arizona Division, Ron Balon and Margaret Chapman, Bev and Marv Hawkes, St. Paul's United Methodist Church of Globe, Edith Pingel, Bernice Fenner, Lutheran Mission School of Bylas, the Cox family, St. Philip's in the Hills, Richard DeBernardis and Perimeter Bicycling Association of America, Tucson-Pima Library, University of Arizona Library, Martha Gore

Arkansas: Ashdown Public Library, Hope Chamber of Commerce, City of Dumas, Marvell Police Department, Bill Grove and family, Louise Lung, Yvonne Schulz

California: The Salzanos, the Eiblings, the AYH Pacific coast hostels, Kenn and Rudi, Lisa, Steve Gouert, Pat Gouert, Fraser Gouert, Paul Gasloli, Inez Hooper, the Penseyres family, Ranger Phil at Agua Caliente Hot Springs Park

Colorado: Margaret Cooley, Cathy Rohne and daughters Holly and Donella, the Ziebarths, Barb, the people of Grand Lake, Jane Goslin and the people of Kremmling

Connecticut: The people of Putnam, the bike shop in Willamantic

Delaware: Wilmington Amtrak station

Florida: WMFE-FM radio and everyone else who helps put on the Florida Bicycle Safari

Georgia: Those peaches!

Hawaii: Chuck Fisher, Kona Lodge and Hostel, Joyce Aros

Idaho: The people of Bliss, the Bilderbacks

Illinois: The Andersons, the Rutledge family, the people of Vienna

Indiana: The Keiths, Thom and Clare Villars, Charli, Randy, my truckers' convoy, the people of Oakland City, the Zabels, David Jenkins and Tina Spolarick, Mary Lou and Alan Ross, Wilbur and Nadine Lord, Dean and Chris Randall

Iowa: The Cornicks, Bill and Kay Perry

Kansas: The people of Rolla, Deerfield, Healy, Gove and Grainfield; Grigston Elevator, the Gruvers, Gertrude Railsback

Kentucky: LaRue Bristoe and the people of Lovelaceville

Louisiana: Dot, Lynn, Lyle and J.P. Reynolds; Margaret Foust

Maine: Trek Across Maine, David and Patty Breed

Maryland: Maryland Department of Transportation, Baltimore Bicycle Club and LAW Rally '84

Massachusetts: *New Age Journal*, Lorry Sorgmyn, the Brehobs, the Hendrix family, the Stewarts

Michigan: Ann Arbor Bicycle Touring Society, Reuben Chapman and his Effective Cycling class, Muriel Lester Cooperative, University of Michigan, "Tour de LAW" contingent, the Hainaults, Bill and Shirley James, Gaylord and Marilyn Hill

Minnesota: Anita and Steve Manders, the Andersons, Linda Palsic

Mississippi: Bea Green and the rest of the Episcopal Church parish in Holly Springs, Tom and Barbara Patton

Missouri: Judy Cureton and family, Jim Hurtle, Velo Girardeau, Margaret of Martin's Grocery, LAW 1986 National Rally

Montana: The people of Baker, Culbertson Public Library

Nebraska: Steve Albright, Don and Carol Morton, the Osborn family, Rev. William and Kathryn Graham, Althea Palmer

Nevada: My rainstorm rescuers, Las Vegas International ' Hostel, Suzy Truax

New Hampshire: University of New Hampshire, Sharon Studio Barn, the people of Randolph

New Jersey: Layton youth hostel, the Millbrook village restoration, LAW GEAR '85

New Mexico: Jimmy Brooks and family, Glenda and Pat, Dave Johnson, the people of Socorro and Vaughn, Jimmy Brooks, Michael Running Wolf and Kat, Mountainair Assembly of God camp, Clovis KOA, the Gladstone store, Mary Steigerwald, *Mothering*, Manasseh House of Albuquerque

New York: LAW GEAR '80 organizers, LAW GEAR '86 organizers, Jim Tompkins, the Muellers, R.T. Simmonds, Jerry and Hillary Schrauf

North Carolina: Yosh Mantinband

North Dakota: The people of Bowman

Ohio: the Vanden-Eyndens, the Hinds family, the Donovans, Charlie Pace

Oklahoma: The people of Boise City

Oregon: United Bicycle Institute, Trinity Church of Ashland

Pennsylvania: William and Kathryn Retallick and Max the dachshund, the people of "Birdland" (aka Penn Wood), the Stehmans, Grace & Nat Brewer, Vernon and Jean Van Dyke, the Tilleys, the Schopps, the Naesers, the City of Pittsburgh, Jane Twomey, the Staleys, the Heinrichses, East End Food Co-op, Mafalda Jones, Western Pennsylvania Wheelmen, Pittsburgh AYH, Cathy Schnaubelt and Schnaubelt Shorts, Pittsburgh Pro Bicycles

Rhode Island: Pulaski State Park

South Carolina: Bruce and Barb Robertson, J.R. McLeod, Glenn Eberhardt, the Sheorns

South Dakota: Min Patenode, the people of Harding County, Tri-State Bank of Belle Fourche

Tennessee: The people of Brownsville, the Kulows, Captain Billy Bob Haas

Texas: Rev. Steven Rogers, the Jacobsons, Dorothy Jones and the people of Hamlin, Mel Cude and family, the Pawls, Douglas Fonville, the Ginthers, Commerce Church of Christ

Utah: Aften and Celia Richens, the Burgess family, the people of Tremonton and Snowville, Father Ed Howlett and St. Peter's Episcopal Church

Vermont: Jean, Tom, Lynn and Chris Gouert, Sleepers River Home Hostel

Virginia: Scotchtown, Kappa Sigma at Randolph-Macon College

Washington: Harold Dille, Greg Mulhair, Ute, Jill, Caitlin, the McWilliams family, the Humphreys, Laurie, Fred and the other wonderful folks on To Hel'en Back '87, John Kelley, "Crash" Lusby

West Virginia: Slim Lehart (aka "The Wheeling Cat")

Wisconsin: North Roads Bicycle Club, the Irlebecks, the Summerfelds, the Kaczmarowskis, the Larsons, Angelina Speckhard, Kainz and Wick, the Retallicks of Eau Claire, Rev. Joseph Jenkins, the Claflins, Rev. Speerstra, Rev. Phillipps

Wyoming: Devil's Tower, the people of Aladdin

CANADA

Alberta: Parks Canada—Banff and Jasper National Parks, the Icefields Parkway hostels, Louise and friends, VIA Rail Canada

British Columbia: Vancouver International Hostel, VIA Rail Canada, the Bellerives

Ontario: The McCormick family, Neill-Wycick Residence, Ontario Cycling Association, Tom Parry, the people of Blind River and Elora

Saskatchewan: The people of Minton, Davidson and Moose Jaw, Saskatoon YWCA, Tourism Saskatchewan, VIA Rail Canada, Sam Farmer

Introduction

This is the story of my bicycle travels in all 50 of the United States of America. In the following pages, you'll read a lot about where I went and whom I met. That's the physical journey. There's also a spiritual journey and a coming-of-age story in here. And if you need to take a break from the narrative or want to know more about cycletouring itself, there are numerous "sidebars" that deal with the how-to stuff.

I covered 43 of the states during three long solo tours: 2,500 miles in the upper Midwest and Canada in 1980; 8,300 miles around the U.S. in 1981-82; and 3,600 miles from Phoenix, Arizona, to Mexico, from Mexico up to Canada and the Pacific Northwest in 1987. The seven states not included in these long tours—Washington, Oregon, Hawaii, Alaska, Maine, Florida and Nevada—were covered during shorter rides in 1986-92.

I've made my journeys without corporate sponsors, foundation grants or government funding—this was out of my belief in paying my own way. However, I owe a tremendous debt of gratitude to all the people who've helped me along the way. They've given freely of themselves without thought of reward, offering meals, places to stay for a night or longer, and rides and bike repairs when I needed them. One Arizona family hosted me for four months while I worked to replenish traveling funds during my 1981-82 journey. This book is as much about the people who supported my efforts as it is about me.

What's the moral of my story? Actually, there are three. First, be careful of what you say in casual conversation. I had no idea that doing something as simple as stopping to chat with another cycletourist in July 1980 would inspire me to pedal every state in the Union, but it did. Second, ignorance can be a useful tool. When I first started cycletouring, I had no idea that it would be considered so dangerous, especially for a lone woman. Had I known better, I probably would have stayed home. Third, if I can do the whole United States on a bicycle, so can you. I speak from personal experience when I say that you don't have to be a gifted athlete to achieve such a feat. What you do need is perseverance. And you have more of that than you think.

Throughout the narrative and the sidebars, you'll encounter references to various products and services. None of of the purveyors of those things paid me to mention them. Any recommendations I make are based on my personal experience or that of other cyclists whose judgment I trust.

I hope this book inspires you to go out and get to know this country better. I'd be delighted if you did so on a bicycle, but that's up to you. In the course of your explorations, you'll find plenty of evidence to dispel the stereotype of Americans as violent, selfish and materialistic people. I certainly did! You'll also be helping to combat prejudice, which I believe comes from our tendency to avoid interacting with people who aren't "our own kind," whatever that may be. As a cycletourist, I dealt with all sorts of people. I had to—I needed their help! I hope that you will also be fortunate enough to find yourself in the same situation.

NOTE: In order to protect their privacy, the names of some individuals mentioned in the text have been changed or part of a name has been omitted.

• 1 •

Be Careful of What You Say in Casual Conversation

I f it can be said that fateful moments happen in the strangest places, then mine happened in a place whose name I can barely pronounce.

It was July 1980, and I was just a year out of college, in the midst of a 2,500-mile bicycle journey through the upper Midwest and Canada. I was heading west across Michigan's Upper Peninsula, bound for Minneapolis, where I hoped to revive my temporarily stalled journalism career. I had just passed through a town called Ishpeming when I saw something I hadn't seen in weeks: another cycletourist.

Jeff was riding home to New Jersey, having begun from the West Coast. He told me about another cyclist he had met during his cross-country journey, a man who intended to ride in all 50 states. Jeff said he wanted to do the same.

"Me too!" I replied, not at all realizing what my spur-of-the-moment announcement would mean. But I never made it to Minneapolis, and I've been discovering America ever since.

When I was young, I never thought I'd do anything like this. I was too afraid to get on a bicycle until the fourth grade, and it took countless sessions with my father running along-side, then a year of training wheels, before I could balance a two-wheeler. By that time, the rest of the neighborhood kids had graduated to ten-speeds.

All through school, my clumsiness was legendary. I was the one nobody wanted on the team because I was a sure strikeout in softball, a turtle in the relay races, and seldom got anything near the goalie in field hockey. Once, during a tenth-grade basketball game, I got the ball, took aim at the basket, and launched into what I thought was a layup shot. Instead, that ball came right back down and hit me on the head—provoking a chorus of jeers from everyone else in the class. I wanted to melt right through the floor.

I longed to be fleet-footed, graceful, and strong, instead of being that shy, gawky kid whose intelligence felt more like a curse than a blessing. After all, the other kids cheered loudest for the one who scored the most points on the basketball court, not the history exam.

The high school varsity letter I did earn was for academic excellence, and it had an embroidered lamp of knowledge instead of a fleet foot. At home, I papered my walls with honor roll certificates. My grade-point average put me in the top tenth of my class, and filled the mailbox with wooing letters from colleges all over the country. I chose my parents' alma mater, the University of Michigan at Ann Arbor.

One of my main reasons for going to Michigan was that I didn't have to take physical education to graduate. But it wasn't the nonathletic university I had so ardently hoped for. It was home to the sportingest people I'd ever seen, from the sell-out crowds that packed into the 100,000-seat Michigan Stadium for every home football game, to the continuous parade of runners, joggers, roller skaters and bicyclists all over campus.

I quickly learned that many of my very active classmates had been living lives much different from my sheltered, linear existence. For as long as I could remember, I'd been programmed to make top grades all through school, do it again in college, then go straight out to work. Any deviation from this path was considered very suspect indeed.

But now I was surrounded by people following myriad "suspect" paths—and they were enjoying their journeys immensely. There was Bob, who had spent several face-numbing winters up near the Arctic Circle building the Alaska Pipeline and putting himself through school on the money he made; Dan and Barb had taken time off to live on Israeli kibbutzim; Linda had done coursework of a very different sort while raising goats on a homestead operated by Western

Michigan University; and Zelda, an American Indian, had come of age in San Francisco's Haight-Ashbury district in the late '60s and was just beginning college as a middle-aged single mother.

The presence of all these non-linear lives in mine prompted me to develop the vague notion of getting my degree-with-honors, then becoming a lighthouse keeper along some remote part of the Great Lakes where I could contemplate my place in the world before going out to join it. It was a pleasant dream, one I shared with no one. Yet as I nurtured it, I felt like the little kid who wanted to run away from home but lacked permission to cross the street. I was looking all around for some parent or other authority figure who'd allow me to act on my dream, not realizing that I was now old enough to give *myself* permission to do so. I abandoned my dream when I found out that most lighthouses had become automated and no longer needed human keepers.

Shortly after I began my senior year in September 1978, I was befriended by a bunch of sports lovers who relentlessly prodded me, a bookish economics major, to get some exercise. They had an annoying habit of inviting me to come along whenever they were heading out to the pool or the jogging track. I couldn't *do* sports, I'd wail, adding that I'd *never* be an athlete. They countered that the only thing stopping me from being as athletic as they were was my negative attitude. Once I banished the phrase "I can't" from my vocabulary, I could do anything, they assured me.

One night in October, my friends talked me into going lap swimming with them, something I hadn't done since my summers in junior high when I ran up a long string of last-place finishes on the swim club team. By the time I finished thirteen laps, I was so exhausted I could barely drag myself out of the pool and crawl back into the locker room. But in that pool, there was no one else trying to beat me; there was no one else to compete against but myself.

In myself, I found a formidable opponent, one who urged me to go back to the pool, swim more than a couple laps without stopping, go for a quarter mile, then a half. By the end of the semester, I was comfortably swimming a mile, something I never thought I could do.

When spring came, my friends switched to a different sport: bicycling. Like everyone else in town, they pedaled ten-speeds with pencil-thin saddles, turned-down handlebars, squeeze brakes, and skinny tires. To me, those bikes seemed as if they were designed to torture the human frame like a medieval rack. I swore I'd never ride a ten-speed. I was sticking to my comfortable Schwinn one-speed, which my parents brought out from Pennsylvania after I graduated in April 1979.

I stayed in Ann Arbor to take a job as assistant editor of a small magazine. On my days off, I tooled around town on my bike, while my friends rode all over southeastern Michigan on theirs. I envied them, and they knew it. After explaining for the thousandth time why his ten-speed was so much lighter, faster, and more efficient than my beloved old clunker, my housemate Paul handed me a well-worn copy of his favorite book. For several days, I immersed myself in *Richard's Bicycle Book,* an exhaustive treatise on the hows, whys, and wheres of cycling. Author Richard Ballantine helped me swallow my doubts about ten-speeds, and by June, I was ready to go out and buy one. Paul gave me the name of his favorite bike shop, which was just around the corner from the house we shared with several others.

I bought a bottom-of-the-line Peugeot—perfect for a beginner like me, the salesman said. After writing a check for $189, I pushed my bike out the door and walked it over to a quiet side street. From there, I planned to ride home. Unfortunately, that ride lasted long enough for me to swing my right leg over the saddle, plant both feet on the pedals, and tip over. Tearfully, I got up and pushed the bike home.

Paul was in the kitchen cooking supper and rushed out to inspect my new machine as soon as I arrived. He nodded his approval, then noticed my downcast expression. I told him I'd fallen off the bike because it was too big. Instead of sympathizing, he threw a fit. "There's nothing wrong with that bike!" he insisted. "You just have to get used to it." He stormed back into the kitchen.

It took a couple hours of coaxing from two other male housemates before I got back on that bike again. They held it steady and gave me a push, then I was off and pedaling on the fastest ride of my life. I lost count of how many times I circled the block before darkness chased me home—to a dining room filled with all six of my housemates, who were still wondering what it was that made me miss supper.

That bike took over my life. I spent most of my free time roaring down the streets and alleys near my house, or the sidewalks on the university campus. When I wasn't riding my bike I was tinkering with it. That Peugeot was the first mechanical thing I'd ever worked on. I rarely had any idea what I was doing, and left a trail of mashed bolts, stripped screw threads, and snapped cables in my wake. I enlisted the aid of my more mechanically adept housemates—until they began to avoid me whenever they saw my grease-stained hands and puzzled expression. Through trial and plenty of error, I progressed from fixing a flat tire to overhauling the entire bike.

In July 1979, I joined the Ann Arbor Bicycle Touring Society. I showed up for nearly every Sunday morning ride, from the slow, chatty thirty-milers to one of the many glacial lakes outside the city, to the brisk eighty-milers in which we seldom shifted out of high gear, rode in tight single file, and stayed glued to our saddles for hours. Whatever our pace or destination, our conversation rarely focused on the rolling pastures or cornfields around us, but on some club member's recent ride in Europe, Canada, Mexico or the American West.

At home, there was a United States map on the wall outside my bedroom. In the evenings, I'd trace some the routes my fellow club members had taken. And I'd chuckle at the funny place names like Walla Walla, Washington; Truth or Consequences, New Mexico; and Pawtucket, Rhode Island. I'd wonder how a town got to be named Flagstaff, Arizona; Cut Bank, Montana; Normal, Illinois; or Painted Post, New York. Somehow, I had to get to all of those places.

Paul loaned me a stack of *Bicycling* magazines with a series of articles by John Rakowski on his 1977-78 ride around the edge of the continental United States. I don't know if Paul had anything in mind when he let me borrow them; he wasn't the sort to reveal his motives in any situation. He was probably so tired of my endless barrage of questions about cycling that he gave me some magazines in exchange for a few days of peace and quiet. His strategy worked. I immersed myself in Rakowski's narrative, took notes on it, traced it on the map, and began wondering if I, too, could make such a journey. The opportunity came sooner than I expected.

When winter came, I heard that the grant funding for my job was about to be cut. The magazine's budget wasn't big enough to absorb my salary, so my boss said she'd have to let me go in June. I quickly calculated how much time was left until then, and started saving as much as possible from my remaining paychecks. I decided to start my two-wheeled explorations right in my own back yard: the Great Lakes region of the upper Midwest and Canada. In addition to my recently having joined the Touring Society, I'd also become a member of a national cycling organization called the League of American Wheelmen (LAW). LAW was having a rally in upstate New York over the July Fourth weekend and I'd heard that an American Youth Hostels group from Detroit would be riding over for it. Did they have room for one more from Ann Arbor? Sure, and after sending off an entry fee to cover the cost of camping and group meals for a week, I was part of the "Tour de LAW" group.

Another check to LAW got me room, board, and a spot on as many day cycling expeditions as I could handle in and around rally headquarters in Geneseo, New York. I'd placed a "touring partner wanted" ad in the LAW bulletin, hoping I'd find some older, more experienced cycletourist to accompany me in my travels after Geneseo. As much as I hoped that someone would materialize to shepherd me along, no partner came forward. I felt like a baby bird being booted out of the nest, but deep down, I knew I'd have to continue on by myself.

So, I ordered some county maps from the province of Ontario to plot my northward trek into Canada. Eventually, I'd turn west toward Minneapolis, a place I'd visited while attending a friend's wedding the summer before. Minneapolis seemed like a congenial place, and since I was looking for a new city after almost five years of Ann Arbor, why not try it out for a while?

As for my Peugeot, it didn't get to go with me because I sold it right before I left Ann Arbor. Although I loved that bike, every ride on it left me with aching knees and shoulders. From the Touring Society's experts, I learned that it was indeed too big. To get a bike that fit my five-foot, one-inch body, they suggested that I order one from Ann Arbor's premier custom framebuilder, Mark Nobilette. I did.

On Tuesday, June 24, I brought my frame home from Mark's basement workshop. I spent three days figuring out how to transform two wheels, several boxes of small parts, and the frame into a working bicycle. Total cost of this machine: almost $1,000. Three days later, I left Ann Arbor and began exploring both the U.S. and Canadian sides of the Great Lakes.

•2•

Initiation

Detroit's "Tour de LAW" contingent turned out to be a lot faster and more competitive than I was. This 350-mile ride was just another weeklong time trial for them. For me, it was quite a Herculean effort. I chased their back wheels across Ontario and upstate New York for a week. Each night, I collapsed into my sleeping bag, totally spent. We didn't see much of each other once we got to the LAW rally, but we all got together for one last time right before it ended. Then, the rest of the group drove back to Detroit, covering in one afternoon the distance we had cycled in a week.

As for me, I was finally alone—and terrified. By bicycling, hitchhiking, and taking a ferry across Lake Ontario, I made it to Toronto, where I promptly checked into a hotel. I stayed there a week, wondering what I'd gotten myself into. I had no long-distance cycling experience, and the longest solo ride I'd ever done was a 30-mile day trip.

Out on the road, I would be on my own as I'd never been before. As well as acting as my own engine, I would also have to be my own mechanic, dietitian, meteorologist, physician, and navigator. I was completely self-contained, which meant that if I really needed something, I'd better have it with me. I couldn't run back into the house to get it—I was *pedaling* my house! Unlike my ride to Geneseo, there would be no support van to come along and rescue me if I encountered any bike or body problem I couldn't solve on my own.

Having entered such unfamiliar physical and mental territory, I turned to something I hadn't tried in years: prayer. I prayed that a grocery store would materialize whenever I was hungry, that all roads I took would be clearly marked on my maps, that the only mechanical problems I encountered would be the ones I knew how to fix, and that all cloudbursts would hold off until I found indoor shelter for the night. Sometimes those prayers were answered, sometimes they weren't.

I also rode for two hours in a northern Ontario downpour, miles from any kind of indoor shelter. My cycling shoes were still wet two days later. On two other occasions, I pitched my tent at the end of a sunny day, only to be rudely awakened in the middle of the night by a ferocious thunderstorm. I learned the hard way that it's impossible to get any rest in a soggy sleeping bag.

The Trans-Canada Highway was all too clearly marked on my Ontario map—it was the only road between Espanola and Sault Ste. Marie. In 150 miles, I narrowly missed three head-on collisions and came within inches of being sideswiped by countless logging and mining trucks. After three days, I crossed the Sault Ste. Marie city limits, truly grateful that I was still alive. I had planned on riding all the way around the Canadian side of Lake Superior, but that meant staying on the Trans-Canada, so I fled back across the border to Michigan's Upper Peninsula.

I tried to true my wobbly back wheel, an insidiously simple-sounding process that involves tightening and loosening spokes with a special wrench. I managed to send that wheel more out of true than ever before. It took two bike shops and several days' traveling money to get it back to just a slight wobble. But more often than not, my bike seemed to maintain itself. That old cyclist's nemesis, the flat tire, struck only once during my 2,500-mile journey.

As a woman traveling alone, I was repeatedly warned about robbers, rapists, and murderers, warnings that were usually accompanied by long lists of horrible "what-ifs." Before I left Ann Arbor, I had no idea that my going solo would be considered so risky. In the Touring Society, you weren't really a serious cyclist until you'd done a long tour—whether you went alone or with a group was up to you.

During my four-month journey, I was nearly hit by several cars and trucks. I'll never know if those drivers were being inattentive or malicious, and I quickly lost count of all the people who hollered at me as they sped by. But no one ever laid a menacing hand on me. Nor was I ever looking down the barrel of a gun.

Instead, I met a far more diverse, curious, and generous world than I ever dreamed of. I was befriended by college professors, ministers, housewives, airline pilots, dairy farmers, and iron miners.

There also were those two boys in the bike shop in Blind River, Ontario, who invited me home for the night. All through supper, their burly father pounded the table with his big fists, insisting that if our President Carter had any guts at all, he'd send a squadron of B-52s over to "Eye-ran" and bomb the hell out of it until we got our hostages back.

He was just as sure that the answer to the energy crisis lay in nuclear power. Blind River was on the edge of some of the largest uranium deposits in Canada, and he'd moved his family here to capitalize on the many business opportunities in this boomtown along Lake Huron. Later, while the two of us did the dishes, his wife confided that she hated this roughneck town and wished they'd move back to Toronto.

Then there was the couple I met while camping on the shores of Lake Superior in Munising, Michigan. Upon hearing that my bike's rear derailleur wasn't shifting properly, they drove me 40 miles to a bike shop to get it fixed. And how could I forget the Seventh-Day Adventist village of Arpin, Wisconsin, where the woman who waited on me in the grocery store followed me outside, took my hands in hers, and offered a prayer for my safe journey home.

•3•

Pedaling Infinity

In late October, I returned to Ann Arbor and collapsed into bed with a nasty chest cold. I was too weak to lift my head off the pillow, let alone cycle. By the time I was well, the first snow had fallen, but I had already decided that this would be my last winter in Michigan.

Come spring, I would be leaving on another bicycle journey—this one around the United States. I planned to follow the Mississippi River down to the Gulf of Mexico, cross the Deep South, and head up to New England. From there I'd cycle west across the Appalachians, the Great Plains, the Rockies, and meet the Pacific. I'd ride south on the Pacific Coast Highway and stop somewhere in California or Arizona to get a job and replenish my traveling funds. In spring 1982, I would head north again. When finished, my route would look something like an infinity symbol. It also would take me through at least half of the 50 states.

I started training in February 1981, when the icy winter winds cut right through my long johns and made my nose run nonstop. My workouts focused on the steepest hills I could find on Ann Arbor's east side. I took each hill, broke it down into sections, devised strategies for each one, then attacked, over and over again. I practiced coasting downhill, bent over the handlebars, hands on the drops, elbows tucked in tight a perfect human bullet. After I stopped riding, I was so exhausted I could hardly stand up.

To stay fed and sheltered, I worked odd jobs around town, including stints as a paste-up artist, foot messenger, election poll watcher, and freelance writer and photographer. My personal financial strategy was to live cheaply, save as much as I could, and not tap into the money that was left over from the previous summer's travels. In keeping with this strategy, I rented a room in a cooperative house, a rambling old mansion on the edge of the university's fraternity row. Two hundred dollars a month plus four hours a week as a dinner cook and dishwasher got me all the food I could eat, a telephone, television, game room and a daily newspaper.

Most of my 50-plus housemates were students, as immersed in their classes and exams as I was in preparing to return to what I reverently called "the road." Their mailboxes brimmed full of letters from the university, law schools, MBA programs, credit card companies, and corporate recruiters. Mine was loaded with travel brochures, campground guides, and maps of all 50 states. Our relationship was strained, and we argued often. I marked my departure date on my calendar—Sunday, May 3, 1981—and in March started counting the days remaining until then.

In addition to the physical preparation, I did a lot of mental training for my ride. I'd gained some insight into what cycle-touring was like from my previous summer's travels. The journey I was about to make would cover four times the distance and last more than a year. What would it be like out there? I wouldn't know until I began riding, but I spent many months in the Ann Arbor public library, searching other cyclists' accounts for clues.

My favorite was a book called *Full Tilt: Ireland to India with a Bicycle* by Dervla Murphy, who had pedaled alone from her native Ireland to India. Along the way, she was attacked by a wolf in the mountains of central Europe, and fell and broke several ribs in the Middle East. In that part of the world—not known for its enlightened attitudes toward women—Murphy was delighted to find that Middle Eastern men accepted and treated her as one of them.

Running a close second was *The Long Ride* by Virginian Lloyd Sumner, who rode 24,000 miles around the world, through the American West, the Australian Outback, southeast

Asia, Africa and Europe. I also studied the library's back issues of *Bicycling*, paying particular attention to British cyclist Ian Hibell's expeditions across the Sahara desert and the Central American jungle, and John Rakowski's European adventures. Rakowski noted that most long-distance cyclists traveled by themselves. "They may have been natural loners," he continued. "Or perhaps bicyclists with the combination of time, money, inclination and similar interests can be found only through a computerized data bank." Rakowski also found that a similar note of despair eventually crept into all of their journals.

I spent my last day in Ann Arbor packing all of my worldly goods into boxes to ship to my parents. At first, they had balked at my idea of riding alone around the country, even though I planned to visit them when I came up the east coast. "You better fly out this way," my dad warned. "It's too dangerous to ride around here." I assured him that after all I'd experienced the previous summer, I could certainly handle southeastern Pennsylvania. Following that telephone conversation, I heard no more resistance from them.

That night, I couldn't sleep. In the darkness, I wondered: would this be the last night of my life? What if I got hit by a car tomorrow? What if I fell off the bike and broke my neck? What if I lost my brakes coming down a mountain pass? What if I inadvertently steered off the road and went over a cliff? None of those fears ever materialized, but they would haunt my nights for many months to come.

•4•

The Numerical Trap

On Sunday, May 3, I left Ann Arbor. My wish for no rain had been granted, but I should have made another one about the wind. The gentle breeze in my face at sunrise soon became a headwind that made every inch of forward progress a hard-won battle. Achieving my goal of 70 to 100 miles a day seemed all but impossible.

Nonetheless, I wrestled 80 miles out of my first day on the road and stopped for the night in the tiny farming community of Weston, Ohio. There I stayed with Tom and Jane Vanden-Eynden, a young couple who'd listed themselves in the League of American Wheelmen's hospitality home directory. This directory lists more than 1,000 people who offer simple overnight accommodations—usually a shower, a meal, and a bed—to their fellow LAW members. I used this directory during my 1980 tour, and planned to rely on it again while I pedaled around America.

My quest to pile up mileage and hurry south almost stopped my journey on Day One. Pushing high gears to go faster made my right knee feel as if there were knives under the kneecap, stabbing on every downstroke. Off the bike, I could barely walk. Tom and Jane insisted my sore knee would heal with a couple days' rest, but I was determined to press on.

Monday morning, my knee still throbbed, but I mounted the bike and headed out, right back into that wind, which slapped me in the face for 60 miles across flat Ohio soybean fields until I called it quits at a gas station on the outskirts of

Lima. I dragged a chair over to the pay phone in the office, sat my aching body down, and called Lois Hinds out in Cridersville. The Hinds family was Stop Number Two on my hospitality home list.

From my recitation of landmarks outside the Sohio station, Lois deduced that I was still 12 miles away from her house.

"I can't go on anymore," I said, fighting back tears as I rubbed my knee.

"Want somebody to come out and get you?"

"YES!!!"

So ended my quest to make this a completely self-powered venture, but I really didn't care. Just standing up was torture. I was only too happy to load my bike into the Hinds's car and drive that last dozen miles with Lois's daughter, Barbara. She looked to be about my age and averaged about one joke per sentence. Barbara seemed genuinely thrilled to be rescuing me from my predicament.

"You'd have never made it," Lois declared as I hobbled through the back door. All through that cloudy Monday evening and rainy Tuesday, she assumed the dual role of nurse and benevolent dictator, ordering me through a regimen of hot baths, plenty of heat rub on the knee after I dried off, then the heating pad. She had plenty of experience at this—several of her sons had played high school football and the entire family rode their bikes hard.

I saw very little of Barbara after she brought me home. She spent most of her time in bed. Lois told me that Barbara needed a kidney transplant. Lois had just gotten out of the hospital herself. She'd been suffering from some mysterious ailment that affected her balance. Now she was waiting to hear her doctor's word on whether she could ever bicycle again.

The weather cleared on Wednesday, and the winds became northerly, 20 to 25 miles an hour. Over breakfast, I joked with Lois about putting up a sail and coasting all day. Outside the house, she took a picture of me astride my loaded bike. We hugged each other, then I was off. We've corresponded only once since then—she never mentioned what the doctor told her.

The glob of Soltice balm I smeared all over my knee that morning blocked out most of my pain, but not all of it. Shortly after arriving in Richmond, Indiana, I hobbled into Ernie

Keith's Schwinn bicycle shop, bragging about the 100 miles I'd just done. Ernie immediately spotted my poorly disguised limp and delivered a stern lecture.

"Young lady, if you don't slow down, you're not going to be riding anywhere," he said. "A hundred miles a day? That's no tour, that's a *race!* You better not do more than fifty miles a day. Get yourself into condition, then build up your miles."

After closing his shop, Ernie loaded my bike into the back of his pickup and drove me out to his house for the night.

"What'll you do if you can't go on?" his recently divorced and living-back-at-home daughter asked me, eyeing my rigidly outstretched right leg. I couldn't answer. I hadn't thought of giving up for a minute, but her father was right. It was time to slow down.

Since leaving Ann Arbor on Sunday, I'd been in such a rush that I'd forgotten my reason for being on a bicycle—to explore the America that motorized travelers miss. An automobile could cover in one month the territory I planned to cycle in a year. But why should I try to emulate the automobile, which insulates its passengers from everything around them? All too often, drivers get locked into a world of numerical accomplishments: miles made each day, hours behind the wheel, rest stops taken, gallons consumed, and money spent. I had unwittingly fallen into the same trap.

The next day I began to slow down. I stopped. I savored. I stood along the roadside below Richmond and gave a speech about my ride to a herd of beef cattle. As if they were well used to hearing the pitches of traveling salesmen and campaigning politicians, the cattle pressed against the barbed wire fence at the edge of their pasture, scrutinizing me closely through big round eyes as I announced that I was headed south, then north, then west, then, finally, east and north back to where I came from. "So far, I've come two hundred miles and then some," I continued. "Killed my knee doing it, too. Got two big lumps on it now. Looks like I've got two kneecaps—two of 'em!

"This guy I was gonna stay with last night gave me his address as Chester Boulevard. That's where the Richmond city hospital is! All I saw along that street were doctors' offices. I was petrified! Always been afraid of doctors. Thought for sure this Ernie Keith was some M.D. who'd take one look at my knee and tell me to give this thing up—just go home. Well, I woulda told that doctor where to go and what to do when he got there!

"Turned out Ernie Keith owned a bike shop on Chester Boulevard. And he lived out in the country. Last night, he told me to slow down, not quit, just slo-o-ow down. So I'm just doing thirty miles today. Down to Brookville, and that's it. If I can only do twenty miles tomorrow, I'll do it. Anything to save this ride, 'cause I want this ride and I'm not gonna give it up!"

In my mind, I imagined a sellout crowd leaping to its feet to give a standing ovation. But my audience just stared at me, thoughtfully chewing their cuds, not comprehending a word I said.

In a phone booth in Brookville, I chatted the morning away with a coworker of my hospitality home host for the night. Outside, a truck loaded with newsprint rolls as wide as I am tall rounded a curve too fast, and one roll fell to the pavement. The truck went on, the driver unaware that anything had happened. I abruptly ended my phone conversation. I was shaking so hard I could barely hang up the receiver.

Like a high-speed movie camera, my mind spun out the events of the morning. If I'd left Richmond later, if I'd given the cattle a longer speech, if I'd tarried longer on the hill above Brookville, admiring that field of wildflowers, I could have been right behind the truck—under that newsprint. And here I was instead, trembling all over, but still alive. Meanwhile, several men had wrestled that runaway roll into the back of a pickup, and it took off after the newsprint truck. The whole morning reminded me of that Bible passage about the battle not belonging to the strong, or the race belonging to the swift. Instead, time and chance happen to us all.

The following morning, my go-for-it-regardless spirit returned, and my knee cooperated for most of the 70 miles to Madison, Indiana, on the banks of the swift, muddy Ohio River. There I took three days off to wait out a couple of back-to-back storms. The enforced rest was just what my knee needed.

It healed in time for the roller-coaster terrain of southern Indiana. On Wednesday, May 13, I was inching up a steep grade on Highway 56 north of Jasper when I heard an engine growling and grinding behind me. Even without looking, I knew it belonged to a truck, but it sounded more like a freight train. The beast lumbered by, giving me a wide berth on the narrow road. It was a truck all right. Its twin chrome stacks belched acrid black smoke. Far above me in a hopper the size of a backyard pool were tons of coal.

I'd been warned about the coal haulers by friends who'd biked in Kentucky. Those guys were paid by the load—pile it in, run like hell, and let nothing get in the way, especially "bah-sickles." But this trucker passed me without blasting my eardrums with his horn or running me off the road. Surely a fluke, I thought. Then another one went by, followed by several more. All were as courteous as the first driver.

I stopped at a gas station in Haysville, a tiny settlement at the crossroads of Route 56 and U.S. 231. That handful of coal haulers I'd seen on 56 had become a mean looking parade on 231. According to my state map, 231 was the only thing that stood between me and lunch in Jasper. I asked the attendant if there was any other way to go.

"Nope." He was glued to his TV set. A news bulletin was on.

"Some guy just shot the Pope," he said.

"What? The Pope?" Why would anyone want to shoot the Pope? I mean, uh, well, he's...the Pope." I stammered through a few more half-formed sentences, then left.

The coal beasts on 231 turned out to be quite tame. Their drivers were non-union, as the United Mine Workers were out on strike. All the trucks traveled in pairs, and each had an extra man aboard. Sometimes I could see him holding a shotgun. They were prepared for the worst, but gave me plenty of road space.

In Jasper, I stopped at a Wendy's and went straight for the salad bar. I filled my plate with a mountain of lettuce, spinach, tomatoes, carrots, onions, eggs, croutons and a dollop of blue cheese dressing on the peak, then staked out the last empty table in the crowded dining room. I was about to dive into my creation when a man sat down across from me. He was wearing a baseball cap, T-shirt, and jeans with a "Preston—The 151 Lines" belt buckle. Tatoos covered his muscular arms.

"Are you that bah-sickles I saw back there on the road?"

"Uh, yes." I braced myself for the inevitable lecture: he and his trucking buddies had put up with my presence long enough. Now—if I didn't want to get hurt—would I please get off their road and ride somewhere else?

"Where you headed to?"

"Down south. Toward the Gulf."

"You been to Kaintucky yet?"

"No." Wasn't planning on it, either.

Turned out Mr. Preston 151 was from Louisville and quite proud of it. He launched into a long discourse on the wonders of the bluegrass country—Mammouth Cave, Fort Knox, and Dale Hollow Lake—that would do the Department of Tourism proud.

And of course his hometown hosts the Kentucky Derby. "You like to party? You oughta come to Lou-ah-ville during Derby Week. I'll tell you, you're really missing it all by staying up here. You oughta see Kaintucky."

We chatted a while longer. He probably had a schedule to keep, and I didn't want to delay him. I mentioned my positive experience with the coal haulers that morning. So far on this journey, the long distance truckers had been just as polite, and I told him how much I appreciated it.

We went our separate ways after lunch. The last I saw of him, he was easing his eighteen-wheeler away from the loading dock of a factory down the street and talking on his CB radio.

That afternoon, I was back on U.S. 231 and later, on State Highway 64. I'd just cleared the Jasper city limits when the driver of an approaching semi-trailer really leaned on the horn and waved at me.

Another one came toward me. Same greeting. The coal haulers started waving too. My convoy lasted three hours before a downpour forced me to halt in Oakland City, "where northern vitality meets southern hospitality," the Baptist minister told me. He took me to a motel near his church and paid the owner for my night's lodging. The TV in my room brought the news that Pope John Paul II barely survived the attempt on his life.

The rain went away the next day, but the hills kept on coming. As I entered the Shawnee National Forest in southern Illinois, I spotted a hazy blue ridge on the horizon. Smog from

Evansville or Paducah, I thought. The closer I got, the more it looked like a mountain ridge I wouldn't be able to avoid. Then I geared down for a long ride up the side of a cliff. Sweat burst out of every pore and rained off me. My heart pounded and I silently begged my aching legs to keep pumping just a few more yards, feet, then finally, inches. From the top, I could see all the way to the next ridge. I rocketed down into the valley and halfway up the other side. Then back to the grind, over and over again.

At a tiny store, I bought a dusty quart bottle of grape juice and downed it in two gulps, while the man behind the counter gleefully told me that those monsters I was climbing were the foothills of the Ozarks. "There's a place near here called Ozark, Illinois," he added. "If these are the foothills I'd hate to see the mountains," I replied.

After a hot Friday afternoon in the Ozark foothills, I dragged my weary body into the state campground at Dixon Springs. I had the place to myself and felt pretty smug about my good fortune until a battered blue Pinto station wagon pulled in and a couple and their two children claimed a picnic table next to my site. The mother immediately began making supper and the boy invited me to join them. I declined. That grape juice had done such a thorough job of flushing out my bowels that I wasn't feeling terribly hungry, but I went over to their site and chatted while they ate.

Their grime and body odor put my one day away from soap and water to shame. We introduced ourselves by first names, which we promptly forgot. They were from Gadsden, Alabama, where the father had worked in the steel mills. Considering the depressed state of the steel industry, I gathered he had been laid off, but he never mentioned what happened to his job. Lately, they'd been collecting bottles and cans along the roadside and cashing them in at recycling centers. Home was their Pinto pulled off the road, or cheap campgrounds.

Despite their outward appearance, they had a certain dignity I couldn't ignore. The son and daughter called their parents "Sir" and "Ma'am" and did as they were told without complaining, and their parents didn't nag.

"I'm teaching her the ABC's," the mother said, motioning toward her daughter. Neither child was enrolled in school, and

I wondered how much time they really had for lessons, because they worked from sunup to sundown just like their parents. The college-educated Ann Arbor liberal in me felt angry because these people had been forced to survive on our society's jetsam. If they had any resentment toward their fate, they certainly didn't show it.

Instead, the father bragged about how they got the bottles and cans others would pass up. "We drive 15 miles an hour—my wife does," he said. "And I'm out there with the kids pickin' 'em up—all of 'em."

So far, they had made enough money to pay all their travel expenses. "We're gonna see Canada and the west before we go back home," the father said. The rest of the family beamed, obviously thrilled at the prospect of visiting places they'd never seen before. Once back in Alabama, the father hoped to resume working in the steel mills and the mother would go back to being a housewife.

"Any woman who marries me stays home. I'll make her livin' for her," he said. It took every ounce of willpower I had to keep my feminist mouth shut.

The next morning, I left Dixon Springs before my neighbors were even stirring. I had the Mississippi River in my sights for that day, and I managed to cross the river into Cape Girardeau, Missouri, just ahead of some storm clouds that settled in for the rest of the weekend. I was adopted by members of the Velo Girardeau bicycle club while I waited out the rain.

Monday night, Judy Cureton and I shared a pizza while listening to tornado-watch alerts and soggy-weather forecasts for Tuesday. An art teacher in Benton, Missouri, Judy was as determined to pedal to her last day of school as I was to ride to Arkansas.

At 6:30 a.m. on Tuesday, we awoke to the drumming of raindrops on the roof, and pulled on our foul weather gear. Judy's outfit included a pollen mask improvised from a bandana worn cowboy style. We were soaked just half a block from her house, and slogged 15 miles south on U.S. 61 before the rain let up. We said goodbye on the edge of Benton, where I caught a strong north wind and headed away from the Ozark foothills and into the flat Mississippi River Delta.

•5•

The Great River Road

After bidding Judy farewell, I continued south along Highway 61. Green and white signs bearing the logo of a sternwheeler within a ship's steering wheel told me that this bumpy stretch of pavement was part of the Great River Road, a 1,000-mile network of highways from the Great Lakes to the Gulf. I craned my neck and gazed over the fields and woods to my left, trying to catch a glimpse of that great river.

The previous summer, I had ridden for a week in the Mississippi valley up in Minnesota and Wisconsin. It was a glorious week, just the tonic I needed after hundreds of miles in the north woods of Ontario, Michigan and Wisconsin. As I pedaled past tall, rocky bluffs, I watched tugboats push huge blocks of barges up and down that powerful stream, and raced the Burlington Northern freights that lumbered along beside the road. Those chuckling engineers knew their locomotives had enough power to beat me many times over, but they played right along, slowly letting out the throttle as I pumped harder and harder. Ultimately, the train would reach a straightaway and pull ahead for good, and I'd churn along at ten miles an hour, sweaty and happy with my momentary triumph over the iron horse.

Now, nine months later in southern Missouri, I was a dozen miles away from the Mississippi, which was locked into its course by levees, earthen embankments built along its banks to control flooding. Even small streams had levees, and the highest hills around were overpasses on Interstate 55, which ran parallel to Highway 61. From now on, I would only see the Mississippi when I crossed it.

Within an hour of leaving Benton, I found myself in a land of sharp contrasts I had never seen before. There were no in-betweens. It was either rich or poor, black or white, high land or low land. I rode by ornate ranch houses set far back from the road on wide, grassy lawns—the white landowners' places. There were many more shacks tottering on stilts, shingles falling off the rooftops, windows stuffed with newspaper to replace the glass that had fallen out long ago. The yards were full of junked cars in various states of decay, old wringer washers, broken bottles, rusty cans, rotting mattresses, 55-gallon drums, chickens pecking at the ground, and mangy dogs scratching themselves. The human residents were invariably black. I rode on by, not even waving—all the better not to rub in the fact that I was just passing through, and they weren't going anywhere.

I remembered from my eighth-grade history classes that Missouri had been a border state during the Civil War, home to Union and Confederate sympathizers. The day before, Judy Cureton's mother told me I would soon cross that invisible line between North and South. The rebel flags I'd begun to see on pickup trucks, store windows, and baseball caps told me I had done so. The people's accents had changed from Judy's Missouri twang to a drawl that moseyed along through words, sentences, and paragraphs, in no hurry to end the conversation.

While a Northerner would let me go about my business, a Southerner would be eager to make my acquaintance. In Marston, I ducked into the grocery for my lunch, which I planned to send right down to my grumbling belly, then jump back on the bike. At the cash register sat a portly, middle-aged woman who planted her ample girth atop a milk jug. I was used to the stares of small-town folk—since seeing a long distance cyclist wasn't an everyday occurrence—but this woman scrutinized me so thoroughly I thought I was being X-rayed. After an eternity, she spoke. "What kinda helmet is that?" Her curious eyes were focused on my Bell Biker helmet, with its reflective stripes, triangular ventilation holes, and the rainbow I'd stuck on the front after the trademark fell off.

"It's a bicycle helmet."

"Never seen such a thing before. You by yourself?"

"Mmm-hmm." Ever so subtly, I could feel my Yankee reserve crumbling away. This wasn't going to be a five-minute lunch stop.

"Honey, you sure are a brave girl. 'Specially with all that meanness out there now. Just had a prison break over at New Madrid—that's just a few minutes away from here. Pretty dangerous men, too, honey. You better watch out. Don't you ever get scared being by yourself?"

"Well, sometimes. Not too often. I just like the solitude. I can keep my own pace and not have to worry about anyone else's, stop when I want to, set my own schedule. I guess I'm sort of a loner. I was an only child, and I learned that being alone isn't the same as being lonely. You can be lonely in a crowd, too." But she was adamant. "You really should have someone along with you—for protection. Safety in numbers."

Then I told her about what happened on a bike club ride a couple summers before. We were riding single file, close together, when a teenaged hotrodder roared by and tossed several beer bottles at us. One missed my helmeted head by inches. That was the worst harassment I'd ever encountered—and I was in the midst of a crowd. Ironically, our destination for that day was Hell, Michigan.

"Honey, I still think you're pretty brave to be out there all alone," she said sympathetically, as if it had been my misfortune not to find someone else to ride with. I recalled what John Rakowski had said about companionship, that he wished he could rub a crystal ball to produce riding partners when he wanted them, then make them vanish when he needed solitude.

On that damp, cloudy afternoon in the Missouri bootheel, my crystal ball had produced a most unlikely companion, yet I knew her concern would stay with me for a long time. She urged me to set a spell, here's a spoon for that yogurt and peanuts. C'mon, just pull up one of those chairs by the counter and tell her about my ride.

I started to tell her everything that had happened since Day One, but my usual recitation of states and dates seemed less urgent than sharing how this journey was affecting me. Starting from Day One, May 3, and shaking free of Ann Arbor and those familiar roads of southeast Michigan. My knee, Lois Hinds and Ernie Keith. That paper roll in Brookville. The southern Indiana truckers' convoy. Those dirty, but dignified trash-pickers. Those strangers on bicycles who flagged me down at the edge of the Mississippi River in Illinois as they were finishing their club ride and loading their bikes into the back of Jim Hurtle's pickup. They treated me like a celebrity biker, and Jim and his buddies drove behind me into Cape Girardeau, fending off the heavy traffic on that narrow, two-lane bridge over that river I'd follow all the way to Louisiana. Then they took me in for the rest of that rainy weekend.

Over and over, I was seeing the best of America, I told her. Sure, there was meanness out there. I watched the TV news, too. But how distant that world of robberies, rapes and murders seemed to me. As if protected by some special power, I felt immune from that TV America. It might have been 10,000 miles away from me as I sat in that little store.

"Don't worry about me," I assured her as I got up to leave. "I'll be okay." As if she wanted to erase her remaining doubts about my pedaling about the country by myself, she nodded vigorously. Then she wrote something on a scrap of paper and handed it to me. In a firm, businesslike script was her address: Martin's Grocery, Marston, Mo. 63866, then underneath, her name, Margaret.

"Now you be sure and write me when you get to Loozey-Anna," she ordered. "I want to know you're all right. I'll be thinking about you. Now, y'all come back now, y'hear?"

We shook hands, then I plunged back into the biting chill. The bike had been leaning against the mud-spattered storefront, beneath the big "For Sale" sign that told me Margaret probably wouldn't be here when I came through again.

Margaret's jailbreak story convinced me not to camp out that evening. Instead, I stopped in Hayti and rented a room in an aging Missouri-Mexican style motel called El Rancho. El Rancho's exterior was done in adobe colored stucco, with cut logs simulating roof beams. The overall effect didn't fool me at all. Inside my room, surrounded by 1950s vintage institutional furniture and the inevitable television and Gideon's Bible, I plunged into my day's end routine of wiping off the bike frame, cleaning grit out of the chain with toilet paper from the bathroom, showering the crud off me, then going to bed.

Early the next morning, I got back into my mud-encrusted cycling clothes, and headed out into a sultry Delta morning with broiling sun and waves of humidity shimmering up from the rice fields. Just outside Hayti, I pulled off the road to check my maps, which prompted the driver of a passing pickup to pull over and stop, too.

Oh, no, I thought, here's that meanness Margaret warned me about. This guy's gonna beat me up, rob me, rape me, then toss my broken body into that cottonmouth snake-infested ditch along the wayside. I stood motionless as the smiling stranger—clad in Sears' Best work khakis, seed company cap, and mud-caked boots—strode toward me.

"Hi, ya lost? Need a ride?"

"No, thank you." I really wanted to get going again.

"Where ya headed?" He seemed genuinely interested in helping me. Ever so slowly, I let down my guard.

"Well, I'm coming from Ann Arbor, Michigan, near Detroit, and I'm riding around the United States. I'm going into Arkansas today. That'll be my sixth state so far."

"Well, now ain't that somethin' else. All by yourself, too. I don't think I could make it as far as Arkansas. Here, let me see your map."

I handed him my Conoco Touraide road map. He studied it for a moment, then launched into a set of directions that were full of entreaties to be sure and see this and not miss that. Like a connoisseur describing the taste of a fine wine, he strolled through a list of the towns I'd be passing through: Braggadocio, Steele, Rives, Hornersville, and, finally, Arbyrd, "just a short piece away from the Arkansas line. I sure do wish you luck. You come back this way again, y'hear?"

"I will." Despite my suspicions, all that guy wanted to do was make friends.

As a white suburban kid growing up in the 'sixties and 'seventies, my image of the South was limited to the TV shows' portrayals of the good ole boys and girls below the Mason-Dixon line as barefoot, illiterate racists, six o'clock news clips of civil rights marchers being hosed down by burly sheriff's deputies, and Martin Luther King dying on a motel room balcony in Memphis.

I grew up outside Philadelphia, in the fox hunting country along the Upper Main Line. Our neighborhood was all white, but our grade school was integrated. Almost every kid who attended Penn Wood Elementary during the late 'sixties had Mrs. Martin for music. A tall, slender black woman, Mrs. Martin was a strict disciplinarian who had no qualms about using the paddle, or picking us rowdy boys and girls up by the ears to restore order to her classroom. But not even the threat of her firm hand kept us as quiet as that day she told us about her previous summer's trip to the Carolinas. Barely concealing her anger, she recalled the day she stopped at a laundromat with a "Whites Only" sign out front.

"I went inside that place, asked to speak to the manager, and I told him how hurt I was about that sign out there. I knew he was a Christian—just like me—and I gave him the Gospel. I told him nobody had the right to treat their fellow man that way, because I'm a person too—just as much as him. I asked him why—in 1967—did he still have that sign up, but he couldn't answer me. Just couldn't say a word."

I had to pinch my arm to remind myself that it was nine-teen *sixty* seven she was talking about, not nineteen *thirty* seven. But I wasn't at all surprised that our Mrs. Martin had confronted that man over his sign.

Fourteen years later, I had no idea what happened to that determined lady, and I wondered if in a few weeks I'd happen upon that laundromat, with its "Whites Only" sign painted over. Heading further south into Arkansas, I looked carefully for the remnants of Jim Crow: the segregated restrooms and drinking fountains, or even a park bench with those senseless words "Whites Only" hidden under a hastily applied paint job. But it was all gone, erased forever as if the practice had never existed.

In September 1957—two months before I was born—Arkansas Governor Orval Faubus called out the National Guard to prevent the federally ordered integration of Little Rock's Central High School. President Eisenhower responded by sending U.S. Army troops into Little Rock to ensure that a handful of frightened black students could safely attend their new school. The Army stayed for the whole school year, as did the black students. Now, almost 24 years later, nearly every town I passed through had its public school and Christian academy. I'd heard them referred to as "segregation acade-mies," and I could see why. The kids I saw frolicking in the academy playgrounds were white—the public school play-grounds were predominantly black.

"We have to have these academies around here," insisted a preacher's son in a crossroads hamlet a few miles from the Mississippi River bridge at West Helena. "The public schools are just so bad, you wouldn't believe it. No way would I go to one of them."

His father looked on, silently nodding his approval. I got the distinct impression that this man's congregation would consider him a fool if he chanced his son's education to the public schools.

Why he'd feel just like the lone grain of salt in the pepper shaker, the boy told me. He'd also be the only white kid on the basketball team. His academy team was all white.

"You know, in every town down here, there are places where we whites don't go," the preacher said. "We've got one street here—it's called 'Boogie Alley'—and let me tell you, if you or I went in there on Saturday night, we wouldn't get out of there alive. It's just not our territory. And there are places where blacks don't go either. We stay on our side of the tracks and they stay on theirs."

In that town—just like every other—I saw blacks and whites in stores and on the streets greeting each other like long-lost friends. Those honks from passing cars, hearty waves, and firm handshakes looked too real to be an act. But each night they went home to their own separate ends of town, never the twain to meet. Deep down, I hoped things would be different across the river in Mississippi, but I knew they wouldn't.

"A few rich white men own this state," the caretaker of an oil tank farm just across the river from West Helena told me. "The rest work for them. You could call it a modern form of slavery. A lot of these little towns along the river are named for the landowners. Take Stovall down the road here—that's the next place you'll go through. All the land around there belongs to Mr. Stovall. Sherard, same thing."

It was exactly as he described it, many rickety shacks like I'd seen on the other side of the river, and a few big mansions with wide, manicured lawns. All around were thousands of acres planted with rice and soybeans. Only a handful of farmers were growing cotton now, for its market price barely cleared the growing expenses. The roadsides were dotted with the rusting hulks of bankrupt cotton gins.

Nonetheless, the owners still called their spreads "plantations." Almost all the fieldhands were black, as were the highway workers and gas station attendants. The black man's work was still the dirty work—a modern form of slavery.

Since I was out doing something that few of these Delta blacks would ever dream of, I fully expected to encounter resentment and hostility. Over in Arkansas, a school bus full of black high school students passed me, and all eyes were fixed on me with that same dark, penetrating stare me and my University of Michigan friends used to get as we drove through Detroit ghettoes on the way to Cobo Arena rock concerts. Then one of those kids pelted me with gravel. The sharp little stones stung my flesh, and as the bus pulled away, I heard jeers and mocking laughter. I had no proof it was racial, maybe just youthful high spirits, but I'd never know.

In Mississippi, I found surprisingly little hostility, just the same smiles, waves, and friendly greetings from blacks walking along the road that I got from whites driving by in their pickups.

"Where you going?" asked the black foreman of a crew patching potholes outside Stovall.

"Around the United States."

"Well, God bless you. You'll get whatever you want out of life."

Clusters of black children surrounded me whenever I stopped at stores and they were full of questions.

"Where you from?"

"Ann Arbor, Michigan."

"Where's that?"

"Near Detroit."

"Dee-troit? You rode that thing all the way from Dee-troit? How come you ain't tired?"

"Oh, I get tired sometimes. Real tired."

"Where's the motor on that thing?"

"It's a bicycle. *I'm* the motor."

"You mean you're just *pedalin'* that thing? How far you goin'?"

"Around the United States. About ten thousand miles."

"Ten thousand miles? Ten *thousand*? Are you kidding?"

If I hadn't had more miles to make before sundown, I'd still be answering questions in Mississippi.

Not that the climate made moving on easy. When I left Ann Arbor, winter had just given way to spring, and it was finally possible to go outside in a light jacket instead of a down parka. The day I left, the thermometer labored mightily and nudged the 70 degree mark. Now, almost three weeks later, it was into the eighties by midmorning. The wind off the Gulf felt like a blast straight from hell, and it got stronger as I pedaled further south. While I sweltered, the locals complained about the cold spell that was holding up the planting season. Out on the white cement roads, the sun beat down on the pavement, which radiated the heat back up at me. I felt like I was pedaling through fire.

On our last ride before I left Ann Arbor, my bike club buddies jokingly warned me against getting cinched by the Southern Bible Belt. "Watch out, or they'll baptize you in a watering trough and turn you into a holy roller," my friends quipped. We were anything but pious. Our main ride of the week took place on Sunday morning, and most of us didn't include church in our day's itinerary. I certainly didn't—church was something I left behind in high school. Down South, our behavior would be considered socially unacceptable, my friends said. Southern religion was everywhere, they added.

Now, three weeks later in the Mississippi River Delta, I could see exactly what they meant. Southern religion was everywhere, no escaping it. There were the well-thumbed Bibles and stacks of tracts next to cash registers in grocery stores, "Praise the Lord" bumper stickers, tent revival notices plastered all over telephone poles, and billboards asking in big, bold letters if passersby were SAVED. Then there were the TV shows, featuring those immaculately tailored evangelists with good ole boy names like Billy, Jimmy, Joey, and Bob.

On the Sunday before Memorial Day, I started out before seven to get a jump on the heavy holiday traffic on Highway 61 between Greenville and Vicksburg. I stopped at a tiny store to get my morning rations. The man behind the counter didn't pay me the slightest attention. He had his TV turned up loud and the preacher was just beginning to hit his stride. "Homosexuals!" he cried, "God *loves* you, but he *hates* your sin!"

I had several gay and lesbian friends back in Ann Arbor—some of them regular churchgoers—but none of them watched these programs, except as a joke. So much for getting them to repent.

Brother Television quickly moved on to a more important topic: money. Yes, friends, it took hundreds of thousands of dollars to run this ministry, many hundreds of thousands more than it was taking in. He was just praying for all of us good, God-loving people to come through to keep the word of the Lord on the air. Tears filled his eyes and perspiration rained down his cheeks and dripped on his custom tailored suit, and I had visions of pensioners sending their life savings to some guy named Jimmy Swaggart.

•6•

Loozey-Anna

Once out of Vicksburg, Mississippi, I was out of the flat, dusty Delta and into forested hills. The trees were covered with Spanish moss and lush, leafy kudzu vines. The kudzu also draped itself over shrubs, telephone poles, rocks, old houses, guardrails, and almost anything else that didn't move.

I liked kudzu because it softened the edges of everything it covered. Southerners hate the stuff. Kudzu was originally imported from Japan to control soil erosion along steep highway embankments. There was no problem in getting it to grow here—the problem is getting it to stop. Kudzu can grow several feet a day, right across the road if there's one in the way. Once this strong, hairy vine gets something in its grasp, not much will make it let go. Kudzu has been known to wrap itself around buildings and pull them down. The Southern states have spent millions on kudzu eradication programs, but the vine's still winning.

Memorial Day ended in a deluge that soaked me before I slammed my motel room door behind it in Natchez. In three weeks and one day, I'd come almost 1,100 miles and was closing in on my first milestone: reaching Baton Rouge. Originally, I had planned to go all the way to New Orleans, but now Baton Rouge was far enough.

The reason for this change of heart boiled down to two words: saddle sores. The trouble began in Indiana, got worse in Illinois, and how glad I was to take those three days off in Cape

Girardeau. Up there, each sore was a nagging pinprick. All day, I'd shift and squirm, trying to settle my weight on a pain-free part of my posterior. Gradually, those little sores merged into one excruciating red patch. Sitting on it was sheer agony, but I had no choice.

My leather saddle and black wool cycling shorts hadn't helped the situation. The saddle came presoftened with mink oil, but the oil had worn off, leaving the saddle about as resilient as a brick. My shorts had a chamois crotch insert to cushion the ride, but after absorbing lots of sweat and repeated washing and drying, that chamois was in tatters. To make matters worse, my back had developed heat rash.

I showered, didn't get dressed again, slathered my back and rear with Vaseline, and got into bed for a few hours of relief. The itch and soreness came back as soon as I mounted the bike the next day, Tuesday, May 26.

Immediately after crossing the Louisiana border, I felt distinctly unwelcome. My presence on the road provoked a cacophony of honking horns. Highway 61 was now a busy four-laner, with a paved but gravelly shoulder. I stayed on the road, but as close to the shoulder as possible. I kept the passing lane pretty busy.

Just south of Saint Francisville, someone behind me really laid on the horn. I shrugged it off. Then a van came alongside and forced me onto that gravelly shoulder.

"Git off the road!" the driver shouted. I slowed down to let him get ahead and engraved every detail about that van into my memory. Robin's egg blue van. Louisiana license plate. Mirror tinted windows. Bumper stickers saying, "I'm proud to be a Union Man," and "Join Your Local Co-op Affiliate." I got back on the road. He pulled over up ahead and got out of the van. His face was scrunched up and beet red.

"Git off the #@*& road," he bellowed, shaking his fat fist at me. "You're s'posed to be ridin' on the #@*& shoulder.!"

I steered well around him, shifted into high gear, and screamed, "I got as much #@*& legal right to be on this road as you do, so %@*# off!"

His wife and kids sat in the van, immobilized. I was trembling. The long stream of traffic that had backed up behind me was starting to pass, so that van would be trapped on the shoulder for awhile. An official state car passed me as I approached a bridge. It was going too fast to stop, so I did an angry pantomime, with lots of fist shaking and pointing at the pavement, the shoulder, and behind me. Two cars later, the van passed without incident.

I'd memorized his license number and I wanted to call the cops and have his license yanked. But I'd entered a long stretch of road bordered by oil refineries behind tall chain link fences. There were no public phones for miles in any direction.

On that busy highway, I felt very alone and very afraid. What if he pulled over again? How could I call for help? Almost an hour passed before I reached a store. The manager let me use his phone to call the state police. There was nothing they could do, the dispatcher told me, unless I knew what parish it happened in so the case could be prosecuted locally. All I could say was that it happened south of Saint Francisville. I slammed the receiver down.

I stormed outside to the pay phone and dialed the number of a man on my hospitality home list. Down in Baton Rouge, a woman answered the phone.

"Hugh Reynolds, please?"

"He just left on a bicycle trip. This is his mother speaking." I explained that I was a cyclist too, and asked if she minded if I came to visit. Yes, it was all right with her, and from where I was calling, it was about eight miles to her place.

An hour later, I was pushing my bike up to Hugh Reynolds' house, set way back from the street in a veritable jungle of tropical vegetation. A soft-spoken woman answered the door, introduced herself as Dot Reynolds, and invited me in.

Her son had left just a half hour before I called. She showed me pictures of a rotund fellow with a beard and a big grin standing next to a heavily loaded bicycle—there was even a guitar strapped to the back. There were more pictures of mountains and deserts and the same cheerful fellow everyone called Hugh Baird, just like his late father.

Dot told me that Hugh Baird Senior had been a prominent attorney, but when he died, he left a big house with a big mortgage. Dot paid it off herself, but wanted to leave now. She'd grown weary of Louisiana's steambath climate and longed to return to her native Oklahoma. When Hugh Baird came back from his trip out west, he'd help her fix the place up so she could sell it.

I put the bike in the shop for an overhaul, and stayed almost a week with Dot. She also had her newly separated daughter Lyle and Lyle's son John Paul—alias J.P.—living with her until they found their own place, but they were seldom around.

Dot rarely left the house, and when we went out, she seemed afraid to go more than a few blocks away. She was perplexed at how easily her children ventured so far away while she worried so much about them. She anxiously awaited some news from Hugh Baird. To her, this cycletouring business was far too dangerous, and she was sure my parents were worried sick about me. Lyle's twin sister, Lynn, lived 100 miles away in New Orleans, which seemed light years away to Dot.

Dot was a professional seamstress, and spent as much as 12 hours a day at her sewing machine doing alterations. I removed the decaying chamois from my bike shorts and she replaced it with a flannel pad. It would dry faster, for in the steamy South, the chamois took two days to dry, and that dampness aggravated my saddle sores.

Unfortunately, those saddle sores got some company. During the previous Sunday, I had stopped at a Mississippi roadside rest area because I was in dire need of an outhouse. But the only facilities there were some bushes full of the lushest poison ivy I'd ever seen. In Baton Rouge, rashes bloomed in places where it isn't socially acceptable to scratch. The chino pants I wore off the bike were too hot and compounded my agony. Dot gave me a pair of light cotton drawstring pants Hugh Baird hadn't wanted, and I mailed the chinos back to my parents. She also gave me some ointment left over from the time when she didn't know what poison ivy looked like and included it in a floral arrangement. She came down with the worst case her doctor had ever treated.

J.P. played Little League baseball, and on Wednesday night, Lyle and I drove him up to North Baton Rouge for his game. The other team was all black. They arrived together in the back of a pickup, which was closely followed by a procession of cars full of their parents, friends, and relatives who quickly packed the first base bleachers. The kids began a crisp fielding and throwing drill that would put the Major Leaguers to shame. Then they paused for a group prayer. J.P.'s team was all white except for two players, and they straggled in by ones and twos. A few of them tossed baseballs back and forth while the others watched.

Lyle and I spread ourselves out on the largely empty third base bleachers. We chatted about her MBA courses at Louisiana State, jobs, and résumés. She got out a legal pad and began polishing her résumé. She gave me some paper, and I poked around at mine, but couldn't find words to connect college, an assortment of briefly held jobs, and cycletouring, so I gave it up and watched the game.

The Chicken Shack machine had J.P.'s team beaten from the start. They could hit, they could pitch, they could field, and they could throw. J.P. came up late in the game, struck out on three swings, walked back to the bench, and slammed his helmet down.

"Number twelve!" The umpire called him back to the plate. All eyes were riveted on J.P. "You don't do that in this league!" the umpire bellowed.

J.P. trudged back to the bench and started horsing around with his teammates. Final score was 11 to 1 or 2. I didn't pay closer attention because it was too painful to watch. Soul music filled the parking lot as we walked back to Lyle's VW beetle. J.P. sniffled and mumbled something about hitting a hard line drive back at the pitcher.

J.P. moped around until the weekend, which was reserved for Baton Rouge's annual Fest For All. Lynn drove up from New Orleans, and on Friday night and Saturday afternoon we all drove downtown to join in a real "Loozey-anna" party. There were mock medieval battles on the Old Governor's Mansion lawn, symphony concerts by the river, and rock groups, blues singers and jazz ensembles everywhere.

From the Moorish Old State Capitol with its art exhibits and unique, self-supporting spiral staircase, to Interstate 10 a mile away, North Boulevard was closed off for a crafts fair. Most of the crafts were the inevitable macramé, leatherwork, stained glass, and woodcarvings, but there were a few standouts, like the dulcimers crafted by a portly man from Florida named Loran Harmon. Loran talked me through a fumbling version of "Twinkle, Twinkle Little Star." I had no idea what I was playing until he told me.

I wandered around the fair, consuming beer, nachos, foot-wide chocolate chip cookies, Pennsylvania Dutch funnel cakes and more beer to wash it all down. After we got home Saturday evening, I rode over to the Louisiana State campus. Still full of all that food and drink, I rode sluggishly, and my tuned up bike felt like a stranger, not the trusty machine that had brought me so far.

SELECTING A
CYCLETOURING LOCALE
••

After spending twelve and a half years in two-wheeled explorations of this country, I'm convinced that the bicycle is truly "the best way to see the whole U.S.A." I also hope that after reading this book, you'll be inspired to go out and undertake your own bicycle adventures in America.

Where should you start? I suggest that you start the way I did, in your own back yard. Get to know your town, your county, your state. An excellent way to do this is by joining your local bicycle club. When I first got serious about cycling back in the summer of 1979, I was fortunate to be living in Ann Arbor, Michigan, home of the Ann Arbor Bicycle Touring Society. The Touring Society taught me the craft of cycling on rides in and around Ann Arbor, and they also inspired me to venture much further afield. They freely shared what they'd learned on their own rides in New England, the Colorado Rockies, and the Mississippi River valley, information that proved invaluable as I pedaled those areas myself.

How do you find a bike club? Ask at your local bicycle or outdoor shop. You'll find that the smaller clubs—those with a few dozen members—tend to specialize in certain activities like racing, mountain biking or social recreational riding. Larger clubs—those with several hundred members—tend to offer the full menu of activities.

If your area doesn't have a club, consider starting one. There's a national organization called the League of American Wheelmen (LAW) that can help you do so. LAW was founded during America's first big bike boom in the 1880s, hence the anachronistic-sounding name. Speaking as a bicyclist of the female gender, I'm not too crazy about the name, but I've been a member for a long time because I believe that no other national cycling organization offers as much to its members. For starters, LAW protects the rights and promotes the interests of bicyclists, provides information about bicycling for its members and others, serves a nationwide network of affiliated bicycle clubs and organizations, and sponsors bicycle rallies and other activities. It currently has more than 23,000 members. Write or call:

League of American Wheelmen
190 West Ostend Street, Suite 120
Baltimore, Maryland 21230-3755
(410) 539-3399 or (800) 288-BIKE

I also recommend LAW for lots of other reasons. Each year, members receive the *Bicycle USA Almanac*, which is loaded with information on the bicycling conditions in all 50 states. Want to join an organized ride in Rhode Island, find maps of bicycle-friendly roads in Oregon or find out if it's legal to ride on interstate highway shoulders in Michigan? It's all in the *Almanac*. The *Almanac* also includes the LAW's nationwide network of ride information contacts. These very knowledgeable volunteers can tell you everything you'll need to know about cycletouring in Nebraska, Vermont, Alabama, Texas and those 46 other states. I've found them to be so helpful that I consider them to be bicycling's equivalent of Triple-A.

The LAW also has a network of hospitality home hosts who are ready and waiting for you to come visit them during your tour. And there are the annual bicycle rallies, held in some of the most scenic areas in America. LAW rallies are a very affordable way to sample the cycling in upstate New York, the Pennsylvania Dutch country, the Kentucky Bluegrass region or the Pacific Northwest. If you're going to get into cycletouring in the United States, the League of American Wheelmen is a must-join. And a reasonable one, too. At this writing, individual memberships are $25 per year, $30 for families.

Another organization worth looking into is Bikecentennial, which got its start during a transcontinental bike ride organized to celebrate the U.S. bicentennial. Since then, Bikecentennial has gone about the business of compiling the best cycletouring maps anywhere. They also run low-cost, self-contained bike tours and sell an extensive array of books and other products of interest to cycletourists. The organization currently has more than 33,000 members. Individual memberships are currently $22 a year. Write or call:

Bikecentennial
Post Office Box 8308
Missoula, Montana 59807
(406) 721-1776

•7•

A Southern Fried Yankee

I left Baton Rouge on Sunday morning, May 31. Outside the Reynolds' house, there were lots of long goodbye hugs and invitations for me to visit Lynn in New Orleans during Mardi Gras, Lyle and J.P. in Baton Rouge, and Dot wherever she ended up. Next time, I'd get to meet Hugh Baird, they promised. Obviously concerned for my safety, Dot insisted that I write her the moment I arrived at my parents' house in Pennsylvania. She had already asked for their address and phone number, "just in case I need to get ahold of them," she said gravely.

Baton Rouge on Sunday morning was as sound asleep as Ann Arbor had been a month ago. In less than an hour, I was on U.S. 190, a straight-arrow two laner that sliced through swamps and bayous full of mosquitoes, alligators, water moccasins and cypress trees with splayed out roots and limbs draped with Spanish moss.

Along the shoulders were neatly constructed mountains left by fire ants, which the locals matter-of-factly declared would "eat yore ass alive," if I indulged in my quaint Yankee custom of sitting down to study my maps.

The warm, damp morning melted into a hot, steamy afternoon, with storm clouds drifting inland from nearby Lake Pontchartrain. They left no rain to cool things off. All day long, sweat burst out of my pores, combining with my gooey sunscreen to form a coating that clung tenaciously to my skin. There was no place for sweat to evaporate to in that humid air, and my sticky skin served as a perfect medium for trapping

gnats, mosquitoes, and other flying insects. I felt sure the pro-
prietor of some roadside stand would ignore my request for
iced tea and instead grab me and hang me from the ceiling like
fly paper.

I spent the night in the Abita Springs cycletourist hospitality home of Margaret Foust, a schoolteacher on summer vacation. She'd turned her attention away from lesson plans and
test papers to her other vocation of raising purebred poodles.
One of her females had just whelped, and she barked menac-
ingly whenever I got too close to her tiny flotilla of suckling
newborns. The entire house smelled doggy, something the
Fousts had obviously gotten used to years ago, just like the tiny
brown piles that made a walk in the backyard seem like a trip
through a minefield.

Margaret insisted that this particular stretch of country was
too dangerous for me to travel alone. Life was cheap here, she
said. This was drug running country. Louisiana's innumerable
swamps and bayous provided the perfect cover for marijuana
and cocaine smugglers coming in from South America. Most of
their boats and airplanes escaped detection.

"Around here, you mind your own business," she stated.
"You don't ask too many questions—that's the last thing you
want to do. You ask the wrong person the wrong thing, and
bang!" She made her thumb and forefinger into a gun, pointed
right at me.

Everybody in this part of Louisiana either knew or knew
about those elaborately dressed young men and women with
no obvious means of support who tooled around in Mercedes
and BMWs. She continued, "They're always going on trips, but
they never say where."

And woe to those who got too curious about their interesting lifestyles. The local papers were full of stories of undercover
agents whose bullet-riddled bodies were later found in some
god-forsaken bayou, if the alligators didn't get them first. Then
there were the innocent and the naive: the hikers who'd blun-
dered down the wrong marshy trail and fell into a Vietnam-
style booby trap near a secluded airstrip, and the fishermen
whose discovery of a cove full of catfish was greeted by semi-
automatic rifle fire from the bushes.

For the Fousts, this whole ugly business hit home when Margaret returned from school to find a police stakeout in front of her neighbors' house. She knew little about those people, but thought their comings and goings at odd hours a bit strange. Like the Fousts, they kept to themselves and minded their own business—the drug trade. They were arrested, tried, and convicted. About their current whereabouts—what prison they were in and for how long—Margaret knew nothing. Around there, you didn't ask too many questions.

"Martha, I really hope you're carrying a gun with you," she said, locking her gaze on me. "I can't tell you how lucky you are to make it this far without any trouble. You're really taking a big chance."

I quietly confessed that no, I didn't have a gun, and skipped my usual explanations that a gun was just another heavy thing I'd have to haul uphill and into the wind, and that it could easily be yanked out of my hands and used against me. Since I was run off the road, I'd begun to think about carrying some sort of protection. Over supper, Margaret suggested that we go out and get one of those pocket-sized canisters of Mace, but we never got around to leaving the house.

I slept fitfully that night. My dreams of screaming, cursing rednecks opening fire on me along deserted backroads were punctuated by lightning flashes and thunder.

Monday, June 1 dawned gray and rainy, a perfect day to stay in bed and forget that the idea of bicycling around the United States ever entered my mind. But those rattling dishes in the kitchen and the muffled barking reminded me that this wasn't my house. I was just passing through, as I'd done in so many other places. I was going through an endless succession of revolving doors, shuttling in and out of other people's lives. The only constant was the moving on, always moving on. Outside, a strong south wind had come in from the Gulf and was pushing the storm clouds away. After sharing a light breakfast with Margaret, I headed north with that wind.

After Abita Springs, I turned inland, and headed northeast toward the thick steamy forests of Mississippi. After getting thoroughly lost in Bogalusa, I found my way onto Louisiana Route 10, which dropped down into the swamps along the Pearl River. Just across that swift, muddy river was Mississippi, the first of several states I'd go through twice on this journey. While my mind wandered off to plot the logistics of a ride around America that wouldn't cross any state more than once, a beat up old red Chevy pulled up beside me. The car passed me with only a few inches to spare and the driver leered at me as he went by.

Thanks for nearly running me into the ditch, I thought. Up ahead, he pulled over onto a dirt track beside the river. He opened his car door as I rode by, leered that same lecherous leer, blew wet kisses and pointed at his open fly. I gave him the finger, then ran like hell into Mississippi.

I repeatedly looked back, hoping to heaven and hell that I wouldn't see that awful car gaining on me. With my dream of riding solo around America turning into a nightmare, a voice inside of me screamed at my legs to pedal faster, faster, faster! After sprinting for five hilly miles, my body ran out of adrenaline. I stopped the bike, tumbled off, and half sat and half leaned against a guardrail. Like a vanquished fox, I waited for that hunter in his red car to move in and finish me off. Fortunately, I never saw him again.

U.S. 11 was my first Mississippi road north, an endless series of ups and downs through pine forests interspersed with hardscrabble farms where mule-drawn plows tilled the thick red clay and little towns with no-nonsense names like Poplarville, Lumberton, Hattiesburg, and Richton. Then I turned east into Alabama.

Those Mississippi and Alabama forests were abuzz with the sound of chainsaws. Logging was a major industry, and any tall pines that caught the fancy of the lumberjacks were quickly cut down, piled on the backs of trucks, tied down with chains, then driven away at breakneck speed to the pulp mills.

The trees had most of their branches trimmed off, but the ends dangled far beyond the backs of the trucks, even to the point of dragging on the road. Unlike the Indiana coal haulers, the loggers didn't honk to say hello—these guys meant "Look out!" Again and again, I made it to the ditch just in time to see an untrimmed branch go by, sticking out like a scythe to behead me if I'd stayed on the road.

I was lucky with the logging trucks. I almost wasn't so lucky the morning of Thursday, June 4. It happened right after I left a campground along the Alabama River near Camden. Guess I should have kept a closer eye on that car and the pickup following it, but I figured they were just another couple of oncoming vehicles. Then the pickup pulled out to pass—and came right at me. I froze, and we missed a head-on collision by less than a foot. I ran off the road and nearly tumbled off the bike before I stopped. I was gasping and shaking so hard I collapsed to the ground.

Like a helpless puppy, I panted and whimpered, unable to lift myself out of those thick weeds. My mind replayed the terrible sequence of events that nearly happened: the pickup racing toward me, the sickening crunch of metal on metal, a scream...

Only the slenderest of margins kept me alive that morning. Just a small jerk on the handlebars or a nervous twitch of the hips could have sent me right into the path of that pickup. If I'd paid more attention when it was creeping out from behind the car, I could have run to the shoulder in plenty of time. I concentrated extra hard on the road for the rest of the day, and I remember very little of that 45-mile stretch from Camden to Greenville except the yellow center line.

In Greenville, I bought a pint of neatsfoot oil for my saddle. I retreated to a public campground outside town and dumped the entire can onto that rock-hard leather. It was soft as putty the next morning.

So were the roads that took me back into Greenville. The heat didn't let up at all during the night. As I stood outside a supermarket eating my yogurt and granola breakfast, I stared at the time and temperature sign at the edge of the parking lot, not really comprehending the numbers as they went through their mechanical repetition: 78 degrees at 7:58; 78, 7:58; 79, 7:59.

The early morning haze blocked the sun for another hour, then it was back to the inferno. All day long, my sweat poured out, then pooled on my skin. I drank water a quart at a time, bloating my stomach but not relieving my thirst.

Country stores became a refuge from the heat; their red and white Coca-Cola signs were beacons of hope along the roadside, signaling the last outpost of bearable temperatures for the next five miles. The folks in Rutledge, Luverne, and Vidette must have wondered what they were getting when this sweaty, dusty cyclist burst through their doorways, but the best seat in the house—the one next to the air conditioner—would be immediately offered to me. Set a spell, they'd say. Had I eaten dinner yet? Here's an ice cream bar. Oh, no, no. You put that wallet away. This one's on the house. Did I need some water for that canteen? I'd be offered endless refills until I was water-logged, then they'd pack my water bottle with crushed ice— one for the road. The ice turned to soup within a half hour.

To endure the heat between country stores, I devised my own portable air conditioner by soaking a bandana in cold water, then tying it around my neck. Relief was immediate, but short-lived.

I didn't take a midday break for fear I'd never get started again. Early that afternoon, I found I could pedal no more. Somehow, my rubbery fingers squeezed the brakes hard enough to stop the bike, and my wobbly legs carried me over to the ruins of an old house. I sat down on the cool concrete slab that had once been its foundation and swallowed the last few sips from my water bottle. I stared back at the busy highway, and right before my eyes, it became a wide, wonderful, shimmering ocean full of sailboats drifting back and forth. The live oak that shaded me had become a swaying palm, and how I wanted to lie down and rest my weary body on this sandy beach.

"You're hallucinating," someone said, but I looked around and saw no one else there.

"Get out of here, you can't stay here," the voice ordered. My tropical fantasy world was rapidly dissolving back into the trash-strewn vacant lot in which I'd stopped to rest.

I got back on the bike and climbed the long hill up to the city of Troy. Near the center of town, I stopped at a fruit stand to get a quick boost for my sagging metabolism. The outside thermometer read 96 degrees. A bushel of peaches the size of softballs immediately caught my eye—peaches are my favorite fruit.

"First of the season, ma'am," said the short, potbellied pro-prietor. He'd been watching me all along.

"Those are Chilton County peaches," he bragged. "Best in 'Bama, the best anywhere."

I picked one up and took a bite. He was right. I ate the rest of it, and reached for my wallet.

"Now don't you worry 'bout that," he said. "You needed that peach more than I did. My treat."

Feeling a surge of energy inside my weary body, I thanked him profusely.

My legs carried me just ten more miles that day. Outside Banks, I stopped at a country Baptist church and asked the pastor's wife if I could camp between the church and the parsonage. Her husband, Max, wasn't home, but Ann Kelly was sure he wouldn't mind.

"But ma'am, that lawn behind the church house is just fulla mo-skeetahs," she said. "You'll get eaten up out there. You come on in and stay with us." I was only too happy to be hustled inside by this big, dark-haired woman with bright, laughing eyes. Several of those big 'Bama mosquitoes had sunk their stingers into my legs while I stood on the porch.

Max and Ann Kelly had one child, seven-year-old Cary, who had severe cerebral palsy. He couldn't walk, talk, or sit up. Unable to control himself, he still wore diapers. Cary communicated in grunts, squeals, and chirps. He spent the hot summer days lying on a blanket Ann spread out on the living room floor. All he wore was his diaper—it was too hot for anything more. His baby soft skin was covered with big red welts from mosquito bites.

"He can't defend himself," Ann sighed. "He can't swat those skeetahs away like the rest of us. And he whimpers so when he gets bit. Sometimes I want to cry along with him."

The Kellys readily attested that their deep faith in God allowed them to carry on with the enormous task of caring for their helpless boy-baby. Max and Ann Kelly derived as much joy from Cary as other parents would from a normal child.

"He's been a real blessing to us," Ann said as she held Cary in her lap. "He's really brought the family closer together. Brought us closer to the Lord."

The biggest thrill in Cary's simple world was to be held by Max or Ann—preferably by both. "Gimme some sugar," they'd say, and he'd respond with many wet kisses, interspersed with chirps of delight.

Cary would frequently look over at me and smile—I was just another family friend to him—but I had to force myself to smile back. I'd never been around anyone so severely handicapped, and I felt very uneasy.

Like many country pastors, Max had a fulltime job. He managed the produce department at the Troy Piggly Wiggly. Before he took that job, he had worked in a convenience store that sold more beer than anything else, which irked Max because he didn't drink. For this brawny man with a country-western singer's rugged good looks, becoming a produce manager was the answer to his prayers. "But there's one problem," he said, showing me his big thick hands. There was a thick layer of dirt under his fingernails that could only be removed with lots of scrubbing. But then again, most members of his congregation were farmers with the same condition.

The four of us got up way before six the next morning, a Saturday, usually a pastor's morning to sleep in. But Max had to go to work in Troy, then perform a wedding in the afternoon. Before fixing breakfast, Ann insisted I join her on the front porch for her favorite morning ritual: listening to the birds. I sat and fidgeted on the hard cement stoop while next to me, Ann wore a beatific smile as she softly imitated the bird calls from the forest behind the house.

By the time that wedding started, I was settled in at a campground on Lake Eufaula, 50 hilly miles away. It was a good afternoon to watch the lizards scurrying around my tent, take a dip in the pool, and do my laundry. The only laundromat casualty was my cycling jersey, which was worn and faded when I left Ann Arbor, but had since become so holey that it looked like Swiss cheese. I hoped it would last until I got to my parents' house, but it looked like it wouldn't make it across the causeway into Georgia.

A huge thunderhead passed over camp, which spurred into action two gray-haired women from the motor homes across the road from my site.

"Honey, you're gonna drown if you stay over here. It's gonna rain buckets!" one warned me.

Then the other made the offer I couldn't refuse: "Why don't you jus' come an' visit with us tonight? Stay inside an' be dry, honey!"

I gathered my drying laundry, rolled up my tent, loaded it all onto the bike, then walked everything over to the motor homes.

The women introduced themselves as Betty Jo Self and Felton Griffin, from nearby Hurtsboro, Alabama. They spent almost every summer weekend at Lake Eufaula. Their husbands, Bob Self and Gomer Griffin, were out fishing on the lake.

Bob and Gomer came back empty-handed, so we all went out to dinner in the town of Eufaula. "We're gonna teach you to eat Southern style," Betty Jo and Felton promised. They piled my plate high with all sorts of fried delicacies: onion rings, french fries and hush puppies, little cornmeal dough balls. They instructed me in the proper pronunciation of "y'all." A true, born and raised Southerner says "yawl," but the best I could manage with my hybrid Pennsylvania-Michigan accent was a hopelessly nasal "yahl," which broke everyone up.

After we returned to the campground, I learned why the Griffins and the Selfs were so nervous about storms. At 2 a.m. on April Fool's Day, a tornado had torn through Hurtsboro, reducing most of it to rubble. Two months later, the town was busy rebuilding. I spent the night in the Griffins' motor home, and both couples huddled around the kitchen table, chain smoking and talking in loud, agitated voices about the tornado.

They recalled the wind that sounded like a freight train and pulverized everything in its path. Afterward, people crept out from their ruined homes, calling the names of friends and relatives, not knowing if they were alive or dead. When you heard the others answer, you got down on your knees and thanked God, my hosts said. Their stories were partially for me to hear, but more to help them recover from that night's trauma. They repeatedly glanced out the windows, searching for signs of the storm that never came.

That storm found me in Georgia the next day. I waited more than an hour on the Preston public library's front porch while lightning bolts danced all around. The wind blew sheets of rain under all sides of the porch roof, reducing my dry haven to a small crescent around the book return box. When the storm diminished to a drizzle, I was off to the next town, Plains. Plains looked like so many other Southern hamlets I'd seen.

The railroad tracks divided it in half, with U.S. 280 on one side and Main Street on the other.

But Plains counted a former President of the United States among its 600 inhabitants. Unlike other towns in the heart of Georgia's peanut country, its main industry was tourism. But that was starting to change. Billy Carter's infamous gas station was shut down, and a big sign out front announced a forthcoming auction. Billy had moved to Alabama to do public relations for a mobile-home company. Stores on Main Street had Jimmy Carter plastic-covered placemats, peanut ashtrays, and "Where in the hell is Plains, Georgia?" tee-shirts marked down for quick sale.

It was easy to tell Jimmy Carter's place from the rest—it was the only house with a tall wooden fence around it. There also was a long driveway with a gate and guardhouse by the road. The gate signs said, "Do not stop—keep moving." I stopped. I leaned the bike against a telephone pole next to a newly installed Southern Bell switching box that warned of a $10,000 fine and a ten-year prison sentence for anyone caught tampering with it. I ambled over to the empty guardhouse and took pictures of my reflection in a wide-angle mirror.

Almost on cue, a chubby, red-faced guard approached, with a raincoat draped over his shoulder, shirt tails hanging out and barely covering his potbelly, and black work shoes covered with red mud.

"So this is it, eh?" I flashed him a big, 200-watt smile, hoping that I could somehow wangle an invitation to stroll through that gate and meet the man I reluctantly voted for in the last election.

"Ee-yep," the good ole boy guard replied. He was obviously annoyed that he had to come out into this rain to shoo me away.

Hoping to restart our stalled conversation, I confessed that I was surprised that I hadn't seen an endless procession of billboards touting Plains' tourist traps. I had seen just one billboard all day, and it was just a friendly little reminder to motorists to drive safely. "We want to see you again at Billy Carter's gas station," the sign said.

"Used to have a lot more ah them signs," the guard said. "But they outlawed them. Too much clutter."

And that's all he said. He crossed his arms and glared at me. I took the hint and left.

I felt sorry for Jimmy Carter, and I felt sorry for Plains. This little town had seen it all: heads of state from all over the world, journalists from every major newspaper, wire service, and TV network, and countless tourists. In the stores, cashiers wordlessly handed back my change, then stood there until I left, just like Carter's guard. Starting a conversation was out of the question. They just wanted to be left alone.

Usually, I don't like to ride in the rain, but the rain I rode in on Friday, June 12, outside Columbia, South Carolina, was a blessed relief. For a couple hours, the searing sun disappeared and the air was cool. I was never happier to be soaking wet in my life. But alas, the sun broke through the clouds as I entered West Columbia and coasted downhill into the Congaree River valley. After crossing the river, I entered South Carolina's state capital and embarked on a long uphill climb. Near the top, I dismounted and walked the bike along. Hundreds of American Legion Boys' State finalists converged on the grounds of the domed state capitol building as I strolled by. It was hard to tell which was the bigger local sensation, Martha in her soggy cycling garb pushing her mud-spattered bike, or the traffic-stopping swarm of high school boys being directed across Gervais Street by the police.

Just for me, the swarm blew big, wet kisses and sent forth a chorus of wolf whistles.

"Hey, babe! Nice legs ya got there!" shouted one lust-filled adolescent.

"C'mon and ride a few miles with me," urged another.

"Naw, I'm the one you really want," insisted a third. Like all the rest, his hometown American Legion post had nominated him for these finals, based on his outstanding leadership and citizenship.

I kept my eyes forward and my mouth shut and continued walking with my bicycle.

On the east side of Columbia, I rolled up to a red light and stopped next to a big white luxury car bearing a single-digit license plate, the kind reserved for high state officials, I surmised. A little motor whirred into action, letting down the tinted window on the driver's side. A man in a custom-tailored suit studied me and my bike.

"Where are you from?" he asked.

"Michigan."

"How long have you been on the road?"

"Six weeks this Sunday."

"Good luck."

Up went the power window. The light changed, then we were off on our own very separate ways. Had I just spoken with the Governor? I'll never know.

The city gave way to the suburbs, with their shopping malls, tract houses and industrial parks. Gaps of woodland and fields began to intervene in the suburban sprawl. The wall-to-wall traffic with its honking horns, squealing brakes and rumbling motors gradually fell away behind me. The four-lane highway dropped back to two lanes and I was out in the country again, heading north on U.S. 1.

Back before World War II, U.S. 1 was truly number one, *the* north-south highway on the populous eastern seaboard. Stretching some 2,362 miles from Calais, Maine on the Canadian border to Key West, Florida, U.S. 1 is one of the longest highways in America. Although its role as the premier highway of the east has been usurped by the interstates, it's still a busy road in spots. U.S. 1 was Baltimore Pike, the crowded four-laner that ran behind our house when my family lived in the Philadelphia suburb of Media. All the neighborhood parents warned us kids never to walk across the Pike, for if we lived to get to the other side, we'd never survive the spanking for doing so. They had a point—Baltimore Pike took a heavy toll on the more adventurous neighborhood cats and dogs.

But U.S. 1 in South Carolina was just a quiet country road. The restaurants, motels and gas stations from its glory days were slowly decaying beneath a thick mantle of kudzu and poison ivy. On Saturday morning, I stopped at a peach processing plant near McBee. Baskets of freshly scrubbed peaches were set out in a sales room which doubled as the employees' break room. One of the women on break began asking me the usual where-have-I-been and where-am-I-going questions. Seizing an opportunity to hide from the sun for a few moments, I gave her the best travelogue I could muster. She excused herself, then returned with her boss, J.R. McLeod, who was just as amazed as she by my adventure. And there was no way I'd be permitted to buy any of his peaches. "Help yourself," he insisted. "Take all you want."

J.R. then called his friend Glenn Eberhardt, the newspaper editor up in Chesterfield. Eberhardt, a jovial transplanted Yankee, met me up the road in Patrick. We adjourned to an air conditioned gas-and-grocery store for an interview that really was more of a chat. I fueled up on packaged cups of ice cream and tinned fruit juice, quite grateful for yet another cool refuge from that heat outside.

After the interview, we went outside for a Martha-astride-bicycle picture. I gave Glenn my parents' address in Pennsylvania, and he promised to send them a copy of the newspaper with my story. I'd just dropped my folks a postcard saying that I expected to see them around Father's Day.

We parted on Glenn's warnings not to speed through police chief Jim Foster's territory. "He's a real law and order man," Glenn laughed. I envisioned the chief as a muscular six-footer with sun-bronzed skin, cold, steely blue eyes and closely cropped hair. This guy Foster had to be a real live Buford Pusser, the tough southern lawman immortalized in the film "Walking Tall." When I got to the edge of Patrick, I spotted the chief, a black man, writing a ticket as he leaned against a car pulled off to the side of the road.

GETTING YOURSELF AND YOUR BIKE TO THE START OF YOUR TOUR

● ●

Unless you're going to just roll yourself and your bike out the front door and start riding, you're going to need to do some advance preparation to get both of you to the start of your tour. The amount of preparation depends on what mode of transportation you choose.

I've gotten to the start of most of my tours by plane, but in summer 1980, I hitched a ride with friends. My friends knew how much I valued my bike, so they carefully stowed it in the trunk of their car for the duration of the drive. I appreciated their concern, as that was a brand new, never-toured Nobilette they were carrying.

Despite all the horror stories circulating about airline baggage handlers, I've never had a bike damaged during air travel. The problem I have is with the cost: the major airlines currently charge an oversize baggage fee of up to $55 one-way! For a budget-minded traveler like me, that really hurts. However, there are a couple of ways to get around these high fees. The first is called USAmateur, which offers members free airline boarding passes for sporting equipment, including bikes; discounts on airfares, hotels and car rentals; and free emergency medical air transport in case of injury. Memberships are $74.95 for one year, $127.50 for two years, and $180 for three years. Write or call:

USAmateur, Inc.
275 East Avenue
Norwalk, Connecticut 06855
(203) 866-1984

The second way is the League of American Wheelmen's recently established program that offers members free bike passes on partner airlines when tickets are purchased through the Sports National Reservation Center. LAW memberships are

$22 per year for individuals. The organization's address is on page 39.

After you've joined USAmateur or LAW, you'll still need to package your bike for airline travel. There are two schools of thought on how to do this, and I've done it both ways. Simply put, they are the "box it" and "don't box it" philosophy.

Proponents of the "box it" philosophy maintain that boxing the bike protects it from damage during transit. I'd like to add that it also keeps your dirty bicycle chain away from the other passengers' luggage. The airlines will provide you with a free box (it's the handling that they're charging a king's ransom for) and then you get to provide the free entertainment for the other people waiting in the check-in line. You'll need to take your pedals off—bring a pedal wrench or a crescent wrench for this—and turn your handlebars around sideways. Some brutes have enough force to turn the bars sideways without any tools. I prefer to use a 6mm hexagonal wrench to loosen the stem binder bolt, and then give the bolt a couple whacks with a U-lock to loosen the stem so that the bars rotate freely. The aforementioned procedure is best suited for elderly bikes with tight-fitting stem and front fork combinations. I've found that the stem bolts on newer bikes—especially mountain bikes—don't need to be clobbered. Loosening them with the hex wrench is all that's needed to free the whole stem and bar assembly.

Okay, so you've gotten your partially dismantled bike into its box, you're both on your way, but wait! What if those airline baggage handlers are in a bad mood? It happens. I once saw one stand on the box holding my bike as he was stowing suitcases into the hold directly under me. And I yelled so loud that I think he heard me. This leads me to the philosophy espoused by those who wish to go the "box its" one better. They advocate the use of special bicycle travel cases. They're a great idea if you're traveling to some event and coming back home via the same airport. If you'll be pedaling from point A to point B, stick with the airline box unless you plan to tow the travel case along behind you. I've used a travel case, but I sold it because it took up too much space in my closet. If you have the space to store one, my cycling grapevine says the brand to get is BikePro. For your nearest dealer, write or call:

BikePro USA
3701 West Roanoke, Suite A
Phoenix, Arizona 85009
(602) 272-3588 or (800) 338-7581

Now for the "don't box it" philosophy. I know of plenty of people who just roll the bike up to the airport checkout counter and hand the thing over to the airline personnel, who in turn roll it into the plane's baggage compartment and away it goes. The reasoning behind this philosophy is that if the baggage handlers see what they've got to work with and can roll it rather than pitch it, they'll be nicer to it. I've shipped my bike as is and it has survived every time.

I've spent a lot of time talking about airlines, but the same caveats also apply to shipping bicycles on Amtrak trains and long distance buses. If you want to go Amtrak, you'll need to get a box for your bike—check your favorite local bike shop—or purchase one of theirs for $5.00. Also be aware that Amtrak only accepts bikes at stations with baggage service. As for the long-distance buses, I've heard more horror stories about them than I've ever heard about the airlines, but I can also tell you that last summer I took a 100-plus mile bus ride from Tucson to Phoenix and the bike came through with nary a scratch. I did't box the bike and and I loaded and unloaded it myself. Maybe I have a future in baggage handling.

•8•

Loss

I left the South long before I crossed the Mason-Dixon Line. It was around Richmond, Virginia, that I noticed the change. Those friendly little gas and groceries vanished. Once again, stores were places to dash in, buy something, then dash out again. Chat with the clerks? Never! It was rare enough to hear them mumble "Thanks" when they handed back the change.

I was never closer than 25 miles to either city, but the suburbs of Richmond and Washington had crept out into the woods and farmland, bringing with them people for whom rush hour was not an event, but a way of life. The locals no longer slowed down or stopped to chat when I pulled over to check my maps. Instead, they blasted by at 80 miles an hour or more. Back in rural Alabama and Georgia, I could hardly keep both hands on the bars for all my waving back at people. Now my waves were met with shocked stares and my hellos went unanswered.

The third week of June was a blur of states and places, of camping beneath the busy final approach to Washington's National Airport, being driven across the Chesapeake Bay Bridge outside Annapolis, then let off the state highway department truck on Maryland's Eastern Shore on U.S. 301, a six-laner full of speeding trucks, cars, and buses whose drivers glared at me as if to ask what I was doing on *their* road. Several trucks just missed clipping my left leg—deliberately, I think. I took their hint and gladly left that highway at Queenstown.

Cut off from the rest of Maryland by the Susquehanna River and the Chesapeake Bay, the Eastern Shore was essentially a separate state, and, some would say, a separate state of mind. "Don't give a damn about the rest of the state of Maryland," the locals' bumper stickers proclaimed, "I'm from the Eastern Shore." I pedaled past broad expanses of corn and soybeans that seemed straight out of Ohio, and the southern drawls and "Y'all come back now's" were as hearty as the ones I'd heard in Mississippi. I had to keep reminding myself that I was in *Maryland*.

On Friday evening, June 19, I found a secluded campground in the pines near the Chesapeake Bay. I pitched my tent on a thick bed of pine needles and let the breeze whispering through the branches lull me to sleep.

Later that night, a bright flash wrested me away from a dream. Then a thunderclap as loud as a cannon volley erased the rest of my sleepiness. I zipped up my tent flap and waited for the storm to pass. Silence and darkness settled in again. Good, I missed it. Then came the raindrops—gently at first— then with such a fury that I thought they'd pound right through the tent walls. The rain eventually tapered off, and I drifted back to sleep. Between sleep and restlessness, I rolled over into a puddle, which jolted me wide awake.

I gathered up my wet sleeping bag and crawled out into the darkness, which was still punctuated by lightning flashes. My perfect campsite was now a soggy mess. Those soothing breezes of the previous evening were now blowing cascades of droplets off the branches and on to me. That soft pine needle bed was now a squishy wet sponge. Groggily, I packed my wet gear, headed out to the road, and started riding in the predawn gloom.

Ahead of me was another storm moving in from the Bay. A thick pile of slate-gray clouds was plowing inland along the Chester River, and that front sent a stiff wind into my face. I rode across the river, right through those clouds, and only caught a few drops. North of the river, the wind became southeasterly, and pushed me past cornfields, barns, still darkened farmhouses, and historical markers announcing the sites of Indian camps, Revolutionary War officers' birthplaces, and treaty signings.

I rolled up to a restaurant in Galena just as the owner was unlocking the front door, and I gave him the first big breakfast order of the day. As I devoured my scrambled eggs, pancakes, and orange juice, the local farmers began filing in. I heard one say an inch of rain came down in one hour last night.

"Yeah, I was in it," I said, not lifting my bleary eyes from my plate.

"Your bike out there?" someone asked.

"Yeah."

"You're gonna get rained on some more today."

"Thanks."

The gray clouds stayed right with me, sending down an occasional sprinkle, but no more deluges. Overcast Saturday or not, the race to the beach was heating up on Maryland Route 213. The cars towing boats were out in force, as were the station wagons packed with coolers, blankets, tents, stoves, beach balls, and umbrellas. They all rolled southward, like cannonballs fired out of Wilmington and Philadelphia. Few drivers honked at me—most stared straight ahead. What lay ahead was their goal. What was passing by their windows was only to be gotten through, not tarried in, mulled over, or recalled later.

After Elkton came the Mason-Dixon Line and a sign urging me to respect Pennsylvania's traffic laws. Then I plunged downhill on a road so potholey into a valley so steep that I clung to my brakes for dear life and pleaded for the descent to stop. The other side of the valley stopped it cold, and I jumped out of the saddle and cranked my hardest. My chest heaved and my heart pounded so hard I thought it would hammer right through my ribcage. Halfway to the top, I had to get off and walk, although I really could have crawled.

But I was back in my home territory, Chester County, where I grew up. And it would only be a few more miles before I'd see my parents. After covering nearly 2,000 miles in seven weeks, I felt entitled to a break from this ride.

My parents were out working in the yard when I pulled into their driveway.

"Who's that?" my mom gasped. She'd just come face to face with a grinning, mud-spattered bicyclist with the jersey rotting off her back and hanging down below her backside, which was barely covered by a pair of sagging shorts.

"It's Martha!" my dad shouted, and then it was time for lots of hugging and catching up on the latest news from the road since I'd scrawled them a postcard the week before.

Having never seen me after a long, sweaty day of riding, my parents were shocked at my disheveled appearance. Even Max the dachshund hesitated to let me into the house, and he sounded a few warning barks before bursting into a fit of tail wagging and face licking. My next stop was the shower.

I stayed there almost a month, slept in until noon every day and hardly rode at all, except for a morning jaunt into Delaware with the local Brandywine Bicycle Club. I turned my parents' basement into a workshop, stripped my bike down to its nuts, bolts, and bearings and removed seven weeks' accumulation of crud from every place I could get at with solvent, toothpicks, dental floss, and toothbrushes. I retired my tattered cycling togs to the rag bag after purchasing new ones in Philadelphia.

The night before I left, my dad and I went for a swim at the YMCA. Mom met us at the door when we got home, and she handed me a telephone message.

"Dot Reynolds called. She said she got your postcard." Three weeks ago, I'd written to assure her that I had made it to my parents' house.

"Oh, good! How's she doing? She say if Hugh Baird got back yet?"

"He didn't. He was killed in Kansas crossing a bridge over the Arkansas River. A 77-year-old man hit him. Mrs. Reynolds hasn't heard a thing from him. I talked to her for awhile."

I kept calm. I went upstairs. I gathered up my things. I packed them up again. But I didn't get much sleep that night. I left the next day, Tuesday, July 14. Mom and I cycled a mile together, then we hugged long and hard, like we'd never see each other again. Hugh Baird's death showed just how possible that could be.

The tree-lined country lanes and horse farms on the way to Valley Forge didn't charm me at all. My mind was back in Louisiana. Just a half-hour before I called Dot from that store in Scotlandville, Hugh Baird had left on his trip. How close I came to meeting him then. Having missed that opportunity, I hoped to see him on the road later in the summer. That wouldn't happen either.

I was full of questions that had no answers. Most of all, I wondered why I was chosen to go on while he wasn't. It could have happened to me. After all, I'd come within inches of getting killed back in Alabama. Even though we never met, I felt like I'd lost a close friend.

Inside Valley Forge Park, I could no longer hold back my tears, and I didn't care if I ever stopped crying. People in the visitors' center milled around me, but no one came forward to ask what me what the trouble was.

I pressed onward into New England. My legs automatically turned the cranks and my hands shifted the gears and worked the brakes, but my heart was no longer in this ride. The hilly country roads bordered by stone fences, groves of white birch, and 300-year-old houses covered with gray shingles—those New Englandy things all the guidebooks rhapsodized about—didn't move me. I just felt obliged to say I'd been through this part of the country.

My body was dead tired, but my mind was going 90 miles a minute. I thought back to all the months of preparation before this ride. I remembered that snowy January night in Ann Arbor when I told the bicycle club president of my plans to ride around America. "Yeah, that's about 10,000 miles," he said nonchalantly. "Takes about a year." Later, I measured my planned route on a U.S. map. Ten thousand miles it was. Almost halfway around the world.

Now, in the middle of July, I'd just passed 2,000 miles. I felt like I'd been riding forever, but I was barely into New England. The Appalachians, the Great Plains, the Rockies, and the Pacific coast still stood between me and my break in the Southwest. This ride would never end, and I was getting tired of it. I was tired of getting up at dawn and moving on—always moving on—but never lingering anywhere. I was tired of the uncertainty, of being at the mercy of the wind, rain, hills, heat and traffic. I was tired of the constant pain in my knees, butt, back, elbows, even my thumbs. I was tired of the people and all their questions, the same ones, over and over. Where was I from? Where was I going? Did I ever get scared? What kind of bike was that? What if I got a flat tire?

I wanted to go home, but where was that? I'd left my place in Ann Arbor and shipped all my things to my parents, and I hadn't lived in West Chester for more than a few months at a time since high school. I couldn't return to either place and call it home.

I stopped for a few days in Boston and wrote a note to Dot Reynolds while I was there. It started out as a sympathy note for her loss, then it became a sharing of my own anguish, the anguish of a 23-year-old who'd just discovered that not even she was immortal. I finished the note by telling Dot I'd complete my ride for Hugh Baird and dedicate it to his memory.

A year later, after the ride was done, I wrote letters to the people I'd met during my travels. Dot Reynolds' reply came on a postcard showing a paddlewheel steamer on a lake in the Alps. Her note consisted of a few joyful sentences about the European tour she'd decided to take, and concluded with the question, "Can you believe I ever got this far away from home?"

Absolutely, Dot. Absolutely.

THE BEST TOURING BIKE FOR YOU

Long distance tours have been done on every kind of machine imaginable, from unicycles to high wheelers, tandems to tricycles, and of course, on those trusty metallic burros known as touring bikes.

Exactly what is a touring bike? Simply put, it is a bicycle that is built strong enough to carry your gear and is comfortable enough to ride all day long. Ideally, touring bike frames should have built-in eyelets for mounting the racks on which you'll be hanging your panniers. Fender eyelets are also useful if you're planning to do a lot of touring in rainy areas. Touring frames also should have enough room to fit at least two water bottles.

Touring bikes tend to have long wheelbases and relaxed frame angles. The combination of these two attributes helps the bike absorb the road shocks, rather than your body. They also should have a wide range of gearing—18-speed or 21-speed drivetrains are optimal—so you can pedal in all kinds of terrain. Traditional touring bikes tend to have dropped handlebars, whereas the newer species of bike known as the "hybrid" tends to come with upright bars. The drop bars are nice to have, especially when you're hunkering down against a headwind. And last but not least, your touring bike should have a comfortable saddle.

Touring bikes aren't as widely available as they were when I first got serious about cycling, but they certainly haven't disappeared from the marketplace. My personal favorites? Here goes:

Cannondale, whose fat-tubed aluminum frame bikes have been piloted around the world several times. I own two Cannondale bikes, a racing bike and a mountain bike, and I like them a lot. Like their racing and mountain brethren, Cannondale's line of touring bikes feature well-built frames and high quality components. And hats off to Cannondale for creating manufacturing jobs in my home state of Pennsylvania. Every Cannondale bike frame is produced in Bedford, Pennsylvania, 100 miles east of Pittsburgh. For the name of your nearest dealer, write or call:

Cannondale Corporation
Friendship Road, RD #7
Bedford, Pennsylvania 15522
(800) BIKE USA (In Pennsylvania, 814/623-2626)

Terry Precision Bicycles for Women, Inc. It's been known for a long time that women are built differently from men, but you'd be amazed at how long it's taken the cycling industry to realize this fact. Georgena Terry is an avid cyclist and mechanical engineer who believes that the industry hasn't done a good job of serving the needs of women cyclists. She notes that most bike manufacturers produce bikes designed by men for men, who tend to be longer in the torso and narrower in the hips than women. These "industry standard" bike designs can make cycling a very painful experience for women, especially short women. (My own trouble with an "industry standard" bike is described on page 6.) Terry's bikes have solved the comfort problem for many short women cyclists and have thus turned cycling back into the enjoyable activity that it should be. For the name of your nearest dealer, write or call:

Terry Precision Bicycles for Women, Inc.
1704 Wayneport Road
Macedon, New York 14502
(800) 289-8379

If off-the-shelf touring bikes just aren't going to fill the bill for you, I'd like to suggest two more options. First, you could have a custom frame made by a builder. I happen to know a terrific framebuilder in Longmont, Colorado, by the name of Mark Nobilette. Tell him the Lone Rider sent you:

Nobilette Cycles
1616 South Horseshoe Circle
Longmont, Colorado 80501
(303) 682-9146

The second option involves a much greater amount of participation on your part: building your own custom frame. Not only will you have a bike frame to show for your efforts, you could also use the knowledge you've gained in your own framebuilding business. For information on framebuilding classes, contact:

Tim Paterek
Paterek Frames
935 Quarry Road
River Falls, Wisconsin 54022
(715) 425-9327

United Bicycle Institute
432 Williamson Way
Post Office Box 128
Ashland, Oregon 97520
(503) 488-1121

Paterek teaches his classes on a one-to-one basis. You can learn how to build a road, mountain or tandem bike. He also teaches frame repair classes. UBI offers group classes on road bike framebuilding with the world-renowned Albert Eisentraut. (He taught Nobilette back in the 1970s.) The framebuilding classes at both of these schools fill up fast, so register as far in advance as possible.

Before I leave you to your stationery or your telephone, a couple of thoughts about using mountain bikes and "hybrids" on long tours. In some parts of this country, Alaska in particular, a mountain bike is the optimal touring machine. The most interesting things to see aren't along the paved roads, so why not use the bike that best handles the back country? For more tips on mountain bike touring, check out *Mountain Bike Action* magazine. They have at least one good touring story per issue.

As for "hybrids," they're those bikes that look like road bikes on steroids or mountain bikes on a diet. Whatever your viewpoint, they're selling like crazy and people are doing tours on them. Nothing wrong with that, but you might find yourself wishing for dropped handlebars when headwinds come your way. If your hybrid comes with a straight bar, trade it for a drop-style. It'll make your headwind battles a little easier. You'll also want to reduce your bike's rolling resistance by replacing your knobby tires with a pair of slick (treadless) tires or tires with inverted treads.

•9•

Turnaround

The sluggishness I had felt when I arrived in Boston was transformed into a renewed sense of purpose by the time I left the city on Monday morning, July 27. I hadn't been this ready to hit the road since I left Ann Arbor.

As the morning rush hour traffic brought the white collared legions in from the suburbs, I headed out. I gazed long and hard at the serious expressions on the faces of the well-scrubbed drivers hurrying into town. Many of them appeared to be in their early twenties like me. What different paths our lives had taken. I could just as easily have become one of them. Out on my bike, I certainly wasn't earning their $35,000 a year—I was living off of savings. But I was free of their car payments, house mortgages, credit card statements and dry cleaning bills.

Unlike many of my commuter counterparts, I didn't need a two-story house and a mini-warehouse unit to store my possessions. What I needed for my day-to-day existence was the 20 pounds of gear I was carrying with me. The remainder of my worldly goods was stowed neatly into a corner of my parents' basement.

Instead of being ruled by an alarm clock by the bedside, then an office clock later on, I lived each day in tune with the rhythms of nature. I got up at dawn and retired at sunset. I spent the better part of each day outside, moving under my own power, in conditions most others tried to manipulate or avoid. But I couldn't. I had no control over the sun, the wind, the rain or the fog. My "job" was to adjust myself and my cycling to whatever Mother Nature dished out. In short, I had taken that proverbial road less traveled. And not for one moment did I want to trade places with those rush hour commuters.

Once out of Boston, I pedaled along the North Shore, right next to beaches jammed with people seeking relief from the midsummer heat. I spent my first night away from the city in the coastal resort of Marblehead, where I stayed with the family of a college housemate who was away on an archeological dig in Italy. Around the dinner table, I recalled all the times back in Ann Arbor when that hard driving perfectionist Jennifer Brehob would get on everyone else's case to keep our communal kitchen and bathroom clean.

"This is a co-op, not a pigsty!" she'd exclaim as she wiped up the ever-present pile of crumbs around the toaster, or scraped crud off the bathtub drain.

Report card time was one of intense agony for Jennifer, and from the basement to the attic, we'd hear her lamenting that one B that tarnished her otherwise sterling record of straight A's. Quite a contrast from her easygoing brothers, Bart and Geoff, who graduated from high school "in a photo finish," according to their father.

Before I left the Brehobs, I took a walk out to Marblehead Point and dipped my toes in the Atlantic Ocean. Three months later, I would repeat this ritual at the Pacific shoreline. But an entire continent still loomed ahead of me, and I was anxious to head west, so I postponed my plans for going into Maine until some future ride. I started west from Durham, New Hampshire, on July 30.

Crossing New Hampshire, Vermont, Massachusetts, New York, and Pennsylvania, I tackled just about every mountain range in the Northeast, along with their interminable foothills. These mountains were short, steep 1,000-footers that had me out of the saddle and stomping on the pedals as I inched toward the top. Then I'd streak downhill, shrieking with terror and delight. On August 13 came the high point of my battle with the Appalachians—2,200-foot Cresson Mountain, a 10-mile climb outside Altoona, Pennsylvania. At the summit, I tumbled to the ground, gasping for breath. There I remained, flat on my back, for almost an hour.

The narrow, winding road down from Cresson was full of half-filled potholes and coal chunks that had fallen off mining trucks. That old state road deteriorated even further as it passed through little towns full of soot-covered houses. Sitting on porches were round-bellied men and women sipping cold cans of Iron City beer, following me with mournful eyes. These were steelworkers' towns, but those jobs were gone now. All that remained for the inhabitants was the waiting—waiting for the unemployment check, waiting to be called back to work, waiting for times to get better and something else to open up, and until then, the slow death by waiting. In Johnstown, the huge Bethlehem Steel plant that once lit up the night sky as bright as day stood silent, closed indefinitely, I'd heard.

As a western Pennsylvania native, I knew well the sulphurous smell that filled the air when the steel mills were operating. I hadn't lived there for almost 20 years, and I strained my nostrils for just a hint of that familiar odor, but the air was very clean.

Two days later, I was standing in a gas station office in West Newton, making a long distance call that the manager generously offered to pay for. Twenty-five miles away, my friend Gary Naeser picked up the phone in the log cabin he and his wife Joanne built together above Washington, Pennsylvania. I told him I was mighty tired of pushing my loaded bike up every damn hill I came to, and had no idea when I'd make it to his place. He told me to stay on the road I'd been traveling all morning, and he'd come out and get me.

We met each other along the banks of the Monongahela River. Gary tied my bike to the back bumper and door frames of his VW Beetle, then we drove off into a downpour that lasted all afternoon. Gary, Joanne, and I spent the rest of the day swapping stories of log cabin building and bicycle touring over a huge meal and endless rounds of beer. That evening, Gary drove me and the bike down to his parents' homestead.

I'd known the Naeser family almost all my life. Gary's father, Curt, was known throughout western Pennsylvania for his storytelling ability, and one of his all-time favorites concerned how he met my father. The Naesers and my family attended the same church when we lived in Peters Township, outside Pittsburgh. Curt and my dad ushered together one morning, something Curt had looked forward to for a long time.

"I'd heard about this guy Retallick, but I'd never gotten a chance to meet him," Curt recalled. "After we'd taken the collection, we were standing in the back of the church with the plates full of money, waiting to be called up front. Retallick stood there, straight as an arrow, eyes forward. Looking at this guy, I felt like I was back in the Army, waiting for inspection.

"He hadn't said a word to me all morning, so I leaned over and whispered, 'How much did you keep?'

"Well, he turned and glared at me, and said 'Pardon me?'" Curt scrunched up his face, mimicking my father's indignant expression.

"I was trying pretty hard to keep a straight face now, but I asked him again, 'How much did you keep?'

"He turned and glared at me even harder and said, 'Nothing, of course!'"

After the service, Curt explained that he was only kidding, and he hadn't pegged my scrupulously honest father as a thief. Curt was only trying to break the ice. That did it.

But if there were ever a case of opposites attracting, this was it. My father, a taciturn fellow who stayed trim by running and lifting weights, was pulled into the world of this pudgy, wisecracking guy who wasn't about to let anyone ignore him. Like that first taste of the forbidden fruit, my dad loved Curt's constant teasing, his off-color jokes, and all those stories. Because my dad has a Ph.D. in chemical engineering, Curt insisted on calling him "Doctor," despite his weak protestations that someone might call on him to deliver a baby.

When I was a kid, Curt never failed to make me laugh. He could make his big blue eyes bulge out like one of those Saturday morning cartoon characters. He could wiggle his ears, and I'd wear out every little muscle on my face trying to wiggle mine. I never could. Curt would take ordinary dime store balloons and stretch and twist them into the shapes of cats, dogs, and monkeys, then present them to me and his three kids. He'd put pennies on the railroad tracks, then instruct us kids to watch carefully as the train went by. After the train was gone, we'd scurry over and retrieve the flattened copper disks, now the size of silver dollars.

My family moved to eastern Pennsylvania when I was six. The Naesers stayed in Peters Township. On the surface, they had it made. They lived in a cozy Colonial house below Pleasant Valley School, where I'd spent some of first grade. The high school was just up the road, an easy walk for Peter, Gary, and Ruthie, who were into everything from drama club to varsity football. An engineering manager, Curt continued to climb Bell Telephone's corporate ladder, and Ruth was the school nurse at Pleasant Valley.

But the Naesers felt trapped. All around them, the dairy farms and wooded hillsides were being turned into subdivisions. Rural Peters Township was rapidly becoming a bedroom suburb of Pittsburgh, a prestige address for the upwardly mobile.

Like many other suburbanites, the Naesers dreamed of building a log cabin in the woods somewhere. In June 1971, they followed their homesteading dream to a wide spot in a creek hollow called Good Intent. Good Intent is just 30 miles from Peters Township, but it seems light years away.

The Naesers constructed their log cabin from used telephone poles Curt procured from his employer. The construction itself was a group project, with friends and relatives coming from all over the country to help.

In November 1971, Curt suffered a heart attack, but work on his dream home continued while he was in the hospital. He went home at Thanksgiving, deeply depressed and not about to share in any of the holiday spirit that had taken over Good Intent. In the kitchen, Ruth treaded carefully through a maze of sawhorses while trying to cook the turkey. My father came out for his annual deer hunt on the adjoining state game lands, and Peter and Gary put his carpentry skills to good use in hanging the powder room door. In the living room, Curt sat bundled up in a warm down jacket, glumly watching his two sons and their college buddies laying stone for the fireplace and chimney.

Curt's doctors said he'd have to take it very easy for the rest of his life. Ruth insisted that her husband would never accept life on the sidelines; there had to be something they could do for him. Fortunately, there was a solution, a new surgical technique called the coronary bypass. If it was successful, Curt might be able to resume an active life. But with such a new and risky procedure, they weren't making any promises. In April 1972, Curt became one of the first people in western Pennsylvania to undergo bypass surgery. The operation was a success, and Curt bounced back, ornery as ever.

Like every other visitor to their homestead, the Naesers immediately put me to work. Several weeks before, Ruth broke her arm while running for the phone, so I took over many of her tasks. For a week, I washed the dishes, chopped vegetables from their organic garden, fed the chickens, and gathered their eggs for our breakfasts. Unfortunately, another homestead guest, their daughter Ruthie's Alaskan malamute, killed one quarter of the chicken flock and sent the rest into hiding for a couple days. Curt gave that dog a good thrashing, and tied a dead chicken around his neck. Frostie learned his lesson well—he steered clear of the chickens after they returned.

Curt and Ruth intended their country lifestyle to be as self-sufficient as possible. They were fully prepared to live without outside electric power. There were numerous candles and lamps around the house to provide light during power failures. They normally used an electric motor to run their well pump, but their water system could also run on gravity. Every appliance in their house could run on a 12-volt battery.

"We can funnel electricity into that battery and store it for later use," Curt explained. "If we ever lost West Penn Power for an extended period of time, we could build a little water wheel on the creek out in front of the house and use that battery as part of our own power plant."

The Naesers maintained that in cloudy western Pennsylvania, solar energy was not a feasible way to heat one's house. "Best alternative energy around here is wood," Curt said, patting the cast iron Cawley LeMay woodstove in the kitchen corner. They used a woodburning furnace and their fireplace to heat the rest of the house.

When the Naesers first came to Good Intent, no one else in the area sold woodstoves. They ordered one from an out-of-state company, then became distributors for that line of stoves. Curt and Ruth called their new venture the Good Intent General Store. Since there was no room in the house to store their inventory, they began selling stoves from their front porch.

Then the energy crisis hit, and heating with wood became enormously popular. Business took off, and was just beginning to slow down. The Naesers no longer sold stoves on the porch. The Good Intent General Store had moved into an attractive two-story log building on the edge of their property.

In 1977, the store was busy enough for Curt to take early retirement from Bell. A year later, Peter and Gary quit their teaching jobs to start Good Intent Log Homes. The brothers quickly developed a reputation for being two of the finest custom builders in western Pennsylvania.

In a year when most builders were glad to have one house under construction, the Naesers had half a dozen going at once. Some were preplanned and precut packages they'd sold to do-it-yourselfers who'd then gain the valuable experience of building their own log home. Then there was the $200,000 luxury model they had begun building on speculation, hoping to attract a buyer as construction progressed. It was a big gamble, big enough to bankrupt them, but a doctor from Pittsburgh bought the house before the foundation hole was finished.

When Ruth didn't need me, I climbed aboard the Good Intent General Store Jeep and accompanied Curt on errands for his sons. Curt skillfully maneuvered the Jeep on the narrow dirt roads that hugged the steep hillsides around the homestead, and with a big chaw of Red Man firmly planted in his cheek, he'd expound on everything from how the family's organic garden was growing to politics. A lifelong Republican and staunch conservative, he could hardly suppress his joy over seeing one of his own occupying the White House after decades of "big spending liberals and do-gooders" whom he believed were ruining the country.

As for my bicycling around America, he minced no words: "You're *nuts*." He very much wanted to talk about what I was planning to do with the rest of my life, but he also understood what motivated my quest.

"I guess you're a lot like our daughter, Ruthie," Curt said. "She got restless living down in Good Intent with us old folks, and she wanted to get out on her own. So she joined the Air Force and they trained her to be a jet mechanic and stationed her up in Alaska." Ruthie met her husband up there, and had a baby just a month before I left Ann Arbor.

Yes, I was restless, I said. I had grown up in the affluent suburbs of Pittsburgh and Philadelphia, where everything from grade school music lessons to my college education was paid for and given to me by my parents. Of course my parents hadn't gone as far as some in the neighborhood, and given me my own phone line or a sports car for my sixteenth birthday. I had led a very sheltered life, and at age 23, I felt I had to test my mettle out in the world. My parents did give me some money when I first graduated from college, and that money bought me my first ten-speed bicycle. But they did not pay one cent toward the $1,000 price tag of my Nobilette bike. Nor did my parents give me any money to finance my two-wheeled travels. It was all my own money, and I wouldn't have it any other way. I had vowed from the start that this venture would have only one financier: me.

Even after hearing this explanation, Curt was still adamant. "You've got to get down to the business of making a living. What was your major in college?"

"Economics."

"With that I can get you an interview with a bank vice president I know up in Pittsburgh. They'd snap you right up."

I squirmed in my seat as the thoughts I wanted so badly to put into words twisted themselves into knots. Yes, this ride had to end someday. I was hoping that in the course of my travels I'd find a place to land, a place I could call home. A part of me sensed that I had already found it. After what seemed like an eternity, I was able to speak.

"Pittsburgh will still be around when I finish riding, won't it?"

"Sure!"

"I guess you know that after my family moved east, I never really felt at home there. I always wanted to come back here."

"So, what's stopping you from doing that?"

"Nothing. Nothing at all."

No matter where we'd gone or what we'd done, the highlight of Curt's and my day came when we returned to Good Intent, and we'd all settle into the soft, cozy chairs on the porch to watch the creek gurgling by. Ruth would pour everyone a glass of wine, Curt would make a selection from their vast record collection, switch on the outside speakers, then fill the valley with Bach organ fugues.

"I don't have to keep up with the Joneses," Curt boasted one evening. "I'm Jones."

But this unique couple had attracted more than their share of would-be Joneses. The Naesers played host to a steady stream of visitors interested in their lifestyle. TV and newspaper reporters had made the 50-mile trek from Pittsburgh to do stories on them.

"All our kids' college friends have come here, and they thought it was really neat," Ruth said, mimicking their young visitors' starry-eyed expressions.

"We think it's real neat too," she continued. "We've never regretted coming to Good Intent, but what we've got here wasn't handed to us on a silver platter."

The credo of the Naesers' country lifestyle could well have been summed up by the little magnetic plaque on their refrigerator that read, "Often, people fail to recognize opportunity because it comes dressed in overalls. And it looks like work."

On that romantic notion of moving out to the country and living off the land, Curt warned that it couldn't be done. "You've got to have a cash flow," he insisted. "If you don't, you'll be flat broke and back in the city within six months."

To keep that cash flowing, the Naesers devoted far more time to keeping their woodstove and log home businesses prospering than they did to putting the final touches on their still unfinished cabin and maintaining their organic garden. The garden had obviously not been weeded in months—the weeds stood taller than most of the crops. Such neglect was all part of Curt's "German philosophy" of gardening: "Grow...or die." Despite its unkempt appearance, the Naesers' garden produced some very tasty vegetables.

On Thursday, August 20, I left Good Intent. Her arm freed from its cast on Tuesday, Ruth fixed us her first big two-handed breakfast. We feasted on omelettes and whole wheat toast to the accompaniment of a German marching band record Curt had selected for this day. For tending the chickens, the Naesers presented me with a Good Intent Log Homes patch, which I sewed onto my cycling jersey's right shoulder. Curt drove me and the bike out to U.S. 40, gave me a bear hug, then I rolled ten miles downhill to Wheeling, West Virginia.

CARRYING YOUR LOAD

If you're taking more than yourself and your credit card on tour, you're going to need to find some means of carrying all your goodies. The most popular way to do this is to let the bike be your beast of burden—with some help from bike racks and packs.

For years, my basic touring setup has been a handlebar bag up front and a back rack to hold two panniers (what the equestrians call saddlebags), my sleeping bag and my tent. That's it. My load usually weighs 20-25 pounds, which makes me a real light traveler among cycletourists. That's okay by me, because I believe that cycletouring provides excellent practice in living without all of those material possessions that are so exalted in our culture. (There's a discussion of what I take on tour in "Trip List," page 222.)

My alltime favorite brands of cycletouring luggage have been the Eclipse Standard handlebar bag and MPacks panniers. Eclipse was cofounded by one of the members of the Ann Arbor Bicycle Touring Society, so I got a good indoctrination in his firm's emphasis on quality while I lived in that city. His products lived up to his words—it took me years to demolish my first Eclipse bag, which I replaced with another. Eclipse no longer makes the Standard model, but they still offer their top-of-the-line Professional handlebar bag. For more information, write or call:

Eclipse USA
3771 East Ellsworth Rd.
Ann Arbor, Michigan 48108
(313) 971-5552

For more information on MPacks, write or call:

Ibis Cycles
Box 275
Sebastopol, California 95473
(707) 829-5687

I'll preface my next pannier recommendation with this caveat: I've never owned the product myself. However, the connoisseurs tell me that Robert Beckman Designs are the ones to get. They're fairly expensive, but I'm told they're worth every penny. I'm promising myself a set for my next long tour. For the name of your nearest dealer, write or call:

Robert Beckman Designs
Post Office Box 6952
Bend, Oregon 97708
(503) 388-5146

Concerning racks, I've been a Blackburn user since I took my first tour. My Blackburn rear rack has been sturdy enough to handle my loads, it's reasonably priced, and it's widely available. Since heavily loaded handlebar bags can cause the front of the bike to oscillate, Jim Blackburn is a strong advocate of using a "low rider" rack on which to hang front panniers. He makes two very fine models for this purpose, but I've never used them. Why not? First, I think that the bag between the handlebars provides more protection for my camera than would a low-riding pannier on the outside of the front fork. Second, my touring loads have never been big enough to require front panniers. (I am careful not to put much more than the camera up front, because my bike does tend to oscillate when the handlebar bag's heavily loaded.)

There are a couple of other approaches to this load-carrying business. The first approach is for the ultra-light types, the ones who'd rather not carry much more than a change of clothes and a toothbrush. That's too small of a load to fill a pannier, but too big of a load to put in a seat pack. So consider the day saddlebags made by Custom Cycle Fitments. They attach to the bicycle seatpost and a special hanger that bolts to the saddle rails. For more information, write or call:

Custom Cycle Fitments
726 Madrone Avenue
Sunnyvale, California 94086
(408) 734-9426

The other approach involves a line of reasoning that goes something like this: rather than hang the load on the bike where it's just dead weight, why not put it on wheels and let it roll too? In other words, put your load in a trailer and tow it along behind you. I use a Burley Tourist trailer for running errands around town, and I'm strongly tempted to take it on tour sometime. Its effect on bike handling is negligible, and it comes with a bright orange flag that's very visible in traffic. People who've done long distance tours with trailers tell me that they can get squirrely in crosswinds, but loaded bikes can also do that. For the name of your nearest dealer, write or call:

Burley Design Cooperative
4080 Stewart Road
Eugene, Oregon 97402
(503) 687-1644

• 10 •

Great Plains, High Plains

In mid-Ohio, the twisting, winding roads of the eastern hills gave way to the straight-arrow roads of the Great Plains. At one-mile intervals, side roads intersected the main highways at precise right angles. In the Midwest, I found myself in a giant checkerboard of corn and soybean fields, the crops fully grown and ready for harvest.

I shared the roads with bright yellow buses full of kids heading back to school. Inside those buses, the eyes of every passenger were fixed on me. Some of the kids giggled and jostled to get a better view of the strange, helmeted creature pedaling down the road, others made faces and gave me the finger while shouting wisecracks out the windows, and one or two stared enviously at me, just like I used to do when my junior high bus passed those scruffy, backpack-toting hitchhikers back in eastern Pennsylvania. How lucky they were, I'd muse. They were on their way to someplace very far away from West Chester. As for me, I was trapped inside this bus, on my way to another day of agony as an awkward eighth-grader at Stetson Junior High. Ten years later, my adolescence was just a bittersweet memory, and now I was the object of envy for a new generation of would-be nomads.

Planted at ten-mile intervals in the Midwestern checkerboard were towns with plain, no-nonsense names like New Concord, Zanesville, and Gibson City. Just like the surrounding countryside, the towns were laid out in a grid, with a square in the middle containing the city hall or county courthouse. From

Ohio to Iowa, I found little variation in the grid-around-the-square theme, but as similar as all the towns appeared, it seemed as if they all were engaged in a great American superlatives contest.

Many had the name and likeness of their high school mascot painted on the municipal water tower. Any state championships won by the local baseball, basketball, or volleyball teams were sure to be proclaimed at the city limits along with the population and speed limit.

Famous townsfolk were prominently mentioned as well. Cambridge, Ohio, staked its claim in history as the birthplace of Mercury astronaut John Glenn, while across the state, a tongue twister of a place called Wapakoneta had produced moonwalker Neil Armstrong. Galesburg, Illinois, described by one of its present day inhabitants as "one of the most boring places on earth," was the birthplace of poet Carl Sandburg.

A "blink and you miss it" crossroads called Batavia, Iowa, compensated for its small size by proclaiming that it was "on the way to everywhere." Then there was Stanton, Iowa, which bade me "Willkomen," and boasted that it was the home of the world's largest Swedish coffee pot.

It was a pot of a different kind that caught my eye in Stanton. Growing in a creek bed on the edge of town was the thickest, lushest stand of marijuana I'd ever seen. Back in Ann Arbor, such a healthy crop would have been picked clean before it was knee high. Out here, it was growing wild and free. Perhaps all those stories I'd heard about Iowa's unsophisticated bumpkins were true. I couldn't believe I'd happened on an entire town that didn't know what marijuana looked like, much less what it could do.

I knew exactly what it could do. Standing on the bridge over that creek, I toyed with the idea of picking some leaves, flattening and drying them in my handlebar bag mapcase, then mailing a sample back to my Ann Arbor friends with a little note bragging how I got absolutely free what they were paying $40 an ounce for.

But the road I'd stopped on was too busy to allow me to carry out my mission. I left the Stanton pot crop undisturbed, a wise move, since the first person I spoke to in the next town of Red Oak was an off-duty state trooper.

I later found out from a streetwise Methodist minister that what I'd coveted was not marijuana, but wild hemp.

"You can't get high off that stuff," he chuckled. "All it does is give you a bad cough!"

On Labor Day weekend, I crossed the Missouri River into Nebraska. Now I had a new carrot to dangle in front of me, to ride into that place the Iowans called "out west." I was headed toward a place I'd only heard about and seen in pictures. Now was my chance to ride into those pictures and see if all those superlatives really fit.

In Nebraska, I began to comprehend the meaning of "wide open spaces." In the east, I was rarely more than ten miles from a town. Now that distance had grown to twenty, even thirty miles. Between towns was the enormous silence of the high plains, occasionally broken by chirping crickets, bellowing cattle, and the wind in the tall grass.

I felt that to talk was to intrude on this silence, and my usual chatter to my bike dwindled away to almost nothing. I glided along as soundlessly as my shadow passing over the grass, gravel and sunflowers on the wayside. Set far back from the road were white farmhouses and barns surrounded by a few scrubby trees. The forests I'd left far behind in eastern Ohio; I wouldn't see them again until the Rockies.

This was the boring Midwest I'd heard about, the endless high plains the automobile drivers whipped through at 60 or 70 miles an hour on the interstates. For them, this was country to be gotten through, not tarried in. This treeless land was simple and spare, devoid of any embellishment. Moseying along at ten miles an hour, I savored every bit of it. This was land reduced to its basic elements: earth, water and sky.

In Franklin County, Nebraska, I hit a ten-mile stretch where I didn't see another person—no one in a car, outside a house, or on a tractor. I listened hard, but heard nothing but my legs pumping the pedals, the chain going 'round, and the telephone wires humming in the wind. I was truly alone, but unafraid. I'd found a place that seemed beyond civilization, a place where I could ride right down the middle of the road, or from side to side, over and over again. After all, only the road would know.

MONEY MATTERS

When asked how much it costs to be on the road, I'd have to say that it depends on what kind of a tour you want to do. When pinned down, I'll confess that it cost me around $10 a day when I was camping out or staying with people I met along the way. When my lodging took the form of hotels or motels, that cost-per-day went up by at least a factor of three.

More confessions. Throughout most of my travels, I was living off of savings, which I converted into traveler's checks at periodic intervals. My *modus operandi* was to call my credit union in Ann Arbor and have them wire me more funds via Western Union. I'd then take the Western Union check to the local bank and convert it into traveler's checks—$20 was the optimal denomination for small towns.

This system worked without a hitch during my first two long trips, but I ran into problems on my 1987 trip, the details of which are explained in the "Fan Letter to a Bank" chapter. Without giving away that whole story, let me say that you should make sure that your financial institution is willing to send funds to you while you're traveling and know what their fund transfer procedures are before you hit the road.

I used no credit cards until 1990, and I didn't figure out how to use my long distance calling card until last year, so I'm not much help there. I do know of other cycletourists who have put a trustworthy friend or relative in charge of paying their credit card and phone charges while they were gone, and they have spoken quite highly of this arrangement.

I carried cash in a wallet that always stayed with me. Traveler's checks stayed inside a plastic pouch that held other important papers such as airline tickets, an address book and my journal. I hid this pouch in various places inside the bike packs, a strategy I highly recommend.

While I've heard stories of other cycletourists being robbed during their travels, this has never happened to me. I feel very fortunate. I attribute at least some of this luck to not discussing my finances with anyone unless I was absolutely sure I could trust that individual with the information. In other words, I rarely talked about money matters. I strongly advise that you also keep mum about your finances during your travels—be safe rather than sorry.

• 11 •

Rocky Mountain Breakdown

I entered eastern Colorado thinking I'd immediately see the snowcapped peaks of the Rockies, but it was home to the same grassy, windswept plains as Nebraska. The ever, increasing elevation figures posted at the edge of every town— along with that shortness of breath I felt at the top of every hill—assured me I was gaining altitude.

Two days and 70 miles into Colorado, I stayed overnight in the village of Akron. I stopped in the library to look up phone numbers of bike shops in the larger towns ahead so I could replace some worn-out parts, and was invited to come home with the librarian after she closed the building. Margaret Cooley also wrote for Akron's weekly paper, which her late husband once published. As soon as we got home, she brought out her camera and notebook, and turned my journey into a feature story for the next issue.

Over supper, Margaret informed me that Akron was situated on the loftiest spot between Omaha and Denver. "Sometimes you can see the mountains from the edge of town," she added. After we finished our meal, we drove to a rise west of Akron to look for those elusive Rockies. No luck.

We drove further west into the prairie, watching the tall grass undulating in the breeze like an inland sea. Far off to my right stood a rock formation with sheer sides and a flat top. It looked like the birthday cake my mother used to bake when I was little.

"That's a butte," Margaret said, sensing my fascination with this thing I'd never seen before. "You'll see lots more of them. They're pretty common around here. That one's called Fremont Butte. When I was a little girl, we used to have our school picnics out there."

"Can you climb that thing?" I asked, picturing myself with a rope around my shoulder and climbing hardware dangling from my belt.

"I suppose you could," she replied matter-of-factly. I gathered that butte climbing had not been within her realm of experiences. I pictured those long-ago picnics with Margaret and the other girls wearing their Sunday best, clothing intended for climbing the local social ladder, not Fremont Butte. When she was growing up, little girls certainly weren't encouraged to climb buttes, much less trees or fences. Rare indeed was the girl who was permitted to ride a bicycle, and those who did never went too far from home.

When I was growing up, the bicycle was something we kids used to get around the neighborhood until we got our driver's licenses. Although the local boys did it regularly, pedaling the three miles between our homes in Westtown Township and West Chester was considered far too dangerous for any girl. Pedaling a bicycle around the country? That was totally unheard of. During my three weeks in Westtown, my former neighbors repeatedly expressed astonishment at my journey, and marveled that I must have possessed a superhuman amount of bravery to be doing it alone.

I assured them that my ride was not as fraught with peril as they thought. In fact, it was quite the opposite. The great majority of my days on the road consisted of long, seemingly endless stretches of repetitive motion. For me, this long-distance cycletouring business had become as routine as another day at the office was for them.

The next morning, Margaret bade me farewell and gave me the address of her daughter, Cathy Rohne, a journalism student at the University of Northern Colorado in Greeley.

"She writes for the local paper. Maybe she'll want to do a story on you, too," Margaret said.

Two days later, I rolled into Greeley, just 35 miles from the Front Range of the Rockies. I still hadn't seen the barest outline of those mountains. The only clue that indicated the existence of any mountains in this state was that silhouette of a snow-capped range on Colorado's license plates.

Cathy Rohne was divorced and raising two grade-school-aged daughters by herself. She was just as interested in doing a story on me as her mother. Cathy sat me down in her apartment's kitchen and sent her daughters, Holly and Donella, away to do their homework and prepare a guest room for me. She proceeded to pepper me with questions, scribbling my responses in a little notebook. I felt like the kitchen was whirling around me, and my stomach heaved and churned. What I really wanted to do was lie down and take a nap on the floor. Cathy had rounded up some of her college friends and they were heading over to the local Pizza Hut for a feast in my honor. I could hear Holly and Donella getting psyched up for some pizza, but the very thought of food nauseated me.

"Cathy, uh, I feel pretty, umm...tired right now," I stammered. "Can I rest up 'til it's time to go?"

"Sure," she said, and escorted me back to my room. I flopped down on the bed and fell asleep. After what seemed like five seconds, Cathy tapped on the door and announced that she and the girls were leaving. I got up, followed them down to the car, and embarked on an excruciatingly long ride to the Pizza Hut. My stomach and bowels had begun turning flips. As soon as we got to the restaurant, I sprinted to the restroom and threw up the hot pepper omelette I had for breakfast at a truck stop. Then my bowels kicked out their own contribution. Pizza was now out of the question, so I watched my newfound friends chow down. Unfortunately, I got to know the restroom far better than any of them.

After we returned home, I spent the rest of the day attempting to sleep and racing to the bathroom, hoping each time that this trip would be the last. Early in the evening, I tottered out to the living room, where the Rohnes were watching TV.

"Look out the window, Martha," Cathy said.

I looked out across the Greeley skyline and there it was, the Front Range. Thirty-five miles away stood a wall, one I'd soon have to surmount. With a mixture of reverence and trepidation, I watched those dark mountains fade into the night sky.

The rest of Thursday, September 17, and the next day consisted of huddling in my sleeping bag, alternating between sweaty, fitful sleep and body-wracking chills, and dashing to the bathroom to empty my guts. All day Friday, I watched the western horizon for my mountains, but the city haze blocked them out. They returned at dusk, and so did my appetite. I nibbled a little supper and prayed my digestive system would treat it kindly. It did.

I left the Rohnes on Saturday afternoon and headed out into a stiff, chilly breeze off the mountains. Still weak from my illness, I pedaled 20 shaky, sweaty miles into Loveland and got my first good look at the Rockies from the edge of town. Thick black clouds hugged the peaks, and sent darts of lightning down the slopes and peals of thunder across the plains. I started asking myself some hard questions about the soundness of my plan to cross that range. On my bike, I'd be a perfect lightning rod.

The rest of the day was devoted to buying the bike parts I needed to replace. While the owner of one shop assembled a workable tire pump for me, I read the 1981 Coors Bicycle Classic program. It was full of pictures of sturdy young men and women with treetrunk thighs pedaling up impossible mountain grades. The owner and his wife ecstatically reeled off the names of European and American cycling stars they'd met when the Coors came through in July.

During all my shopping around, the day had slipped away, and I informed this friendly couple that I needed to start looking for a place to stay. It had to be indoors, since I was still too woozy to camp out, and the overnight low was now getting down near freezing. The locals were saying that the first big snow was due any time.

"We'd invite you over any other night but this one," the owner said with a twinkle in his eye. "Tonight's our wedding anniversary. We want to be together—just the two of us."

Then he got on the phone and called every motel he could think of. As befitting a resort town on Saturday night, every one in Loveland was full. He finally found me a place 15 miles west of town in the Big Thompson River canyon. He also recruited another customer with a pickup truck to haul me up there.

My motel was a rustic group of log and stone cabins along the swift, narrow Big Thompson. The sun had already set behind the steep canyon walls, and darkness came quickly. I went inside and made a cozy cocoon beneath the thick, heavy blankets on my bed.

As exhausted as I was, sleep only came in bits and pieces. I spent most of the night tossing and turning, my mind gripped by terrifying visions of the mountain passes ahead. I wanted very much to believe the stories I'd heard from cyclists back in Iowa and Indiana about the Rockies being easy compared to the Appalachians. But the Loveland bike shop people said I'd be in for some rugged climbing. I wasn't a strong climber, but managed to survive the steep ten-mile ascents back east. Out here, the climbs would be 25, even 30 miles long. I wondered how long I could endure.

After chasing the will o' the wisp of sleep all night long, dawn felt like a relief. Usually, I was famished in the morning, but I could barely force down two little granola bars and the tin of chocolate pudding I'd bought as a treat for the mountains. I'd get my appetite back after a few miles of pedaling, I thought. My motel was at 5,000 feet, with 20 miles and 2,000 more feet between me and the end of the canyon outside Estes Park. I'd have no trouble making this climb, I thought. But the road to Estes turned into four hours of climbing hell. The rock-hard legs that brought me this far had suddenly turned into jelly. Over and over, I stopped and tumbled to the ground, gasping and clutching my chest. A steady stream of cars, motorcycles, and campers with license plates from all over America passed me by. Like me, they were headed for Rocky Mountain National Park just west of Estes Park. None of them stopped to gaze upon the writhing bicyclist on the shoulder. I wouldn't have cared if they did.

I barely got five miles away from the motel when the wind began inflicting its own torture. Icy gusts from the peaks of the Rockies hurtled down the narrow canyon and slammed right into me. In a restaurant parking lot at Drake, I spotted a group of cyclists. Hoping for a congenial bunch to ride with, I chatted with them while they took a break from their own climb. They were from Boulder, and roundly dismissed my claim that this was the toughest road in the world. Why, they did this stretch all the time, and they were anxious to get back on their bikes and drop this pesky flatlander. So off they went, riding in tight single file like a well-tuned locomotive with me on the back, a struggling caboose. They quickly shifted into high gear and sprinted away. I never saw them again, and was reduced to walking even the most level stretches until the wind died down and let me pedal into Estes Park.

Estes Park was surrounded by snowcapped mountains. Their lower slopes were covered by thick forests of yellow aspen and pine. To celebrate my arrival into the Rockies, I stopped at a restaurant done in Bavarian decor and ordered a big stack of blueberry pancakes. My stomach had been screaming for food, but after a couple bites, my pancakes tasted like cold oatmeal, and a whole pitcher of syrup didn't make them any more palatable. I pushed the plate away, paid the hefty bill, and then went into town and rented a motel room. As soon as I closed the door, I collapsed into bed—and stayed there for two hours.

Outside my window was Prospect Mountain, a ten-thousand-footer, according to my Colorado map. All over this town, I imagined that gift shops did a brisk business selling postcards of mountains just like this one to people who'd marvel to the folks back home about the breathtaking scenery. Yeah, it was breathtaking all right. I could barely breathe, let alone move.

Sunday was the day I made my weekly call to my parents. I lifted what felt like a lead weight of a receiver off the hook and with fumbling fingers dialed their number. They both got on the line, and in a high-pitched voice I described my battles with truckstop omelettes and the Front Range. They listened with the same concerned silence that usually resulted in a decision to take me to the doctor when I was a child.

When darkness came, I closed my eyes and sleep soon came, only to be wrested away in the middle of the night. No matter how I tried, I couldn't get it back. Next door, someone was snoring loud enough to wake the dead. I wanted to pound the walls and shout, but didn't want to risk being kicked out of this place. Instead, I yanked my sleeping bag off the bed, threw it on the floor, then pulled off all the covers and threw them down too. Then I crawled into my bag, pulled all the sheets and blankets over my head, and hoped this arrangement would block out that damn snoring. It didn't. I quickly found that the thinly carpeted cement floor was no place to rest my weary body, so I got back into bed, piled all the covers on my head, and eventually fell asleep. I woke up late the next morning, totally exhausted.

The road to Rocky Mountain National Park was mostly level. Even so, I lost count of the times I stopped to catch my breath, trying to gently lower the bike to the ground, but dropping it instead, then collapsing on the shoulder, each time banging a new set of bruises into my hips and palms.

Inside the park visitors' center, I spotted a sign describing the symptoms of altitude sickness: anxiety, dizziness, lethargy, loss of appetite, shortness of breath, and sleeplessness. They described me perfectly, and I wanted to scream it. But I wanted even more to keel over.

The only way out of this park was Trail Ridge Road, America's highest continuous paved highway. In just 44 miles, this road climbs from 8,000 feet to over 12,000 feet, then drops back to 8,000. Crossing the Rockies on Trail Ridge would be quite a feather to add to my cycling cap, but everyone had a different version of how tough a climb it was. Some assured me I'd have no problem at all, while others warned that I faced a steep grade all the way to the top. Since I had enough trouble keeping the bike upright on level ground, I decided to rest a few days and get used to the altitude. I pulled into the first campground after the visitors' center, Moraine Park.

Moraine was full of empty sites, and I could have stayed there for as long as I wanted without paying. The Park Service stopped charging after Labor Day. As befitting its name as the final resting place of glacial debris, Moraine Park was littered with boulders, rocks, and pebbles, which made finding a smooth tent site a tricky proposition.

As soon as I found an acceptable site and got my tent staked in, a storm rolled in and sent me scurrying inside. I tried to pass the time by writing in my journal while listening to the raindrops thudding on the tent walls and feeling the pebbles and stones painfully making their presence known in my back and legs. Outside, huge thunderclaps echoed off the mountains, and I nervously opened and closed the tent flap, hoping to see this cloudburst moving on. Storms come quickly in the Rockies, but they also stop as suddenly as someone turning off a faucet. When the rain ended, I crawled outside and found the grass and bushes soaking wet and the ground as dry as the moment I'd set up camp. I sat on the ground and kept writing while the gray-haired couple sitting outside the trailer across the road watched me with great interest.

"Would you like to come over for a cocktail?" the woman shouted.

I trotted right over. Not being a cocktail drinker, I ended up drinking a Coors beer and being adopted by Emiel and Eldora Ziebarth, retirees from nearby Longmont. They invited me to camp under the protection of their trailer canopy, which I did for a couple days. Emiel put a piece of carpet on the rocky ground, and I pitched my tent over it. Eldora loaned me a winter jacket and several blankets for the chilly mountain nights. During our first evening together, we feasted on Rocky Mountain trout freshly caught by Emiel. That trout brought back the appetite I thought I'd lost forever, and I emptied my plate several times.

After supper, we bundled up and drove to another section of the park, a valley that was closed to humans except for the road running through it. This was the elk mating ground. We humans clustered outside our cars and campers, with binoculars and cameras ready, waiting to hear the first male elk bugle, signaling the start of the evening's romance.

"There he is," Eldora whispered, intently studying a nearby meadow through her binoculars. She handed them to me, and I watched a bull elk emerge from the shadows, holding his antlers high. His lady friend followed, and they began grazing in the tall grass. Then we heard it, "A-yip, a-yip, yee-owww-ooo!" the call from a still unattached male, which was followed by some squeaks and squeals. To me, it sounded eerie, like the recorded songs of the humpback whale.

Far above us, on the mountain ridge at the south side of this valley, a line of headlights was snaking down a narrow road.

"That's Trail Ridge Road," Eldora told me.

"Way up there?"

"It goes a lot higher than that."

"How high up does it go?" I asked her the next morning.

"Up there," she said, pointing at a snowy ridge at the western end of the valley below our camp. With her outstretched finger, she traced the route of the road over the mountaintops. Eldora knew this road much better than the average Coloradoan, for when this old Indian trail was paved during the 'thirties, her father worked on the construction crew.

"My grandparents were sodbusters," she added, explaining that her family homesteaded on the high plains of eastern Colorado during the 1800s. It was then called the Colorado Territory—Colorado didn't attain statehood until 1876. Eldora's family built their house out of sod blocks, hence the nickname "sodbusters." At night the coyotes would climb on the roof and howl, which scared the daylights out of Eldora's grandmother.

"She thought they'd come in after her," Eldora chuckled. "They never did."

The Ziebarths drove me into Estes Park so I could buy food before tackling Trail Ridge Road the following morning. I wouldn't see another grocery store until Grand Lake, almost 50 miles away. I also stopped at a bike shop to replace my cycling shoes, which were about to fall apart. The owner sold me a new pair at cost, explaining that he didn't want any extra inventory since he was about to close for the winter.

The mountain chill drove me into my tent early that night, but I was too excited to sleep. The next day, Wednesday, September 23, I'd take on the toughest cycling challenge I'd ever faced. I was ready to go long before dawn. After breakfast, I thanked the Ziebarths for their hospitality, then I was off.

Unfortunately, my high spirits and newfound energy proved no match for the steep, winding ascent to the top of Trail Ridge. I ended up walking most of the 20 miles to the summit. Signs along the shoulder warned that this was a rough road, and to me that meant more than the bumpy pavement.

At 11,000 feet, the evergreen forest faded away. All that remained were a few gnarled trees, scrubby bushes with a green branch or two, and the gray carcasses of their brethren that had given up the fight to survive on the windswept tundra. Up there, nothing grew tall and leafy, and nothing grew through the grimy, soot-covered glaciers or the ancient lava flows. Clouds drifted close by my head, casually spilling rain as they went. Soon they would leave snow on this bare landscape and this road would be closed until late the following spring. During winter the snow would pile up, gradually burying the long wooden poles the Park Service planted on the roadside to gauge its depth.

Above the timberline, the wind blows hard enough to knock a hefty man off his feet. I leaned way into that icy gale, and it numbed my face and fingers. But I plodded onward, pushing my Nobilette wheelbarrow as my heart and lungs struggled to wrest some oxygen from the rarified air.

At 12,000 feet, even walking became a Herculean effort. At a scenic overlook full of cars and tourists, I let go of the bike and watched it clatter to the ground. Then my dizzy body followed, and I wound up half-sitting and half-lying on the ground.

A young woman came over and marvelled at my riding a bicycle all the way up here.

"Where are you from?" she asked.

"Mish-ah-gin."

"You must be in *great* shape!"

I stared at the ground, panting furiously. I didn't even have the strength to look up and reply.

After what seemed like an eternity, I was able to get back on my feet and walk the last few hundred yards to the summit at 12,183 feet. I found no signs to mark this spot, just the start of a gentle downgrade.

Getting to the top of Trail Ridge took me eight hours. My descent lasted only one hour. On the way down, I swooped in and out of countless hairpin curves, hanging on to my brakes for dear life. The alpine tundra, then the boulder fields and evergreen forests zipped by in a big blur. Several miles below the summit, I streaked past a carved wooden sign marking the Continental Divide separating the Atlantic and Pacific watersheds.

I didn't ride the brakes all the way down the mountain. Instead, I used a technique called "feathering," squeezing the brakes for a second or two, letting go, then squeezing them again. For those steep descents in the Appalachians, I knew that feathering was the best way to keep the bike under control. But the whole way down Trail Ridge, I prayed that all my braking wouldn't heat up the rims and melt the patches off the tire tubes, thereby causing a blowout. Through 20-plus miles, my rims stayed cool, and I rolled into Grand Lake in one piece. I stayed overnight and through the next day at the youth hostel outside town. I needed the break. I was exhausted, but at the same time proud of having overcome the toughest cycling—make that the toughest physical challenge—I'd ever faced.

I got through the rest of the Colorado Rockies ahead of the first fall snowstorms. In Utah, I wasn't so lucky. I had to wait two days for the weather to clear enough so I could climb the last pass of the Wasatch Range before the Salt Lake Valley. After crossing that pass, I camped on the edge of a lake above Provo. I spent most of the night massaging my feet to keep them from freezing.

The next morning, I crawled out of my tent and found it covered by a thin layer of ice. I stopped in Salt Lake City to buy warmer clothing, but it was too late. In northern Utah, the chills started, and in central Idaho, my throat swelled up to the point where I could barely breathe. I spent almost a week in a Glenns Ferry motel room, shivering under a pile of sheets, towels, and blankets. When the fever came, I kicked it all on the floor.

While I was trying to get rid of whatever I had, I had plenty of time to reconsider the events of the last few months. Of course this process triggered an avalanche of the "if-onlies" and the "on the other hands." It went like this: If only I hadn't goofed off so much on this journey, I would have avoided cold weather in the mountains. I would have stayed well. On the other hand, there would have been no stops to visit my friends and family. There would have been no poking around in country stores and small-town libraries, and none of those spontaneous upheavals of my best-laid plans that had made this journey so rewarding. But some days I gave up too soon. And other days I started too late. When the weather looked threatening, I was too quick to take cover. I had planned on being in Phoenix, Arizona, by Halloween. There I'd take a much-needed break to work and save up some money for the homestretch. Halloween was now just a week and a half away and where was I? Flat on my back in Idaho.

Up ahead were eastern Oregon's sparsely populated deserts and mountains, where storms can dump so much snow so fast you'd better know how to dig a snow cave to survive. Meanwhile, the TV weatherman announced that the northwest's first fall snowstorm was moving inland. As much as I wanted to pedal the rest of the way to the coast, I had already pushed my health to the limit. I probably wouldn't survive a mountain snowstorm.

As soon as I felt strong enough, I rode into Boise, boxed the bike, and took the train to Davis, California. Two days after I got off the train, that snowstorm blanketed the mountain passes I almost crossed. I felt vindicated.

DRESSED FOR CYCLETOURING SUCCESS

Time wasn't too long ago when a flannel shirt, cutoff jeans and hightop sneakers were the height of cycletouring fashion. Some people still won't ride in anything else and I say, "More power to 'em."

I've tried biking in similar garb and didn't find it too comfortable. What follows are my suggestions for cycling gear that will maximize your comfort and safety.

I'll start with the single most important item your can wear while cycling: a helmet. Get a model approved by ANSI or the Snell Memorial Foundation and put it on every time you ride. Although I've never crash-tested any of my helmets, I know of several cyclists who have. The worst injury that any of them suffered was a concussion and he swore that he would have been dead without the helmet. So wear it!

Many years ago on a ride outside Ann Arbor, I learned the importance of eye protection when a bug flew into my right eye and pretty well blinded me—and I still had 10 miles to go before I got home. On every ride thereafter, I made a point of wearing regular glasses or sunglasses. I still do. There are some very spiffy and very expensive cycling sunglasses on the market these days. They're mostly plastic, which means they can break out in the middle of nowhere, so take a backup pair if you need to look cool on tour. Me? I use my prescription suns and carry my prescription along with me.

Before we move into the clothing department, let me stress the importance of something you'll need to be wearing in all those places that those clothes don't cover. I'm referring to sunscreen with a sun protection factor of at least 15. As a cycletourist, you'll be out in the sun all day long, so protect yourself from skin cancer.

My basic touring outfit has been a pair of black cycling shorts, a tee shirt or one of those cycling jerseys with the pockets in back, athletic socks, cleated cycling shoes and fingerless gloves with padded palms. Some of these items are specific to cycling and available only through bike shops or by mail order, while others, such as tee shirts and athletic socks, can be had in almost any small town.

Of all these items of clothing, I'm most particular about the comfort of my shorts and gloves. A major concern to women cyclists is how the shorts are lined inside—this can make the difference between an enjoyable ride and one that's sheer hell. Martha's "Comfy Shorts" awards go to Cannondale, Hind, Pearl Izumi and Schnaubelt Shorts. These four companies have taken the time to find out what women really need in cycling apparel and I thank them for it. (Hint to women and men: you'll be the most comfortable in your cycling shorts if you wear them without your underwear. They're designed that way.)

As for gloves, their primary function is to pad your hands and thumbs so that the nerve at the base of your palms doesn't go numb. This happened to me when I was a very new cyclist and it was an experience I'll never forget. My hands and fingers were useless for a couple days after that gloveless ride. Gloves also can keep you from losing the skin on your palms if you take a sliding fall off the bike. When it comes to styles, I still prefer those good old-fashioned Cycle Pro gloves with the generous palm and thumb padding and crocheted back. Newer cycling gloves come with synthetic fiber backing, which tends to get snagged by the Velcro closures on the backs of the gloves. I also like the old-fashioned gloves because they can be repaired with dental floss.

Since tours also happen during cold or rainy weather, let me share a few thoughts about attire for these occasions. For the cold, you'll need to preserve your body heat but not to the extent that you overheat. I like to wear a wool hat under my helmet, a windbreaker/rain jacket over a turtleneck shirt and possibly long john tops underneath it all. I also put a warm pair of tights—wool or polypropylene—over the cycling shorts. As for gloves, I've used leather models designed for motorcyclists and mountain bike racers' gloves and have found that they worked the best.

Feet are a problem area for the cold weather cyclist. During the years when I toured with cleated leather shoes like the road racers use, my feet would turn to blocks of ice when the temperature got down into the 40s. Some cyclists solve this problem by wearing special shoe covers, but I've never been able to find a pair that was small enough for me. Today, my touring bike shoes of choice are the Shimano SPD mountain biking shoes which have plenty of inside room for thick warm socks, a luxury not available inside the more snug-fitting leather racing shoes.

As for rain, I wish I could say that those miracle fabrics that are guaranteed to keep you dry have done so for me, but I can't. I have yet to find a rain jacket able to withstand those storms that seem to find me—even in the Southwest. The reason I persist in wearing the things is because they keep that wet "rooster tail" spray from the back wheel off of my clothes, and their bright colors make me more visible to all those motorists who are wondering what I'm doing out in the rain. (Getting wet!)

• 12 •

California Coasting

finally reached the California coast on Halloween. I dipped my toes in the icy Pacific Ocean off Point Reyes. The water froze them instantly.

After stopping for a couple days in San Francisco, I joined the southbound cycletourists' parade on the Pacific Coast Highway. After not seeing more than a handful of other cyclists while crossing the country, I was delighted to have riding companions from all four corners of America as well as Canada, Switzerland, France and Germany.

Below Monterey, the road traveled through Big Sur's redwoods. I spent a Saturday afternoon in a state park exploring the hollowed-out trunks of those giant trees, sorely tempted to violate park rules by spending the night inside of one.

Instead, I pitched my tent in the special hiker-biker site. It was primitive camping all the way—just a cleared out space among the redwoods with a fireplace and picnic table in the middle for all to share. The water pump, showers, and restrooms were a long walk away. But it only cost 50 cents a night, and the warmth and camaraderie were priceless.

At supper, I let slip that the following Tuesday, November 10, would be my 24th birthday. Right away, the mellow potluck my newfound friends were preparing turned into a rollicking beer blast in my honor. We polished off countless rounds of Coors, drinking toasts to me, my ride, my two dozen years, two dozen eggs, and anything else we could think of. After we had our fill of partying, we fell asleep on the soft pine needle carpet, blissfully unaware of the raccoons that marched in and ate the rest of our supper. We surveyed the damage the next morning as we picked up the overturned pots and pans and shredded paper towels and plastic bags, wishing each other bon voyage. We exchanged addresses and promises to look each other up if we were ever pedaling through New Hampshire, Michigan, or northern California.

As for me, I remembered that promise I made many months before to my cousin, Steve Gouert, and his wife, Pat, that I would visit them when I went through Santa Barbara. From San Francisco, I sent them a postcard assuring them I'd be in Santa Barbara for my birthday. Santa Barbara was still more than 200 miles away, a good three or four days' ride. On this Sunday morning, I felt too hung over to try bicycling the most mountainous part of California's coast.

I was rescued from my predicament by Lisa, a college student from San Luis Obispo. She'd stowed her ten-speed in her Datsun's hatchback and driven up to Big Sur the night before. When she got to the campground entrance, the ranger said he'd charge her four dollars if she drove in, but only 50 cents if she bicycled in. Lisa parked her car outside camp, pedaled in, and joined our party.

"I was going to do some riding today, but I've really got to get back to school and study for my midterms," she said as I was rubbing my head and loading gear back onto my bike. "If you're headed south, I could take you about a hundred miles or so."

I jumped on that offer. Along the coast, I'd seen all sorts of people—young and old—with their thumbs out. They agreed that this was America's premier road for hitchhiking. Since I'd already seen the country as a bicyclist, walker, and train rider, now I wanted to see it as a hitch-biker. Besides, the jagged contours on my elevation maps for this section of the coast looked like the EKG of someone in cardiac arrest. I was only too happy to sit in Lisa's car and watch others pedal.

"This is about the only road I know that's fun to drive," Lisa said as we pulled out of Big Sur.

Indeed it was. To the accompaniment of a Billy Joel tape, we sang and snapped our fingers as we drove along, rounding countless curves and promontories, long narrow cliffs that jutted out into the sea. We climbed long, seemingly endless hills, then swooped back down to the ocean. Those steep descents had me clinging to the dashboard with white knuckles. We stopped every few miles to watch the surf pounding against the rocks below, leaning into the stiff coastal breeze and laughing at the antics of the seals.

At San Simeon, the cliffs gave way to vast, treeless expanses of ranch land, and our quiet little Highway One became a crowded four-laner.

"Here goes," Lisa said, and she floored the accelerator. The grazing cattle, Pacific coastline, and the outskirts of Morro Bay sped by in a big blur. Once in town and under the watchful gaze of the Highway Patrol, she slowed down, and the blur became houses, shopping centers, hamburger stands, and yacht clubs. Lisa let me off outside Morro Bay State Park, and I pedaled in, saving $3.50 as she'd done the night before.

I rolled into Santa Barbara two days later, on my birthday. Santa Barbara was a sunny Spanish-style paradise overlooking the ocean, tastefully done in whitewashed adobe and wrought iron, home to multimillionaires, movie stars, and the late Shah of Iran's sister. Even President Reagan maintained a ranch in the mountains a few miles away. In Santa Barbara, a modest bungalow on a busy street easily went for $100,000, and the palatial estates on the hills overlooking the city sold for at least ten times more.

Steve and Pat Gouert lived on the other side of Santa Barbara's opulence. Steve was a foreign auto mechanic, trying to hang on through slow times at the shop, high rents, and astronomical everything else. They rented a one-bedroom house on a dusty alley for $600 a month. As much as she wanted to stay at home with her three-month-old son, Pat was coming to the painful realization that she'd have to go out and start waitressing again. Pat was also homesick for her native Minnesota. The only time I saw her truly relaxed and happy was when she talked about life in her hometown, Battle Lake, or art school in Minneapolis, where she met Steve.

I stayed five days in Santa Barbara and helped Pat celebrate her own birthday on Saturday, November 14. Baby Fraser wasn't used to having houseguests, and he cried day and night. I left on Sunday, very relieved to get back on the road.

Gagging on auto exhaust long before I reached Los Angeles, I longed for those wide open spaces on the high plains. Those sunbaked deserts east of the Coastal Range started looking awfully good, although I'd heard that finding enough water would be a problem out there.

I used every one of my ten speeds to get off the coast, over the mountains, and into the desert. Water was much more plentiful than I'd anticipated, and the temperature never rose above a very tolerable 80 degrees. That desert turned out to be one of my favorite places in America, not so much for its bright, cloudless days, but for its nights. Unlike the hazy, glowing Los Angeles sky, the jet-black desert sky revealed constellations and meteor showers unlike any I'd seen before. There were no cars roaring by out there—no sound at all except the coyote choruses.

I spent my last night in California in the El Centro KOA. Unlike the hiker-biker camps along the coast, this place was full of people I wanted nothing to do with. On one side of me were two oilfield workers from Alberta with a huge collection of old *Playboy* magazines. On the other side was an older couple sitting in lawn chairs slurping Budweisers. The man was skinny as a telephone pole, while his wife easily topped 250. When she went into their trailer to fix supper, the man came over and propositioned me. I turned him down flat. He trudged back over to his site and disappeared into the trailer. I never saw him again.

During the night, the wind came up, first as a gentle breeze, then a ferocious gale that flattened my Canadian neighbors' pup tent and scattered their girlie magazines all over camp. My tent stood fast, although the wind lifted it right off the ground, and I spent the whole night being tossed about.

East of El Centro, I picked up the Evan Hewes Highway, a bumpy old stretch of pavement that beat my butt into jelly. I wasn't sorry to leave it behind when it merged into Interstate 8. The gale that denied me of sleep hadn't let up a bit, and it gave me a mighty push toward Arizona. But that wind also kicked up a sandstorm that blotted out the bright desert sun and drove sand into my eyes, ears, nose, and mouth. I pulled into a rest area and made a beeline for the drinking fountain. There I filled all three of my water bottles and emptied them into my eyes.

"Are you allowed to ride your bike out on the Interstate?" I heard a man ask.

"There's no other road for me to ride on." I was in no mood to be friendly after a sleepless night.

"Are you all right?"

"I can't see."

"Listen, I've got a pickup here, and my wife and I are driving over to Arizona. We could put your bike in the back and take you too."

I put my water bottles down and looked at him for the first time. He was an elderly man, long and lean, with thinning white hair and a shy little smile. Clad in a Stetson hat, snap button shirt, and dungarees, he looked like the classic westerner. His calloused hands and leathery tan complexion belied many years of hard outdoor work. I guessed he was a rancher.

"Yeah, why not," I said flatly, watching the sand clouds roiling just outside this little oasis.

I helped the man lift my bike into his truck bed. His wife made room for me on the cab's passenger side, then introduced herself and her husband. I promptly forgot their names. They told me they raised horses in the mountains outside San Diego, and were on their way to Arizona to see some mares they were thinking of buying. I sulked silently through the remaining 20 miles of California, coughing, sneezing, and trying to rub the sand out of my eyes. They let me off a couple blocks away from the Colorado River in Yuma, Arizona.

FUELING YOUR POWER PLANT

Your power plant being you, of course. My discussion of nutrition for the cycletourist has two parts: pontification about what your diet should be on the road, then the truth about what really happens out there.

First, the pontification. You've no doubt heard that the standard American diet falls well short of the ideal, which should be high in fiber, low in fat and moderate in protein. We tend to consume vast amounts of processed foods and skimp on the whole grains and fruits and vegetables.

As a cycletourist, you have a wonderful opportunity to make amends to your body by feeding it all those healthy things you've heard so much about. Believe me, your body will run better if you feed it properly. In addition, give it plenty of water. The human body is 70 percent water and its water stores can be depleted very quickly if you're riding on a hot day. So drink up!

My personal on-the-road favorite foods are bagels, bananas (especially with peanut butter) and trail mix that I make myself by foraging in grocery stores for the most interesting ingredients. I've recently experimented with various brands of energy bars, but have found most of them difficult to chew and even more difficult to digest. They're also not widely available outside metropolitan areas.

I generally try to start my day with a high-carbo breakfast like pancakes then snack and nibble throughout the day. I've found that waiting until I'm hungry to eat means that I've waited too long. I've had some pretty spectacular blood sugar crashes as a result of delaying a snack or a meal.

Lunch break often finds me at a salad bar in a restaurant or a grocery store. At times I've explored the outer limits of the phrase "all you can eat" at the salad bar, and I've always paid for it when it was time to get back on the bike. It's hard to ride when you're stuffed!

Supper time is fat and protein time, as I'm off the bike by then and my body can concentrate on processing foods that take longer to digest than carbohydrates. My favorite supper foods are spaghetti with a stick-to-the-ribs sauce and parmesan cheese on top, pizza, ice cream and just about any other sinful dessert you can name.

Which brings me to the second half of my discussion: what really happens to hungry cyclists out there. The reality is that you'll get knocked off your nutritional high horse in a hurry. I've seen passionate vegetarians turn into steakaholics and anti-refined sweetener types develop insatiable cravings for sugar! I'd venture to bet that some of these dietary changes may be driven by practicality. For certain people, the rigors of cycle-touring can cause their bodies to desire high protein foods like steak or that quick burst of energy found in candy bars.

What also happens out there is that you meet people who just have to share their best Texas chili or Pennsylvania Dutch shoo fly pie, and no, you don't say, "No thanks." Your best strategy is to be like a politician on the campaign trail and try a bit of whatever is offered to you. You just might like it!

• 13 •

Snowbird

M y first full day in Arizona was Thanksgiving, with roast turkey, TV football games, and family reunions for everyone else. For me, it was just another day on the road. I marched eastward out of Yuma on old U.S. 80, a straight arrow two-laner beside equally straight lines of telephone poles and railroad tracks.

Early that afternoon, I rented a motel room in the tiny village of Tacna. On this, the most family-oriented holiday of the year, I was alone. The electronically produced companionship of the TV set provided no solace, and soon I filled the empty room with body wracking sobs and wails. I didn't care who heard me, but no one came tapping on the door, wondering what the trouble was.

Friday, November 27 dawned as gray as my mood. A leaden blanket of clouds hung over the desert, and I climbed Mohawk Mountain outside Tacna in a drizzle. On the other side, that drizzle changed to a downpour. Having run out of frontage road, I was back on Interstate 8, getting sloshed by a steady stream of cars, trucks, and buses headed for everywhere except this saguaro-studded desert the Air Force used for bombing practice. Creek beds that hadn't seen moisture in months were swollen with swift, muddy water, and the highway was covered with a foamy brine that saturated my shoes, socks, and wheel bearings.

The welcome sign outside Gila Bend proclaimed that it was home to 1,700 friendly people and five old crabs. Reality was quite different. The town lay just outside the Gila Bend Indian reservation, and the Indians had come into town in droves, cruising up and down the main drag in their pickup trucks, glaring at the whites, who glared right back.

I checked into a motel run by Indians from the other side of the world. Their office reeked of curry, and they spoke to each other in nasal, rapid-fire Hindi. I signed away a couple of $20 traveler's checks, and they handed me a room key. I never saw any of them again.

My primary reason for being there was to dry my gear. I draped my soggy sleeping bag over the desk and chair, hung up my tent in the closet, draped my cycling togs over the shower curtain rod, opened all the dresser drawers and turned them into a drying rack for my street clothes, then wrapped the big warm bed blanket around my shivering naked body.

That evening, the KOOL-TV news from Phoenix was full of pictures of rush-hour traffic slogging along flooded streets. Rain was rare in that desert city, and naturally the top news story. The weather map of the usually sunny Southwest looked positively soggy.

"Winter's finally here," the weatherman chortled. The Arizona rainy season had begun, and for the entire weekend, that happy-go-lucky guy had to insert that rarely used "r" word into his forecast.

I spent all day Saturday watching TV football games and thunderstorms. That evening, I wiped the sand and grit out of my bike's drivetrain, then polished the frame for its last travel day of 1981. Phoenix was just 65 miles away and on Sunday, I would go for it, regardless of the weather.

I was up and gone an hour before the rest of Gila Bend was stirring. I cranked along in the highest gear I could muster and didn't stop until Buckeye, 35 miles up the road. The rain didn't stop until Buckeye either. I slogged into a cafe for a big Sunday brunch, and a local cotton farmer sat down next to me. Was I that biker he just saw speeding up the hill outside town?

"Yeah, and that was *slow* for me." I didn't dare mention that tremendous tailwind pushing me.

"Where you going?"

"Phoenix."

"You're almost home now."

I hoped I had a home in Phoenix. Three months ago, right after I'd crossed the Mississippi River at Burlington, Iowa, I wrote to the Greater Arizona Bicycling Association to inquire about places to live and work in Phoenix for the winter. My letter appeared in their monthly newsletter, and a club member named Don Spalding sent me a letter via my parents' address and invited me to stay with him, his teenaged sons, Brent and Mark, their "lovable, but somewhat undisciplined dog" and "two birds that fly about the house." I accepted.

I let out a victory yell when I crossed 43rd Avenue into Phoenix. With ten miles to go, I wasn't letting anything stop me now—except red lights. An hour later, I was standing on the doorstep of a white tract home in northwest Phoenix, hoping the Spaldings were home, hoping they still wanted to see this soggy cyclist from Michigan.

Don answered the door, Patches the dog barked me aboard, and the racket ended any plans that Brent and his best friend, Chuck Malenfant, had for sleeping any later into the afternoon. The two groggy ones dragged themselves out into the living room for the requisite round of introductions and handshakes, then helped me bring my gear inside. As for Mark Spalding, I wouldn't get to meet him until he came home on semester break from the University of Arizona in Tucson.

The Spaldings not only took me in, they made me part of their family. Within hours of meeting each other, we found we had more in common than we ever thought possible, right down to sharing the same tastes in science fiction books and movies, rock 'n' roll bands, and electronic space music. I was calling Don Spalding "Dad" before the day ended.

Chuck and I endured a frustrating month of December pedaling around northwest Phoenix and neighboring Glendale looking for jobs. I'd arrived too late to hire on as a temporary in the department stores, and the Job Service counselors told me that any kind of work was hard to find. Almost every day, Chuck and I made the rounds of the bowling alleys, hamburger stands, and convenience stores, filling out applications which everyone promised to keep on file.

I finally landed a job in early January. Chuck found one a few weeks later. For the next three months, I worked in the American Cancer Society phone room, recruiting people to go out and raise money. I didn't use my bicycle to commute—it spent much of the winter in the Spaldings' garage until I had enough money to buy replacements for the parts I'd worn out. Instead, I rode the bus to and from work, whiling away the time in transit reading books from Brent and Mark's vast science fiction library.

On the surface, I had settled into a comfortable routine of waking up to the rock-n-roll morning show on KUPD-FM, eating a quick breakfast with Dad and Brent before the bus came, then putting in eight hours at the Cancer Society. But my mind was still very much on the road. While dialing my calls, I sketched the places I'd been in the last year, and brainstormed different gearing setups for the bike.

I gave the bike a complete overhaul in early February, then started getting ready for the road again. Every weekday evening, I'd sprint home from the bus stop, change into cycling clothes, then dash out for ten miles in Phoenix rush-hour traffic. On weekends, I took longer rides down quiet boulevards lined with palm trees and Spanish-style homes set well back on exquisitely landscaped lawns. Man had certainly made this part of the Sonoran Desert bloom, but unfortunately, the grasses and shrubs with which this feat was accomplished produced far more pollen than my allergic sinuses could handle. When things started blooming, my nose ran like a faucet, and I sneezed nonstop while I rode.

The pollen eventually settled down, and so did my sinuses. My allergy attack aside, I felt pretty lucky to be in Phoenix. Elsewhere, people were fighting snowdrifts, ice storms, mudslides, and tornadoes. While the rest of America was enduring one of the century's worst winters, I was savoring my second summer. So were thousands of other northerners, and the locals called us "snowbirds," not an entirely flattering term. A favorite wintertime tune on the local radio stations was Ann Murray's "Snowbird," especially the verse, "Spread your tiny wings and fly awa-a-ay."

This snowbird made plans to depart the Phoenix area by the end of March. I'd be well out of the Southwest by the time the summer heat got fierce again. In fact, I hoped to be back in Michigan by then.

On Friday, March 26, I quit my job at the Cancer Society, rode the bus home for the last time, and loaded all my gear back onto the bike. Dad, Brent, and Chuck rode a couple miles with me the next morning, then I was on my own again, headed for some of the widest, openest spaces in all of America.

COPING WITH REPAIR "OPPORTUNITIES"

For many urban cyclists, having a mechanical problem is no big deal. You just take it to the bike shop and have them fix it. Come touring time, you're 100 miles out of town, something breaks, and presto: you are the bike shop.

A lot of fiction and folklore have grown up around the world of bike repair and maintenance, and before I proceed any further with this discussion, let me assure you that neither of these things are terribly difficult. I learned them without having any mechanical background.

How do you learn to maintain and repair your bike? You can start the way I did: have an incurable urge to tinker with the bike, break things, then beg your more knowledgeable friends to help you fix whatever you broke. The trouble with this system is that your friends soon start avoiding you.

There's a better way to learn that not only keeps your interpersonal relationships intact, but also sets you apart from many of the other cyclists out there. It's called formal instruction, and you can get it through classes, books or a combination of both. The best places to find bike repair and maintenance classes are your local bike shop, bike club, community college or parks and recreation program.

If you want to go one step further and learn the professional standards the bike shops use, may I suggest a couple weeks at bicycle school? I can personally vouch for the high quality of the training offered by the United Bicycle Institute (UBI). UBI takes you through all of the major systems of the bicycle in a two-week introductory course. There's also an advanced course for those with previous professional experience or certification from the introductory course. UBI's courses are oriented toward those who wish to seek employment or start businesses within the bicycle industry, so you'll also spend some time learning about business plans and marketing strategies. Write or call:

United Bicycle Institute
423 Williamson Way
Post Office Box 128
Ashland, Oregon 97520
(503) 488-1121

There are countless how-to books that cover bike repair and maintenance in infinite detail. Here are my four favorites:

Barnett's Manual: Analysis and Procedures for Bicycle Mechanics, Second Edition, by John Barnett. Its outline format is similar to an automotive service manual which allows quick access to vital technical information. This is the reference book the bike shops use. Cost is $129.95. Available from:

Vitesse Press
28 Birge Street
Brattleboro, Vermont 05301
(800) 848-3747

While we're on the subject of expensive-and-worth-it bicycle books, *Barnett's Manual* draws quite heavily on information contained in *Sutherland's Handbook,* by Howard Sutherland. This book is the bicycle industry's bible of mechanical specifications, and you won't get very far as a serious mechanic unless you know your specs. At this writing—mid-1993—the book is out of print. The new sixth edition will be out in early 1994. For more information, contact:

Sutherland Publications
Box 9061
Berkeley, California 94709-9980
(800) 248-2510

Okay, so you'd rather not spend a good portion of next month's rent money on bicycle fix-it books. You might want to try *Bicycling Magazine's Complete Guide to Bicycle Maintenance and Repair.* This one's $24.95 and available from:

Rodale Books
Emmaus, Pennsylvania 18098

A light-hearted look at the subject can be found inside *Anybody's Bike Book: An Original Manual of Bicycle Repairs,* by Tom Cuthbertson. To call this book "original" is an understatement. The $9.95 you spend on this one will probably be the most entertaining $9.95 you'll ever spend. Available from:

Ten Speed Press
Box 7123
Berkeley, California 94707

Now that you've gotten all of this formal instruction, what will you most need to fix out there? Here are my top five bicycle repair "opportunities":

1. The flat tire. If you can go on tour without this happening to you, would you please write and tell me your secret?

2. Broken cables. These tend to happen when you most need to use your brakes or derailleurs.

3. Broken spokes. Really fun when they're on the freewheel side of your back wheel. This malady tends to strike heavy guys who like to carry a lot of gear on tour.

4. Jammed or snapped chain. Yecch! A dirty repair job.

5. Broken luggage rack. You had to bring that kitchen sink along, didn't you? You're going to need a good welder to help get you back on the road again.

My traveling tool kit is included in the Trip List on page 222.

•14•

Land of Enchantment

Of the 36 states I pedaled in 1981-82, I had the easiest time with New Mexico. Not once did I see a raindrop during my two weeks there. I also had a 25 mph tailwind pushing me over mountains, deserts, and grasslands.

Unlike my all-day struggle over Trail Ridge Road in Colorado, I stayed in high gear all the way over the Continental Divide outside Aragon. Then I streaked downhill into a vast, treeless sea of undulating grass called the Plains of San Augustin, where I traveled nearly 50 miles and saw only a handful of people. Take away the black ribbon of blacktop and telephone poles that cut a swath through that place and there'd be no evidence that anyone had ever been there.

Out there, I could see 10, 15, even 20 miles in every direction. Dust devils as tall as ten-story buildings whirled across the open range—sending quietly grazing cattle into panic-stricken flight—then rattled on across dirt roads and dry creek beds before dissolving.

In New Mexico, stopping my bike was harder than keeping it going. I'd straddle the top tube and keep my feet firmly planted on the ground, but the wind would keep pushing the bike forward, the saddle nose butting me in the back like an impatient child. I quickly adopted the practice of clamping the top tube between my legs to keep the bike stationary.

Much of the New Mexico I saw was ranch land, home to many more cattle than people. The New Mexicans greeted me with a curious mixture of reserve and formality I hadn't encountered since New England. Back there, I called it coldness, but then I realized those invisible barriers the people had built up were a defense mechanism brought about by having to share such a tiny corner of America with so many others. But with slightly more than a million people spread out over an area twice the size of Pennsylvania, New Mexico had plenty of elbow room. I concluded that the New Mexicans' cautious friendliness was due to their being more used to seeing wide open spaces than people.

I also found that the West's hottest, spiciest Mexican food could be had in New Mexico. From Glenwood in the west to Clovis in the east, I savored fiery burritos, sizzling enchiladas, and flaming tacos. Waitresses would take my order, then issue that special challenge: "Red or green?" I had to choose between red or green chili peppers. Green was hotter, so I always took red. As soon as I started eating, the locals would chuckle and exchange knowing glances as they watched me down glass after glass of water to put out that fire racing down my esophagus. With an audience watching every bite, I knew I had to empty my plate. I always did. Miraculously, those culinary infernos passed through my digestive system without any problems.

Crossing this big state, I realized that those spicy chilis that set my stomach aflame held a lofty place in New Mexican culture. In town after town, I spotted long strings of fat peppers—ristras—hung out to dry on back porches. Those ristras were a visible sign of wealth, set outside for all to see. In Socorro, I read a newspaper ad placed by someone wishing to trade his ristra for firewood, a scarce commodity in this sleepy desert town on the Rio Grande.

The west wind catapulted me out of the Rio Grande valley, over the Manzano range, then brought me out on the grassy high plains of eastern New Mexico. Effortlessly, I continued eastward, through quiet, unassuming places called Willard, Encino, and Vaughn. Outside Vaughn, I found that even my highest gear couldn't outrun this wind, so at twenty-plus miles an hour, I coasted along, chuckling at my good fortune. No problems could I possibly imagine.

Unfortunately, I encountered a very big one in Fort Sumner, the final resting place of Billy the Kid, and I fear, if things had turned out differently, me too. I pulled into the dairy bar on the west end of town, feeling pretty smug about having made 56 miles in only three and a half hours—usually that distance took twice as long. I ordered a tall chocolate cone and settled down at the picnic table to enjoy my reward.

A bright orange New Mexico highway department truck pulled in, and a dark haired, swarthy man stepped out, greeted me, then strode over to the counter and ordered a hamburger.

Almost as an afterthought, he turned and asked if I wanted anything. He flashed me a 200-watt smile and looked me up and down. There was something about him that made me feel uneasy. He seemed too friendly, and in this state, hail-fellow-well-met types were as rare as rainclouds. I declined his offer to buy my lunch, and returned to savoring my ice cream cone with all the intensity I could muster. I hoped he'd quickly get his order and leave. He paid for his burger, then sat down across from me.

"Where ya headed?" He was still wearing that big smile.

"Michigan."

"Where ya been?"

I rattled off my itinerary like a machine gun: "From Michigan to Baton Rouge to New Hampshire across to Idaho got sick took the train to California spent the winter in Phoenix and left there two weeks ago."

"I think what you're doin' is great," he beamed. "I've always wanted to do some traveling myself. I admire you. I wanna hear about your trip.

"Listen, there's a park in town. I'm going to get something to drink, and then I'm goin' down there. Why don't you come on down?"

"Sure," I said flatly. I sensed bad vibes all over the place. I hoped that park he was talking about was a village square with a gazebo in the middle, an open space with nowhere to hide, a place where I could get rid of him, then find a nice, secluded place to camp.

He got in his truck and drove off. I knew those highway workers only got an hour for lunch, and I figured he could jolly well drink by himself, then go back to work. I moseyed around town for an hour, thinking I'd shaken him off until he pulled over to the side of a street I was about to cross.

"Where were you? I waited at the park and you never came." He seemed genuinely hurt.

"Uh...I got lost!" On purpose, I wanted to add. "Well, looks like I gotta stay here overnight," he said. "I got this job over near Melrose. Gotta find it. I'll finish it up tomorrow. Listen, can I buy ya dinner? Anything you like."

"Well, uh, I dunno what I'll be doing tonight," I stammered. Then he upped his offer. "Could I rent you a motel room so you can clean up a bit?"

"Ummm, you don't have to do that. Uh, no thanks."

He was leaning against my bike, resting his left hand on the saddle. His big diamond wedding ring glittered in the midday sun. He persisted with his dinner and motel offer, which made me hedge even harder. Finally, he backed off.

"Look, meet me in the park around six if you wanna go out to dinner. Anything you want, okay?"

"Yeah."

He put his wedding ringed hand on my shoulder, then we shook hands.

"I wish you luck and I'm glad I met you." He gave me the name of the motel he'd be staying in, then got in his truck and drove off.

As soon as he was out of sight, I trotted over to another motel, checked in, and locked my room door behind me.

I was up and out of Fort Sumner at dawn the next morning. I passed by the park where I was supposed to meet my pesky friend 12 hours before. It was a thickly wooded place, where a strong man could do all sorts of things to an unwilling woman. Then came the motel he mentioned. Its parking lot was full of orange highway department trucks, including his. Melrose would be the next town I'd pass through, and I certainly didn't want to meet him along the way.

My body shook convulsively, and I shifted into high gear, silently urging my legs to go faster. They responded to my commands like rubber bands, and the stiff breeze in my face soaked up even more energy. I snarled and cursed at my rotten luck. Except for an occasional oil tanker headed for Texas, this highway was deserted.

Then came that road construction project—miles and miles of it—the same one he said he had so much trouble finding yesterday. By this time my legs had gotten the idea that this was a race, just like the ones I did for fun back in Ann Arbor. And the wind finally kicked in behind me, and I flew into Melrose—36 miles from Fort Sumner—with a full head of steam and a raging hunger and thirst.

I stopped at a fruit stand and bought a quart of cherry cider. While I drank it down, I told the woman behind the counter about my ardent suitor. Her eyes narrowed and she pursed her lips.

"Spanish guy?" she asked, her voice cutting like a knife through the silent store.

I nodded, dreading what she'd say next.

"Well, you're lucky he didn't force you off the road. He's been in jail for that kind of thing."

"What?"

"Rape."

"How could he serve time for that and still work for the *state*?"

"Oh, they have people who've been in the pen working out there. Once you've done your time, you're a citizen like anyone else."

"Do they have anyone working on the road between here and Clovis?"

"They're out everywhere."

On that note, I sprinted 21 miles into Clovis, a place full of stockyards and grain elevators on the Texas border. I pulled into a campground beneath the busy final approach to an Air Force base and spent the rest of the day watching fighters take off and land. I prayed that guy wouldn't spot my bike and tent from the road. Fortunately, I never saw him again, but it wasn't until I was well into Texas before I stopped glancing at my rearview mirror to make sure he wasn't following me.

FINDING PLACES TO STAY

During my travels, I've stayed in conventional places such as campgrounds, private homes, motels, hotels, hostels and churches.

I've also spent the night in an Arkansas jail and in a college fraternity house in Virginia. The jail crash didn't result from my doing anything illegal—it was set up by a small-town mayor. The frat house crash happened during the course of my wandering around the Randoph-Macon College campus looking for a home for the night. The men of Kappa Sigma offered me couch space in their chapter living room and I accepted. (Don't worry, nothing terrible happened. No bodily contact except handshakes. If anything, they deserve public acclaim for being such wonderful spur-of-the-moment hosts!)

So where will you stay on your tour? If you're going on an organized ride, you won't need to worry, as your lodging arrangements will be taken care of for you. If you're on the do-it-yourself plan, let me offer some suggestions.

Hotels, motels and campgrounds are relatively easy to find. If you're a member of the American Automobile Association (AAA), you're no doubt aware of their network of AAA-approved lodgings. Nothing wrong with using them if you're traveling on two wheels rather than four. Campgrounds? The taxpayer-subsidized variety can be found in national, state, and city parks, national forests, state forests, just to name a few places. Private campgrounds can be located through statewide tourism promotion bureaus and their regional and local counterparts. Chains such as KOA publish national directories. You can also turn to the local yellow pages when you feel the need to call it a day.

Some of my best camping experiences have resulted from asking around a small town and seeing what develops. My favorite "asking around" places are a town's churches, city hall, chamber of commerce and police station. Quite often, I've found that my tent doesn't get pitched at all, as I'm invited home by some local person or family. The friendships that have grown out of these invitations have been among the greatest rewards of my travels.

In the western United States, you can go a long way between towns and you just might find yourself camping out in that proverbial middle of nowhere. I have. My best advice to you would be to get yourself and your bike far enough away from the road that you're not visible. It's best not to advertise your presence. Also, don't even think about camping on land that's fenced off and posted "No trespassing." Rural westerners tend to take private property rights very seriously. Most important of all, the best campers leave no trace of their campsite.

Can you tour without a tent? Absolutely. Let me offer you some additional suggestions on indoor crashes for the tentless. There are four groups that provide hospitality homes to touring cyclists. Three of these, the League of American Wheelmen, Women's Cycling Coalition and the Women's Cycling Network, provide their hospitality home lists to those who've paid membership dues. The fourth list, the Touring Cyclists' Hospitality Directory, is compiled by John Mosley. The catch is that you must agree to be a hospitality home in order to get his list. Here are the addresses:

League of American Wheelmen
190 West Ostend Street, Suite 120
Baltimore, Maryland 21230-3755

Women's Cycling Coalition
Post Office Box 281
Louisville, Colorado 80027

Women's Cycling Network
Post Office Box 73
Harvard, Illinois 60033

Touring Cyclists' Hospitality Directory
7303 Enfield
Reseda, California 91335

You'll find hospitality of a more familiar sort when you visit your friends and relatives. Equally enjoyable variations on this theme are the relatives of friends and friends of relatives.

I'll conclude with a plug for one of the most interesting and reasonably priced lodging experiences available to the cycletourist: the American Youth Hostels (AYH). There are about 200 hostels located in scenic areas throughout the U.S., and they're quite popular with travelers from other countries. Why not make your American explorations into an international experience? Individual AYH memberships are $25 a year for adults, $15 for seniors over 54, and $10 for those under 18. Write or call:

American Youth Hostels, Inc. - National Office
Post Office Box 37613
Washington, DC 20013-7613
(202) 783-6161

• 15 •

Texas Travails

Unlike New Mexico, Texas seemed to go on forever. All the way across the state, I battled a gale at least as strong as the one that pushed me across New Mexico.

The 20 or 30 miles I could cover in an hour in New Mexico became my daily totals in west Texas. I inched eastward across dusty plains dotted with pale green mesquite trees and oil wells. Towns were few and far between, and most were little more than tiny clusters of houses, a church or two, and a general store. The larger towns usually had at least one motel— which charged a minimum of $20 a night for a single room—and was filled to capacity with oilfield workers. As much as I wanted to shower off the dust and sweat, then immerse myself in TV soap operas and sitcoms, I ended up staying in churches, parking the bike in a hallway and unrolling my sleeping bag on the carpeted nursery room floor.

Finding a church to crash in was at least as tricky as finding a motel. Every day I had quite a selling job to do to convince the pastor that I wasn't a penniless bum or a thief.

In Aspermont, the county seat of Stonewall, I found the Church of Christ's front door blown wide open by the wind, but no one inside. I leaned the bike against the side of the building, then went down to the courthouse, hoping to find someone who could tell me where the pastor was.

Unfortunately, the entire county bureaucracy was out to lunch except for a smiling secretary who said the pastor was a "real nice fellah" who attended college in Abilene during the week. Abilene was 60 miles away, and she doubted he'd come home before nightfall, but she gave me his home phone number anyway. I trotted outside to the phone booth to try his number. No answer. I skulked back inside, told that friendly young woman about my bad phone luck, and groused about that east wind that had slowed me down to a crawl.

Well, she informed me that the folks on these west Texas plains thought that wind spelled good news: rain. "It's been real drah here," she drawled, "real dra-a-ah." She added that during the long drought two summers ago, a public prayer for rain was held on the courthouse square. During that scorching summer, it seemed that not even God was on the west Texans' side, for the cooling rains didn't arrive until fall.

As for my staying overnight in the Church of Christ, she suggested I try the local sheriff, who also was the deacon. So over to the jail I went. His secretary said the sheriff was out to lunch, but I was welcome to wait until he got back. I sat down and fidgeted through a couple of magazines, but what really caught my eye was the marijuana plant on the secretary's desk.

"Do you get a lot of comments on what you're growing there?" I asked. "Oh, some, but you'd be surprised at how many people still don't know what marijuana looks like," she replied.

I was about to make some snappy remark about the worldliness of folks here as compared to back where I came from when the sheriff walked in. He was a potbellied fellow in his mid-fifties. With eyes that had obviously seen just about everything, he looked me up and down. He didn't move a muscle on his poker face. I told him who I was, and asked permission to stay overnight in his church. He motioned for me to follow him into his office. He sat down at his desk, then looked at the empty chair next to it. I sat down there. He removed a cigar from his shirt pocket and began chewing on it.

"You got a drah-ver's license?" He measured each word very carefully.

I handed him my Michigan driver's license with a two-year-old address and photo. He studied its every line and letter, then announced that he was going to "run a check" on me. He picked up his phone, made a long-distance call, then recited my name, description, and license codes to someone on the other end. There was a painfully long pause, then he said "thank yew," and hung up. "You're okay," he said without changing his expression. I fought back a tremendous urge to heave a sigh of relief.

Then he picked up the local phone book, which was no thicker than my folded Texas map. He called several church members, greeting whoever answered with a hearty "Who'm ah talkin' to?" I gathered that everyone out here knew everyone else within a 50-mile radius, so formal hellos weren't necessary.

The congregational consensus was that it was okay for me to stay in the church if I checked it out with the janitor. The sheriff directed me to the janitor's son's electrical contracting office, and the son assured me that his dad wouldn't mind.

Having gotten permission from most of Stonewall County, I took the bike inside the Church of Christ, then closed that front door. I slept undisturbed, and left early the next morning.

A bitterly cold drizzle accompanied me out of Aspermont. The long-awaited storm had finally arrived, and I got just as far as the next town of Hamlin, where I again looked in vain for a motel room. It was through a long chain of helpful folks— which included the newspaper editor, a restaurant owner, the Church of the Nazarene pastor, and the proprietor of a second-hand store—that I was introduced to a widow named Dorothy Jones. She offered to rent me a spare bedroom until the storm passed. I accepted.

Dorothy was down on her luck, down on her money, and living in her mother's house while she was in the hospital. "She has cancer," Dorothy said with a trace of weariness. "She could go any minute now."

As depressing as her circumstances seemed, I found no sadness in Dorothy's temporary home. Her cousins, Evelyn and Melvin Butler, were visiting from Fort Worth, and they greeted me like a long-lost friend as soon as I walked through the front door. They were about to have lunch, and Dorothy quickly set a place for me at the tiny kitchen table.

"The Lord brought us someone to share this food with," Melvin beamed, and we all joined hands and asked the blessing. Dorothy had reached far back into the refrigerator to find enough food for everyone, but she urged us to help ourselves freely to everything, including the big block of government surplus cheese the county had just given her.

Dorothy and her family and friends spent most of their time at the hospital with Dorothy's mother. I joined them on several vigils, quietly entering that pastel green room occupied by a tiny sleeping figure who no longer had the strength to acknowledge our presence. Dorothy stroked her mother's forehead and spoke to her softly, as if she was a child.

"She used to be the life of the party," Dorothy would say, turning to the rest of us. "Now she's dyin' by inches."

"Mama's going to be with Jesus soon," her family and friends kept saying.

They talked about Jesus not as someone they went to church for, but as a close personal friend they encountered every day. Their faith was the cornerstone of their lives. They talked a lot about being saved and born again in Christ.

I heard them tell many stories about their growing-up years and present lives. They recounted the times when they were down to their last few dollars, yet a heavy dose of prayer always seemed to pull them through. The Lord provides, they assured me, the Lord provides. These people had been poor all their lives, but they weren't bitter. They were thankful for what little they had, and felt truly blessed to have it.

Back in Ann Arbor and before that, in Pennsylvania, I remember discussing such people with my privileged, upper middle class peers and dismissing them as "Bible beaters" and "holy rollers." We found their brand of Christianity to be overly simplistic. And the political agenda that often went with it? Right-wing reactionary, to say the least.

But those Bible-beating fundamentalists had taken very good care of me while I pedaled about the country. Sure, there were many times when I had to close my mouth and lock it when I heard them singing the praises of Jerry Falwell and Pat Robertson and their buddy in the White House. However, one of the greatest gifts of my travels has been the opportunity to meet—and be helped by—those whose beliefs and opinions are totally different from mine.

I found much to admire in the way that people like Dorothy and her family and friends had personalized their faith. They put it on a day-to-day basis that was much different from the ritualistic, go-to-church exercise I had experienced in my own growing-up years. To me, the rituals felt hollow, and I turned my back on them in my early teens.

In high school, I decided to give religion another try. For about six months, I went to a nondemoninational youth group whose practice of Christianity included lots of rousing songs with plenty of hand-clapping and foot-stomping, and public witnessing. Such things were unheard of in the Episcopal church my family attended, and the contrast between our church and the youth group was jarring. The euphoria that came from joining the youth group and "being saved" quickly wore off, and I drifted away from both the group and the church.

During my stay with Dorothy, my most fervent wish—I couldn't really call it a prayer—was that her mother would hang on until after I left. I also wished that she'd soon be taken away from her pain. I felt extremely uncomfortable in her presence—being around that Alabama boy with cerebral palsy was a lot easier than this. I'd never been so close to a dying person before and I was afraid she'd die right in front of me. Then how would I react? I had no idea. In an effort to hide my uneasiness, I spent much of my time in that hospital room watching the rainstorm that was keeping me in this town. Dorothy's mother lived through my third and final night in Hamlin. The next morning, I paid Dorothy for my room and board, then pedaled out of town, right back into that east wind.

THE TRAINING CORNER

I really don't care for the word "training." I've seen too many cyclists—myself included—become slaves to the numbers: daily mileage, weekly mileage, monthly mileage, target heart rate, average speed—you get the point. All of this is done in the name of fitness, but I think there's a very important word missing from this picture: fun.

So, welcome to Martha the reformed numbers-aholic's laidback guide to getting ready for your tour. Before we start, let's assume that you're in good health—you might want to get a medical checkup to be sure—and that your bike fits you properly. How important is bike fit? Very. The way my Nobilette was set up during my 1987 tour contributed greatly to the left knee problems I developed during that tour. Afterward, my knee problems only got worse. By late 1988, I was ready to give up cycling altogether.

Then I wandered into a bike shop I usually didn't patronize, and told the salesman about my predicament. He asked me if I'd had a FitKit done, and I said "No." FitKit is a procedure in which the cyclist is measured as if he or she is getting fitted for a custom-tailored suit. These body measurements are then used to calculate the proper bike measurements. It's a long, drawn-out process and it's also expensive, which is why I hadn't had one done. But in January 1989, I was ready to try anything, cost be damned.

It was the best $50 I ever spent. The guy raised my saddle, adjusted the saddle's fore and aft position and put me on different pedals that would be easier on my knees. I noticed a big difference during the mile and a half ride between that shop and my house. I can't recommend the FitKit process highly enough.

The methods I've used to get ready for my own tours have varied. Before my 1980 trip, I did a lot of rides with the Ann Arbor Bicycle Touring Society but neglected to practice riding with packs on my bike. I also got the bike I was going to use less than one week before I left town. Moral: get your miles in, but also get to know how your bike handles when it's loaded down. And make sure that you and your bike aren't total strangers to each other. In 1981, I did the equivalent of race training. Big mistake. On my first day out, I tried to ride fast into a headwind and blew out my right knee. Moral: practice at the pace you'll be using on your tour. I think I got the formula right in 1987. I rode all through my last winter in Pittsburgh, so I had a nice mileage base of 300 miles before I left. I also used the Nobilette on my errands about town, so my touring load didn't feel any different than a week's worth of groceries or some library books. Finally, I didn't try to knock down big miles right away—I let my body get used to the idea of being on tour first. After two weeks of this easy-does-it cycling, I began building up my mileage.

As you're preparing for your tour, you'll no doubt find yourself getting stronger, but you'll also discover that cycling doesn't do much to keep you limber. In fact, in my Ann Arbor bike club, we did parodies of super-stiff cyclists in order to remind ourselves to stretch during our rest breaks. For cycling-specific stretches, see the book *Stretching* by Bob Anderson. You might also want to try yoga. I was fortunate enough to be befriended by a wonderful yoga teacher when I lived in western Pennsylvania. Because I wasn't—and still am not—a terribly limber person, my yoga lessons were aimed at increasing flexibility so I'd be a more fluid cyclist. It worked. It might work for you, too. For more on yoga, read *The Complete Illustrated Book of Yoga* by Swami Vishnudevananda and find a beginning yoga class with a patient teacher.

So there you have it. And don't forget to have fun while you practice for your tour, because fun is what cycletouring is all about.

• 16 •

Homestretch

My journey around America turned a year old on Monday, May 3, 1982, in Commerce, Texas. A couple days later, I aimed northward for the last time. I nipped off a corner of southeastern Oklahoma, then re-entered Arkansas.

It felt good to be back in the South again. After three weeks in windy, rainy Texas, that sultry Mississippi River Delta was a blessed relief. Once again, I could hardly keep two hands on the bars for all my waving back at people, from those huge black families in beat-up old station wagons with bamboo fishing poles poking out the windows and a mess of catfish in the back, to those wealthy white men in shiny new pickups bearing the names of their plantations.

The sun beat down on the newly planted rice paddies, sending up great hazy clouds that could turn a blue sky gray by midmorning. The planting of the rice crop provoked the return of a formidable Arkansas creature: the mosquito. Whenever I stopped, the little varmints descended on me in droves.

"The skeetah's our state bird," a farmer told me while I took refuge from the stinging legions in a restaurant along the White River. "Lemme tell you a story. I know you've prob'ly seen some big skeetahs out there, some big ones, haven't you?"

"Uh-huh," I winced, rubbing the latest crop of bites on my arms and legs.

"Well, I know a farmer around here who shot a skeetah that was so-o-o big it took him three days to drag it into the woods."

"No kidding!" I exclaimed, as the locals broke up, having once again pulled the leg of an unsuspecting Yankee.

In my travels, I had stayed in private homes, motels, campgrounds, youth hostels, and churches. In Dumas, Arkansas, I spent the night in jail—not behind bars—but on a mattress in the visitors' room. I procured these unusual accommodations through the town's mayor, who upon hearing that I was looking for a place to stay overnight, offered me sleeping bag space in the corner of the firehouse, adding that it probably wouldn't be the most restful place in town. I agreed. He then introduced me to the police chief, who offered me the jail instead.

I saw no prisoners, only shadows under the bottom of the visitors' room door. From the cells I heard coughs, muffled conversations, and a deep black male voice humming a nameless blues song with no particular beginning or end. Another man repeatedly hollered for a cigarette. The guards turned him down every time.

The guards told me they had "hosted" every kind of criminal, from shoplifters and pickpockets to murderers, rapists, and armed robbers. They fixed me supper and breakfast, and never failed to call me "Ma'am." Even so, I left early the next morning, truly grateful for my freedom and mobility.

Across the river a few days later, I played watchdog in the Episcopal church in Holly Springs, Mississippi. The church had been plagued by a series of break-ins, and I slept on the floor in the vacant rector's office with the telephone by my head. Unfortunately, I did my job too well. Early on the morning of Saturday, May 15, I heard someone rattling a side door, so I leaped out of my sleeping bag and called the police. Then I looked out the window and found I'd blown the whistle on a couple of carpenters who'd begun working on the parish hall's exterior. I was too embarrassed to go out and introduce myself, so I cowered in the office for the rest of the day and read Mark Twain's stories of his steamboating days in *Life on the Mississippi*. Sunday morning, no one seemed to notice that my church clothes were a faded yellow jersey and black wool shorts. I left shortly after the service, taking with me the best wishes of the entire congregation.

Up in Lovelaceville, Kentucky the following Wednesday, the Baptist pastor adamantly refused to bend his "ladies wear dresses" rule and allow me into the evening service. So I went down the street to the Methodists, who didn't mind my cycling togs at all. In fact, they invited me to come up front and sing with the choir.

After church, a 67-year-old widow named LaRue Bristoe invited me to stay with her for a few days. LaRue had been making quilts since she was a girl, and although she'd long ago lost the sight in her right eye, she still quilted for as long as 12 hours a day. Some of her quilts had sold for hundreds of dollars, which deeply puzzled her. "I give most of 'em away," she said.

Just before I came through, LaRue's quilting circle had made the Paducah TV news. "I think they might want to do something on you," she said. She called the station, and they sent a crew to videotape me riding up and down U.S. 62 outside the house. I gave a brief, tongue-tied interview, then the TV crew packed up and returned to Paducah. LaRue got on the phone to tell all her friends that she had a celebrity staying with her and urge them to be watching for me that Thursday. I was the final story on the ten o'clock news, and that was the only time I've ever been on television during my cycling journeys.

On Sunday, the members of the Lovelaceville United Methodist Church welcomed me back like an old friend. They raved about my TV spot, then they showered me with gifts— money, a crocheted cross, homemade cake, a lucky stone, and lots of hugs. The pastor, an energetic, barrel-chested man in his sixties whom everyone called Brother McKenzie, offered a special prayer in my honor. His booming voice shook the rafters in that tiny church, and I'm sure that prayer carried all the way across the Ohio River into Illinois, my next destination.

I stayed with LaRue until the following morning. All through my five days in Lovelaceville, I'd been playing a waiting game with a line of heavy storms that were wreaking havoc across the Mississippi River in Missouri. The weather forecasters insisted those storms were headed our way, but they were in no hurry. Except for a few thunderclaps and sprinkles, no big rains came to water LaRue's parched vegetable garden.

Before I left, LaRue quilted me a patch with a hand-painted cardinal in the center, and sewed it to the back of my cycling jersey. Now my jersey had something from all over the country—a Good Intent Log Homes patch from the Naesers, an iron-on ear of corn from Iowa, an American flag from Nebraska, and mud spots, grease stains, and rips and mends from everywhere.

LaRue has since become the most faithful correspondent of anyone I've ever met in my travels. Her letters just about burst the seams of their envelopes. In a larger town they'd be sent back to her for additional postage, but they've always made it to me with just one stamp. They also tend to arrive when I'm really in need of a lift. They're filled with little tidbits of small town news—this about the church, that about the quilting circle, something about her health and, "Look, it's fixing to rain again, and we've already had so much this year." Once, she sent me letter that included a few lines from almost everyone I had met in Lovelaceville.

As soon as I got back on the road, those heavy storms crossed the Mississippi, and I spent a week slogging across southern Illinois and Indiana, just missing several tornadoes.

The dark clouds finally went away in Ohio, but the storm left behind a persistent headwind. After four days of beating into it, I was thoroughly fed up. On Sunday, June 6, I leaped off the bike, slammed it to the ground, and gave that wind a good cussing out—right across the road from a Catholic church. My outburst must have done some good, because the next day I crossed the Michigan border with a mighty tailwind behind me. On Tuesday, June 8, I crossed the Ann Arbor city limits. Thirteen months and 8,300 miles had passed since I'd seen this place. To celebrate my arrival, I emptied my water bottle over my head. It wasn't champagne, but it sure felt like it.

I visited my old Ann Arbor friends for three days, then said goodbye. During my travels, I'd realized I could no longer call this college town home. Almost a year before, I had told Curt Naeser that I wanted to come back and live in Pittsburgh. At that point, I still had a lot of America to pedal. I quietly committed myself to being open to another place that might have greater appeal. No other place did, so it was back to Pittsburgh for me. But I wasn't quite ready to make that move yet. Instead, I bought a one-way train ticket and went out to visit my parents in West Chester Pennsylvania. I slept off the rest of my road weariness during the first part of the trip, then awoke as the train snaked through the mountains of West Virginia and Maryland. I kept my nose pressed to the glass as I watched swift, rocky rivers and lush green forests flow by. Occasionally, I spotted a road leading back into that tantalizing wilderness, and I felt a faint longing stirring deep inside as I remembered that not too long ago I was out on roads just like it. But that part of my life was over now—I'd said that to anyone who'd listen since Tuesday. But deep down, I knew that wanderlust would never leave me.

DRIVER'S ED FOR BICYCLISTS

During my travels, I was often asked if I was afraid to ride on the road "with all those cars." When the answer came back, "Not really," my questioners were astounded.

My relative lack of fear had come from completing the League of American Wheelmen's Effective Cycling course in spring 1980. Taught by a national network of LAW-certified instructors, Effective Cycling is the biking world's equivalent of driver's ed. The course's premise is that bicyclists aren't so much riders of bicycles as they are drivers of vehicles, and it teaches them to act accordingly. Effective Cycling is based on a book of the same name by John Forester, an engineer and traffic consultant based in Sunnyvale, California. Forester's book—a typewritten, spiral bound thing that definitely wasn't coffee table material—was my class text. (That ugly manual has since become a professionally produced MIT Press book that would be a classy addition to any cyclist's coffee table. It's also one of the best all-around cycling reference books on the market.)

The book and my class instructor argued that riding in traffic wasn't as dangerous as we had been led to believe. Drawing on reams of U.S. accident statistics, the book dispels the notion that most bicycle accidents are caused by cars. Actually, about half of all bicycle accidents result from the cyclist falling off his or her bike. The statistics on car-bike accidents don't make cyclists look much better: About half of these are caused by the bicyclists disobeying traffic laws or riding in a nonstandard way. Number One on the hit parade of cyclist faux pas is not yielding to cross traffic. Numbers Two and Three are riding against traffic and not yielding the right of way when changing lanes.

In short, cars aren't anywhere near the menace to cyclists that cyclists are to themselves. And bike paths and bike lanes certainly aren't the solution to this problem. The book cites numerous studies that have shown them to be much more dangerous than a normal road. What's the solution? Teaching cyclists the principles of vehicular cycling, which is exactly what Effective Cycling does.

The Effective Cycling class forced me to confront my own fear of riding in traffic by arming me with the knowledge and skills I needed to ride my bike like the vehicle it is. I had to prove that I'd learned my lessons during weekly practice sessions covering such skills as lane changing, rock-dodging, panic stops and instant right turns. In addition to the class time, there was "homework," which consisted of riding a certain number of miles each week in varying traffic conditions and terrain. The final exam consisted of a written test and a road test in Ann Arbor traffic. Effective Cycling wasn't an easy course—I had to take it twice before I passed the final. But I can say from my own experience that what I learned in Effective Cycling has saved my life many times over.

The League of American Wheelmen can provide you with additional information on the Effective Cycling program and can fill your order for Effective Cycling books and videos. Write or call:

League of American Wheelmen
190 West Ostend Street, Suite 120
Baltimore, Maryland 21230-3755
(410) 539-3399 or (800) 288-BIKE

• 17 •

Pittsburgh

I spent the rest of the summer at my parents' house, outlining a book about my travels. The bike was exiled to the basement. My year in the saddle had left me with zero motivation to ride. But it did earn me some local notoriety. A reporter and a photographer from West Chester's *Daily Local News* came out to do a story on me. The photographer turned out to be an old mentor—he'd supervised me during a two-week internship at the end of my high school senior year. I don't recall much about what I did for the paper, but I remember the internship as a welcome refuge from school, where my athletic and social ineptitude were the butt of numerous jokes. If my tormentors could see me now, seven years later...

I was brimming full of confidence and ready to take on anything—including Pittsburgh's tight job market. I set about that task at the end of August 1982, when I bade my parents farewell and went out to the Naesers' homestead in Good Intent. They'd generously offered me a place to stay while I looked for work.

Curt insisted that I "earn my keep," so Peter and Gary put me to work in the log home business. They had me washing walls, sweeping floors, taking out trash, even digging ditches. I enjoyed working on the construction crew, but I soon had to yield my place to one of the Naesers' regular employees, a neighbor with a wife and kids and plenty of bills to pay.

After Labor Day, I began job hunting in earnest. I wanted to go back into editorial work and was eager to get on with what Curt had so aptly called "the business of making a living." I'd been out of my field for more than two years, but I was sure that my travel experiences would grab the attention of Pittsburgh's top editors and set me apart from all the other job seekers. Unfortunately, my lofty expectations were no match for reality. Pittsburgh's unemployment rate was edging up toward 20%. The editors I talked with enjoyed my road stories, but they weren't about to hire me—or anyone else, for that matter.

In late September, Ruthie Naeser DeWitt informed her folks that she and her daughter were coming back home to Good Intent. The Naesers gently told me that it was time to move on, so I took up residence in the guest room of my old next-door neighbors in Peters Township, the Heinrichses. Another former neighbor, Bill Staley, drove me into Pittsburgh each morning, then gave me a bus ticket for the afternoon trip home.

In October, I joined an informal job hunters' support group at the Oakland Women's Center near the University of Pittsburgh campus. There was no set meeting time—we'd just wander in and out as we pleased. We'd trade stories, offer advice, and generally try to keep up each other's spirits.

Keeping mine up grew progressively more difficult as my search dragged on. Frank and Helen Heinrichs had been through everything imaginable with their four children, so they understood my unemployed blues quite well. But I was still shocked when Helen said I was getting so depressed I ought to see a therapist.

And I was hurt when Frank told me to stop looking for the perfect job and just find something—anything! He was right. The rest of my bicycle trip reserve was dwindling rapidly. Although my dad had begun loaning me money, he couldn't carry me forever.

Dad told me my job hunt would go better if I took a room in Pittsburgh. I was skeptical, but he sent me a check for the first month's rent. After visiting my parents on Thanksgiving, I moved in with a single mother who'd posted a "roommate wanted" sign on the Women's Center bulletin board.

Her 12-year-old son became my first best friend in Pittsburgh, but she and and I didn't get along so well. She asked me to leave by the end of December.

I didn't have another place to live by then, so I stored my stuff in the basement of the neighborhood church and promised the sexton I'd be back for it in a few days. Afterward, I went downtown to buy an American Youth Hostels pass, like the one I'd used during my travels. Then I spent New Year's Eve alone in the Point Park College Hostel, a 19th floor dormitory room full of empty bunk beds.

The rules said I could only stay three nights, but I had no place else to go. For the first time in ages, I prayed to something—anything—to get me out of this predicament. I prayed all night long—there was nothing else I could do. I was too wired to sleep.

Early the next morning, I got on the Oakland bus and went out to the Episcopal church I'd recently joined. There was a small New Year's Day service in one of the chapels, and everyone else looked positively radiant. I was trying to keep from crying.

I'd enlisted the rector's aid in my housing search, but so far his luck hadn't been any better than mine. After the service was over, I told him I had two nights left at the hostel, then nothing.

He excused himself and went back into the altar guild room for a few minutes. He returned with a short, stocky lady who spoke with a thick Italian accent and offered her Shadyside apartment's extra bedroom. If I liked it, we'd "talk business," and she'd rent me the room. We struck a deal the next day, and I lived with Mafalda Jones for a year and a half.

In mid-January 1983, I began working as a part-time cleaner at the Second Plate restaurant in the University of Pittsburgh's massive Forbes Quadrangle. The Quad was built after the Pirates' Forbes Field was torn down, and home plate had been set into the first floor tiles. The restaurant's second-floor location roughly coincided with the old second base.

For washing dishes, busing tables, sweeping and mopping floors, and taking out the garbage, I made $50 a week. And the Plate offered its employees a very important benefit—free meals. On my work days, I came in a little early and had a bagel with cream cheese and a big salad before my shift. At closing time, Patty the manager gave me the leftovers, which I took home for the next morning's breakfast.

When I first started working at the Plate, I was ecstatic about having a job. I was sure I'd only have to do a few months of this subsistence stuff, then the job market would open up and I'd be back on that editorial career ladder. But the effort of trying to live on $50 a week quickly overrode my optimism. I was tense and irritable and constantly trying to ration my energy when I wasn't working. Staying at home in my room didn't require much caloric expenditure, so I did a lot of that. I occupied myself by writing chapters of my book on the blank sides of used computer paper I'd taken from the discard bin at the Forbes Quad computer center.

I also did a lot of thinking, much of it focused on that philosophy of "voluntary simplicity" that I shared with my Ann Arbor friends. In Pittsburgh, that philosophy and its slogan, "Live simply so that others may simply live," had become my credo for survival.

When Pitt's semester ended in May, Patty informed me that the Plate would have to let me go. I got called back to work a week later, but with reduced hours. My weekly take-home pay was down to $30, and there was no way I could even begin to live on that. Once again, I was on a job search to find something—anything!

In mid-June 1983, I applied for a fulltime job at the East End Food Co-op. This one paid $150 a week, and I felt like I'd hit the Pennsylvania Lottery when I heard that I'd been hired. I spent my last week at the Plate in a state of ecstasy.

The co-op was just a mile north of Shadyside in Garfield, a neighborhood that tottered on the brink of becoming a slum, but managed to retain its dignity. The co-op was in Garfield because it couldn't afford anyplace else. Calling it a shoestring operation would be generous. Bare bones was more like it.

The store's 1950s vintage coolers and freezers broke down constantly, but were somehow kept alive through the mechanical wizardry of John the manager and his cadre of neighborhood helpers. Recycled peanut butter buckets on homemade racks served as bulk food containers, and the herbs and spices were kept in gallon mayonnaise jars finagled from a nearby restaurant. Our single shelf of "grocery store" items like canned soup, cereal, and toilet paper was held together with twist ties and heavy duty paper clips.

You had to be a member to shop at the co-op—joining was as easy as paying $2.00 and putting your name and address on an index card so you could get the newsletter and vote at the annual meeting. I'd joined shortly after I moved into Pittsburgh.

There were about 1,200 members in all—punk rockers, yuppies, gays, lesbians, anarchists, Republicans, strict vegetarians, devout carnivores, Orthodox Jews, born-again Christians, welfare recipients, near-millionaires, and many others who defied description.

They viewed their co-op as more than just a place to shop. It was a social center, and, for many of them, a refuge, one of the few places in conservative Pittsburgh where they could unabashedly be themselves.

One of the co-op's most devoted members was a short, muscular guy named George, who stopped in to buy some fresh fruit almost every day. He also helped us with our nighttime cleanup and picked up the the co-op's weekly cider order at a nearby farmers' market.

George was a long-distance runner with one marathon to his credit, and in his late thirties still did 15 miles a day. The miles he didn't get by running, he walked. On the nights I closed the co-op, he'd tidy up out front while I did the daily cash report in the office. Then we'd head up to Highland Park and walk one, two, even three times around the one-mile circular drive below the city reservoir.

Our first walk totaled eight miles, and I savored the same feeling of accomplishment as I did after my first one-mile swim or ten-mile bike ride. I was immediately hooked. I wanted more walks. John had me closing almost every night, so it was easy to get together with George.

He'd read a lot about nutrition, and freely shared his knowledge with me. George strongly advocated a very low fat regimen with lots of fresh fruit and vegetables and little else. He also took a lot of vitamin and mineral supplements. For him, it paid off. He was five-foot six and 140 pounds of solid muscle.

George took great pride in his training log, which he kept on a calendar in his living room. There he recorded all those rain-or-shine miles up at the park, along with his swimming yardage, tennis scores, and weightlifting and aerobics sessions.

I started keeping my own log, and watched my walking miles build up to 20, 30, even 40 miles a week. I hit 50 once, and was so burned out the following week I could barely drag myself to 20.

George's house was on one of the highest hills in Pittsburgh, with an exquisite view of Downtown's skyscrapers, Pitt's 40-story Cathedral of Learning, the Monongahela River steel mills, and St. Francis Hospital, where I'd been born. He rented his upstairs rooms to people who shared his diet and exercise philosophy, and he repeatedly asked me to move in. In June 1984, I did.

George wasn't the only person trying to broaden my diet and exercise horizons. Ruth Naeser preached to me the natural foods and vitamin supplement gospel of Adelle Davis and *Prevention* magazine while I was staying down in Good Intent. Shortly after I left the Naesers for the Heinrichses, I met Peters Township's foremost health-nut-and-proud-of-it, Jane Twomey. She was a yoga teacher who boasted that she'd once been kicked out of an ashram in the Bahamas because she went up the beach to a casino. Even though her free-spirited ways raised eyebrows at the Sivananda Center, she loved her yoga. She was convinced that it would be just the thing to limber up my skinny body and calm my edgy, hyperactive self. Not me.

"I'm not going to turn myself into a pretzel!" I bellowed.

Jane gently explained that yoga wasn't about weird postures, it was about proper breathing, which ultimately was about meditation. Proper yogic breathing—pranayama—meant emptying the lungs completely, then taking deep breaths that started way down in the diaphragm. She taught me a few basic postures—asanas—to go with my pranayama. They felt suspiciously like the warmup stretches my Ann Arbor bike club buddies kept urging me to do. Jane explained that those stretches were based on yoga.

She encouraged me to practice yoga for its own sake, and I did—to a certain extent. I did as many asanas as I could in my cramped Shadyside and Garfield quarters, and did more elaborate sessions at Jane's.

Almost all the flat space in Jane's house—floors, stairs, counters, couches, dressers, and extra beds—was covered with books, magazines, tapes and pamphlets on nutrition, meditation, organic gardening, homeopathic medicine, massage, acupuncture, exercise—and yoga. She was a compulsive information collector, and we could both laugh about that.

When I teased Jane about being such a health nut, she'd look perplexed and ask if the alternative was to be an illness nut. She loved telling me how she'd overcome chronic internal infections, progressive spinal arthritis, diabetes, and heart murmur with a natural foods diet, vitamin and mineral supplements, yoga, and lots of determination.

In 1973—a decade into her recovery—Jane's husband left her. Jane had been struggling on her own ever since, and barely made ends meet by teaching yoga and running several multi-level marketing businesses. She lived with the ever-present possibility that she might go broke and lose her house.

But Jane wasn't bitter — she was one of the happiest people I'd ever met. "I've got a love affair with life that just won't quit!" she insisted during one of our many late-night telephone conversations, which she liked to call "telephone parties."

I was considerably less enthusiastic about my own life. I constantly longed for that mythical place called "the road," where everything had been better. What I conveniently ignored was that being on the road could also be a tough, lonely business. As mundane as my life had become, I found a lot of comfort in having a steady job, although it was a dead-ender that wouldn't even challenge a high school graduate. But I was only too eager to take the money that it paid me, and spend a lot of my free time socializing with co-op members, who threw some of the liveliest parties in town.

Still, I often felt that something was missing from my life. Like me, most of my fellow Pittsburghers had been born there. They seemed content to spend the rest of their lives there, too. Not me. I felt like a lion that was trapped a in cage that was too small. I wanted out!

Whenever I could, I'd get on the bike and make brief escapes from Pittsburgh. I'd dash 20 miles up the Allegheny River to Tarentum or seek out some thigh-busting climbs amidst the country clubs and estates of Fox Chapel. For a few hours, I'd be light years away from the dead end job, away from the dying Rust Belt city. When I wasn't riding, I often imagined myself loading up the bike, pedaling out over to Fifth Avenue in Shadyside, then heading west, west, west...

In early 1985, I realized my long-held dream of becoming an author with the publication of *Ride Over The Mountain*, the predecessor of this book. Although I'd submitted my story to more than two dozen commercial publishers, none were interested. So I had 1,000 copies printed and sold them myself.

John the co-op manager let me set up a book display by the cash register, and the members quickly became my best customers. Another local author/publisher agreed to be my press agent, and got me on several Pittsburgh TV and radio talk shows. This little media blitz did almost nothing for sales, but it went a long way toward rebuilding the self-esteem I had lost during two and a half years of unemployment and underemployment.

My *Ride Over The Mountain* received favorable mention in several cycling magazines. I placed ads in some of them and soon found myself in charge of a busy little mail-order business. I also sold it in several of Pittsburgh's bicycle and outdoor equipment shops.

Although I wanted to be perched atop the bestsellers list, I was instead given a string of modest successes. My publishing venture even turned a small profit. It also gave me the confidence to do what I most wanted to do—get out of that dead-end co-op job and return to the editorial field.

In January 1986, I became managing editor of an academic journal at Pitt. My job was to annotate newly issued books in business and economics, then assemble the annotations into a quarterly journal.

My office was in Pitt's economics department, two floors above the Second Plate. I got a special thrill out of going down to the Plate and paying for my food, extracting my wallet from the hand-sewn leather briefcase my Aunt Jean had just given me for Christmas, instead of that ratty old blue backpack I used to toss in the corner after punching the Plate's time clock.

I was especially glad to have finally landed something that had eluded me during my 1982 job search: a university job. Not only did Pitt's academic atmosphere appeal to me, the university also offered its employees the opportunity to take courses at greatly reduced tuition rates. This benefit prompted many tens of thousands of people to apply for employment at Pitt each year, a situation that led to the local joke that getting a job at Pitt was harder than gaining admission to Harvard. So I felt very fortunate to have gotten in.

My plans for further education at Pitt centered on expanding the business knowledge I'd gained as a book publisher by studying for the MBA degree. However, those plans faded after a few weeks of annotating the general equilibrium theory of this and an econometric model of that. The business books weren't any more interesting. I was having a hard time staying awake in this job, and Pitt's personnel policy stated that new employees had to complete a full year in one department before transferring to another. The year 1986 looked like it was going to be the longest year of my life.

But the job paid better than any I'd had before—I was up to $13,000 a year. Since I'd grown so adept at living on next to nothing, I was able to save a good portion of each paycheck. I told my friends and family that I wanted to buy a house and really settle down in Pittsburgh. This town looked a whole lot better now that I'd climbed above the poverty line. The ones who knew what I made told me that my salary wouldn't even get me a doghouse. I kept on saving anyway.

In March 1986, I bought a black Cannondale racing bike from three guys who'd taken a bold gamble and opened a high-end bike shop at the top of a steep street in Squirrel Hill. Pittsburgh's narrow, crumbling streets and hilly terrain meant that local cycling was not for the faint of heart or weak of legs. Those of us who rode there took pride in being part of a very special counterculture. At least once during a weekend, we'd show up at Pittsburgh Pro Bikes to brag about how we'd walloped some big hill or grouse about another damn pothole that flattened a tire and bent the rim, too.

My new Cannondale was a fast, flashy machine, one that turned my Nobilette touring bike into a cobweb gathering device. On weekends, I'd sneak out of town on the 'Dale and do my Tarentum run or my Fox Chapel stomp, then come back into town to do some more riding.

To console my forsaken Nobilette and to get out of the stultifying slowness of summertime life at Pitt, I took a late August tour of Washington and Oregon, states 39 and 40 on my roster. I was escorted out of Tacoma, Washington, by a League of American Wheelmen hospitality home host who'd biked 50 miles from his place in Centralia just to meet me. John Kelley was a big redheaded Irishman with a constant stream of jokes and a special affinity for women who rode bicycles. He supported his cycling habit by driving gravel trucks and lived for his annual tour of Baja California. When his last boss wouldn't give him the time off, Kelley quit.

"I'd never quit my job to go biking," I insisted. After all, my bike tours had taken place after I'd been laid off or had come to the end of temporary jobs. Kelley gave me a mischievous look, one that said, "You'll eat those words someday."

Kelley took me out for a Mexican dinner in nearby Chehallis, then drove me to a spot outside town where I could take pictures of Mt. St. Helens. Then back to his place for a tour through the photo album he put together after St. Helens dumped countless shovels full of ash in his backyard.

Two days later, I was put up in grand style by Kelley's friends, Roger and Pat Humphrey, in their big country house outside Vancouver, Washington. Roger and Pat organized an annual late June ride around Mt. St. Helens that was a popular fundraiser for the local American Cancer Society. Kelley joked that the Humphreys probably wouldn't let me go home without making me promise to do To Hel'en Back '87. I told him I had no idea when I'd ever get back to the Northwest again.

Not that the Humphreys didn't try their best subliminal persuasion—gourmet meals, romps in the yard with Gator, their exuberantly friendly pit bull, and a date with a handsome blond Vancouver bike club member who was only too eager to show me the Oregon side of the Columbia River.

Roger drove me to the Portland airport without extracting any promises, but made it very clear that he and his buddies were ready to help in any way if I ever wanted to do To Hel'en Back.

I seriously considered not getting that flight back to Pittsburgh. I'd renewed my acquaintance with that "life on the road" drug, and I wanted more.

I returned to find things at the office just as stultifying as ever. At home, George and I were barely speaking. He was still obsessed with his daily laps around the park and his raw fruit and vegetable diet. I hardly ever went up to the park any more, and I found his diet too restrictive. We were drifting apart, and neither of us wanted to do anything about it.

Over Pitt's staff Christmas break, I briefly visited my parents, then flew out to Phoenix and crashed for a few days on Brent Spalding's floor. In four and a half years, that tall, shy kid who'd been my almost-little brother had become an even taller, still shy but articulate young man who was about to graduate from Arizona State University. He and his ASU buddies were packing up to move out of their rented house in South Phoenix, and Brent was working full time at the university's public TV station.

Chuck Malenfant had already graduated from ASU and had just gone off to teach English in Japan. Brent's older brother, Mark, had come back to Phoenix after graduating from the University of Arizona and was working full time and contemplating graduate school. Circumstances kept Mark and I from anything more than a telephone get-together, and Dad Spalding had to run back to northwest Phoenix after picking me up at the airport and taking me over to Brent's.

What I didn't see of Brent I made up for by riding the 'Dale around Phoenix and Tempe and asking everyone I met about what it was like to live in Arizona. To a man and woman, they were enjoying it immensely, and none of the non-natives confessed any desire to go back where they came from. They especially liked the warmth and sunshine in the winter, and I was enjoying those things so much that I'd lost all desire to go back to Pittsburgh. Deep down, I knew I wouldn't be there much longer.

In mid-January, the journal's computer crashed during manuscript production and I had no idea how to revive it. All I could do was bury my head in my hands. I knew I was finished long before the boss called me into her office.

Her tirade was quick and blistering, then she reverted to conversational tones and her steely blue eyes softened.

"It's obvious that you're miserable here," she said.

"You're right."

She told me to start looking for another job, and I replied that I might as well find another city. She insisted that I didn't have to do anything that drastic, but I'd had enough of things going wrong in Pittsburgh. It was time to move on. I set my resignation for Friday, March 20.

I decided that life after Pittsburgh would start with my taking a few months off for some cycletouring. I figured that my "doghouse" savings and what was left in the book's bank account would last about six months, enough for a tour and getting started in a new city afterward.

Going border to border from Mexico to Canada had long intrigued me—now I had my chance to do it. I mapped out a route that would include five of my final ten states: Kansas, South Dakota, North Dakota, Wyoming and Montana. After the bike trip was over, I'd settle somewhere in the Southwest. I hoped to find my new home during my ride.

My parents were horrified at the thought of my throwing away my life in Pittsburgh for another in a place I didn't even know. Our weekly telephone conversations turned into shouting matches until I stopped calling. Before I left town, they sent a letter that essentially said, "It's your life. Do with it what you will."

During the week after I resigned Pitt, I sold the remainder of my books to a mail order house, had a "bon voyage" dinner courtesy of Jane Twomey, told the post office to hold my mail until I sent for it, and packed my stuff into boxes and stored them with a guy who owned part of the bike shop where I bought my Cannondale. That bike would also be his houseguest for a while. The Nobilette was going with me.

On Saturday, March 28, George and I said goodbye while avoiding each other's eyes, then his two other boarders took me to the airport. Once again, my destination was Phoenix, this time with a one-way ticket.

• 18 •

Can't Believe I'm
On The Road Again

O n the plane, my seatmates were a very curious couple of West Virginians who found my carry-on luggage of bike panniers, a sleeping bag and helmet to be so fascinating that they couldn't resist peppering me with questions about my upcoming journey. My nonchalant replies only provoked more questions, which was exactly the opposite of what I wanted. Having just left a man I wished I'd never gotten involved with in a city I never hoped to set foot in again, I really wanted some quiet time to reflect on the five years that had passed since my last journey. I also wanted to engage in some mental preparation for the journey that was about to begin. It turned out that the quiet time had to wait until I began riding, and I found that the three months of my 1987 ride provided ample time for introspection. But the emotional journey was a difficult one, because I quickly found that playing the "blame game" wasn't going to explain all of the misfortunes I'd encountered in Pittsburgh. What was left was a long, slow playing of the "look in the mirror" game to examine the part I'd played in my misfortunes.

After I got off the plane, I picked up the bike and reassembled it slowly, just to enjoy the process. I was enjoying a freedom I hadn't known in years, the freedom from externally imposed schedules and expectations. From Phoenix's Sky Harbor Airport, I knew I was heading over to Tempe to spend the weekend with Brent Spalding and his friends, then I'd pedal on to Tucson, Mexico, and Canada. Where would I end up and when? I had no idea.

Brent's apartment was in the midst of the ASU student ghetto, and he lived with a bohemian couple who were arguing about what to wear to their weekly pilgrimage to "Rocky Horror Picture Show" when I showed up. Eventually, they resolved their differences and found the attire to make them look sufficiently transsexual at the midnight picture show.

Brent had invited some friends over for a Saturday evening get-together. I'd met several of them during my December visit, and told one that I'd decided to quit my crummy job back in Pittsburgh, go biking for a while, then start a new life in the Southwest.

"Congratulations!" he said without any hesitation.

Back east, that statement had been met with great enthusiasm or great horror—there was no middle ground. To everyone who said I was taking a leap into the great unknown, I expressed my belief that God would lead me to a place where I'd come down on my feet. That statement surprised even me, because I'd never been a terribly religious person. I'd briefly been a member of a church in Pittsburgh, but could not feel any connection with the God presented there.

After leaving the church, I became acquainted with numerous people who'd also been disappointed by their experiences with organized religion. They gave me some advice that surprised me. Rather than rejecting all that religion had to offer, they urged me to form my own personal concept of God. I didn't even have to call it God, just as long as it was something I could turn to for help and guidance. They told me they didn't need any set place or ritual for communicating with their God, they did it while they were sitting quietly, kneeling, feeding the kids, doing the dishes, walking the dog, even while making love. I told them that was fine for them, but it would never work for me. They just smiled and said they'd once been where I was. They told me to keep an open mind and it would come to me. Three years later, it had.

Sunday, Dad Spalding came down to Tempe to get Brent, who needed to pick up some stuff from home. I went along and spent the night in Brent's spotless room, which felt like a shrine that Dad had preserved to remember a teenager who was no longer. Brent slept the night in the living room, where the two of us and his high school buddies used to have theme "camp-outs," complete with sleeping bags, a "moon" we created on the ceiling with a dim lamp, and a tape of the Okefenokee Swamp at night. When I reminded Brent of our living room encampments and all that hanging out everyone used to do in his very cluttered room, which was called "the Center of the Spalding Existence," he winced. Although he obviously didn't want to be reminded of what he'd outgrown, I very much wanted to tell him that my memories of those things carried me through a lot of hard times in Pittsburgh.

Dad ran us back to Tempe early the next morning, March 30, and I gathered up my stuff and loaded it on the bike, the first episode of a morning ritual that would dominate my life for months to come. Brent and I had a brief hug, then it was out into Monday morning rush-hour traffic for me and back to ASU for him.

My destination for the day was a state park near Apache Junction, 20 miles east of Tempe. I pedaled most of the distance to Apache Junction with a big, dopey smile, and made numerous attempts to sing Willie Nelson's "On The Road Again."

Although my singing ability hadn't improved since my earlier cycling journeys, I'd upgraded just about everything on my bike. It now had a crankset with three chainrings—including a small "granny" ring to give me low gears for the mountains, a wider, padded saddle that was far more posterior-friendly than the leather ones I'd previously used, and a computer. Although I'd seen many Pittsburgh cyclists become numbers-crazy after they'd installed computers on their bikes, I reluctantly decided to put one on each of mine. I found that I enjoyed knowing how far I went on my jaunts outside the city, even though my speed never improved. I'd traded the wool cycling togs in for Lycra jerseys, shorts and tights, and the rainbow Bell helmet had been replaced by a designer Vetta model from Italy.

Camp at Apache Junction was filled with people from every state but Arizona. A photographer from Homer, Alaska, offered me the rest of the spaghetti he had cooked for dinner, a New Hampshire couple expressed horror at the local custom of carrying a revolver in one's holster (it is legal in Arizona), and another couple from Washington state asked me and everyone else where the local swap meet was. They had a camper full of smoked salmon they needed to sell, but the woman went ahead and gave me a package to take with me, raving all the while about what a wonderful place the road was "because you meet people like all of us." I had to pinch myself to make sure I wasn't dreaming.

But my "back on the road" high dissolved Tuesday morning, when I realized that my decision not to wear sunscreen the day before had brought me a nasty sunburn. And both the interesting mountain routes and the shorter, but boring, flatland routes to Tucson featured a headwind. I chose the flatlands.

I slugged it out through more than 70 miles of desert and cotton fields until I could take no more and stopped in Picacho, a tiny village bisected by Interstate 10. Home for the night was the KOA Kampground.

I spent the evening pumping quarters into the pay phone, trying to reach the one person I knew in Tucson. Susan had been a volunteer at the co-op and moved west shortly after I started working at Pitt. I'd called her before I left Pittsburgh and I couldn't help envying what her life had become. She'd finally found a job she enjoyed. She was in love with a man she planned to marry. She also bragged about how she and her friends could wear shorts to go hiking in February. Perhaps Tucson could work similar magic in my life, I thought. Maybe I'd move there... Susan had offered me a place to stay while I visited Tucson, and I'd written to tell her that I'd be riding through the mountains to get there. Not anymore. Now I couldn't get ahold of her to tell her my plans had changed and I'd be in town tomorrow. Damn! I banged the phone receiver down and stomped back to my tent. The roar of I-10 prevented me from getting more than a few shreds of sleep, and I crawled out the next morning in a worse mood than the one I'd gone to bed with.

I pedaled along 30 miles of bumpy freeway frontage road before I reached the outskirts of Tucson. I finally got ahold of Susan at her office at the University of Arizona. Even though she wasn't expecting me yet, she took me in for a week.

Since she was busy with her job and her man, I embarked on my own bicycle exploration of Tucson, and fell deeply in love with it. My favorite hangout became the university's grassy mall, where the students gathered at midday. Itinerant evangelists also frequented the mall. They preached at the students, who kept right on eating, flirting or sunbathing. One preacher conducted his sermon from the top of a trashcan, which prompted a student working at an undergraduate humanities benefit cookout to jump into another trashcan and start his own harangue.

"Brothers and sisters!" the student cried. "You feel a hunger, a yearning. You need to be filled!"

All eyes were on him.

"Well, of course you're hungry! It's time for lunch! You need a burger!" He held one up. He looked just like the statue outside a Big Boy restaurant.

By this time, the only straight face on the mall belonged to the flustered preacher, who hadn't moved. Then the chanting started: "Burger church! Burger church! Burger church!" The preacher quit for the day.

The mall was also the starting and ending point for the first annual 65-mile Tour of the Tucson Mountains, a university scholarship fund-raiser. The ride was put on by a local long distance cyclist-turned event organizer named Richard DeBernardis. Before I left Pittsburgh, the owner of the mail-order house to which I'd sold the remainder of my books gave me DeBernardis' address, noting that we'd probably enjoy swapping travel stories. I wrote him a letter of introduction, and promised to look him up in Tucson. When we met, I learned that DeBernardis' specialty was perimeter cycling, and that he'd already biked the edge of America and Japan. To encourage others to try "cycling on the edge," he'd founded the Perimeter Bicycling Association of America (PBAA). PBAA already sponsored a popular ride around the city of Tucson each November, and now it was making a bold foray into southern Arizona's busy spring cycling calendar. DeBernardis made me a guest of honor for the Tour of the Tucson Mountains.

Early Sunday morning, April 5, I pedaled over to the mall from Susan's apartment, fastened numbers to myself and my bike, then got into the back of a very long pack of cyclists. Somewhere in front, a cannon sounded, and we were off and running toward the Tucson Mountains west of town.

I quickly found that the other cyclists' notion of a tour differed markedly from my own. They all sprinted away on their ultralight speed machines and left me behind. I'd come with panniers loaded with bike tools, extra water and my camera. I took lots of pictures of a saguaro cactus forest, chatted with university students working the refreshment stops, and finished thirteenth from last. They'd run out of those medals everyone was supposed to get, but that was okay. A medal was just another heavy thing I'd have to carry up to Canada.

I left Tucson the following Wednesday, vowing that it would be my next home. I took a quick spin through the business district of Nogales, Sonora, on Thursday, April 9, then turned north again.

Thirty miles north of Nogales is a windswept village called Sonoita that sits amidst grasslands that go almost all the way to New Mexico. Each spring, about 200 cyclists converge on this place to participate in a weekend ride sponsored by Greater Arizona Bicycling Association's Tucson chapter. The ride heads southeast through the grasslands, traverses a mountain pass, then descends into the old copper mining town of Bisbee, which cheerfully allows itself to be taken over by cyclists for the weekend. Some of the riders race each other to Bisbee, others try to, and the rest just poke along. I landed squarely in the poke-along category, and was pleased to have plenty of company on Saturday.

My home in Bisbee was a postage stamp-sized churchyard that was occupied by a dozen other camping cyclists. After shoehorning my tent into a corner of the yard, I headed over to the underground mine tour. The mine no longer yielded any copper ore, but did a brisk trade in extracting greenbacks from visiting cyclists' wallets. Within seconds, our group attire changed from shiny black cycling shorts and tee shirts to long yellow slickers and mining helmets with headlamps powered by a battery pack strapped around our waists. Then, it was all aboard the miners' train and off we went into a very dark, very cold mine.

Our guide was a former miner given to lengthy explanations of the proper way to place explosives and how the mine's buzzer system was used to cuss out the guys working on other levels. I thoroughly enjoyed his storytelling, but wished I had worn warmer clothing. I was glad to get back above ground, back into 70-plus degree warmth.

Dinner was an all-you-can-eat lasagna fest hosted by the local Rotary Club. Afterward, I waddled over to the country dance, sat a few minutes with other cyclists who also were too stuffed to dance, then left to walk the tortuous course of the Vuelta de Bisbee bicycle race with an older gentleman who believed as I did, that racing was something better left to the racers. He walked me back to my churchyard home, and I made it back to my tent without falling over anyone else's. I'd just wrapped up the most enjoyable two weeks of cycling I'd ever had—in a place I'd soon call home. I couldn't wait to get back.

On Sunday, the wind picked up, giving the rest of them hell all the way back to Sonoita. For me it was a sidewind that nearly blew me off the bike as I headed north to Benson. It almost flattened my tent in the Benson KOA. After Benson, I took to the shoulder of I-10 and rode that crumbling highway into New Mexico, where smoother pavement welcomed my sore posterior.

In Lordsburg, I camped in a trailer park that was quickly losing its population of winter visitors to the annual migration back to the upper Midwest. The only other campers were a retired couple from San Diego who'd sold all their possessions and moved into their motorhome. They intended to live out their days on the road. While their RV wasn't as luxurious as some I'd seen, they certainly weren't roughing it. They were especially eager to show off their stereo system, starting with the radio. We tuned through the entire AM band and found nothing but static. FM yielded one classical music station from who-knows-where. We gave up on the stereo and tried the portable weather radio, which was supposed to pick up official government forecasts anywhere in the Lower 48. Nada.

Not only was Lordsburg one of the remotest places in America, it also felt like one of the coldest. I spent the night trying to get warm inside my sleeping bag. There was a guy who lived in a trailer at the edge of the park who'd invited me to stay with him for the night, and I really began to regret that I'd turned him down, although I sensed that his motives weren't entirely altruistic.

It took an hour of fast riding on the I-10 shoulder before I warmed up again. Sixty miles of the most nondescript desert

I'd ever seen stood between Lordsburg and Deming, and I spent most of the journey watching the numbers increase on my computer's trip odometer. This stretch of road also included the easiest Continental Divide crossing in the United States: no climb at all, just a big sign. I would have preferred a mountain pass to break up the monotony.

I took a couple days off in Las Cruces, then made the colossal error of starting my trek up the Rio Grande Valley on a raw, windy Easter morning. The combination of battling a ferocious sidewind, finding that my backroads route was filled with hostile motorists, and barely outrunning a snarling mongrel dog put me in a thoroughly rotten mood.

I pulled into a state park overlooking Caballo Lake and was relieved to find that my assigned site was in a deserted part of the park. I put my bike inside the site's picnic shelter, and made a bed on the concrete table with my sleeping bag, air mattress and tent, which would serve as a bivouac sack. Then I crawled inside for a late afternoon nap.

Unfortunately, my nap was interrupted by what I least wanted to have: company. An RV with a British Columbia plate had pulled into the space next to mine. I indignantly strode over to where it was parked, and quickly discovered that what its occupants wanted more than anything else was some company. The couple invited me over for dinner. We talked well into the night, and they saved me from having to pedal 90 miles into a headwind by giving me and the bike a lift up to Socorro the next morning. They gave me their address in a Vancouver suburb, and urged me to come see them later in my journey.

In the five years since I'd last seen Socorro, it had changed from a sleepy little desert town to an upscale place that was infested with yuppies. These people would never stoop so low as to trade firewood for ristras; they'd pay top dollar for both items and use them as decorations in those old adobe houses that had become quite fashionable. In a grocery store, I saw two members of this species greeting each other with a most un-New Mexican display of affection: hugging. Older Socorrans looked on in disbelief. I fled Socorro early the next morning.

I started to head east and retrace my 1982 route through the Manzano Mountains, but once again the wind was firmly against me. New Mexico was more than making up for the easy time I'd previously had with it. Contrary to what its license plates proclaimed, I concluded that New Mexico was truly the Land of Dis-Enchantment and I wanted nothing more than to get out of it. Unfortunately, the nearest state border was at least 200 miles away.

So I directed my bike and my crummy attitude north to Belen, where the campers at the state park had no intentions of leaving me alone to sulk. An Indian wearing braids and beads came over to my site and asked if I'd like to join a nature walk. I forced a friendly smile and said I'd love to. The other walkers were a very pregnant woman, her husband, and their two small children. We all piled into the family's ancient van and drove into the desert east of town. We parked alongside the road, then walked until we couldn't see the van anymore.

Our guide, Michael Running Wolf, was a member of the Micmac tribe from New Brunswick, "the only tribe that never came under control of the Canadian government," he said proudly. The elders of his tribe began instructing him in survival skills and the use of wild plants as medicine and food when he was nine. He told us that hard times lay ahead for everyone, "harder times than we have ever known. That's why I decided to share the knowledge of my people.

"I've never been to college myself, but I've taught at many of them," Michael said. "Right now, I'm doing an outdoor survival class at the University of New Mexico up in Albuquerque."

Much of our walk was devoted to identifying edible plants and medicinal herbs, tracing animal tracks, and finding a suitable spot for our silent meditation. With the rest of the group, I sat down in a clearing amidst the sagebrush, closed my eyes, and as Michael put it, "listened to the earth." When we were finished, Michael informed us that the land on which we had walked sold for $10,000 an acre. "But the earth is our mother," he said. "How can we buy her and sell her?"

This area had been discovered by people wishing to escape from Albuquerque and find a country lifestyle. "What would you do out here?" Michael challenged us.

"Dig a well," answered the man.

"Build a house," added his wife.

"Get a job, plug into the money economy," I said with a not-so-subtle hint of sarcasm.

"Yes, but when the Father throws the tomahawk from the sky and there is great trouble in the world, then how would you manage?"

I had no answer.

Later that evening, Michael and his girlfriend, Kat, gave me a bag of trail mix and another one full of chia seeds. "Chew on these, let your saliva mix the juices well, and they'll draw out the natural adrenaline of your body," she said. "The Apaches used chia when they ran across the desert in 110-degree heat."

I chewed those seeds nonstop all the way to Santa Fe, the highest and oldest capital city in the United States. The chia made my climb to Santa Fe much less strenuous than my previous high-altitude efforts in Colorado and Utah. Even so, Santa Fe's 7,000-plus foot elevation curtailed my motivation to go out and explore its history. I spent almost all of my time there hanging out in the offices of an alternative magazine. The night before, one of its editors had hosted me at her adobe cottage in the Sandia Mountains north of Albuquerque.

The magazine staff wore natural fiber clothing and spoke to each other in soft, breathy voices. They kept their refrigerator and cupboards well-stocked with health foods. The radio played meditative instrumental music. Being a confirmed Type-A person, I found all this Type-B behavior a bit hard to take.

As that Friday afternoon drew to a close, the magazine folks drifted out in ones and twos, wishing me a restful night's sleep in whatever place I found comfortable. Once they were all gone, I tuned the radio to a hard-driving rock-n-roll station from Albuquerque, but I quickly found it as grating as that afternoon's laid-back overdose. So I shut the radio off, dragged my sleeping bag into an office and slept until dawn.

Saturday morning, April 25, brought me a good, stiff climb through Glorieta Pass in the Sangre de Cristos, then a long descent into the grassy plains of northeastern New Mexico. The wind that pushed me across the state in '82 had returned, and on Sunday I was delighted to find myself coasting along at 22 mph. I could easily do 30 when I pedaled. Mentally, I took back every negative thing I had thought about New Mexico in the last two weeks.

My luck ran out the next morning. I'd just finished climbing out of the Canadian River valley east of Springer, stopped to photograph the wagon ruts from the old Santa Fe Trail, then wham! the east wind hit me like a wall. I struggled 30 more miles into Gladstone, which consisted of one store and a handful of houses. I shared my predicament with the lady running the store, who proceeded to buttonhole everyone who came in and asked them to give me a lift to the next town, Clayton, 50 more miles to the east. My saviors came in the form of a mother and son who were on their way to Missouri. They completely unpacked the back of their tiny Toyota Starlet to make room for me and my bike, reloaded their stuff, put my bike on top of everything, then we were off. After they unloaded me at the Clayton KOA, I tried to offer them gas money. They wouldn't take it.

On Tuesday morning, I crossed the border between New Mexico and Oklahoma. A few miles up the road, I caught a strong tailwind that blew me all the way to Rolla, Kansas, 102 miles from Clayton.

FINDING TOURING PARTNERS

Hey! What's the Lone Rider doing talking about touring partners?

Now, just because I've done most of my cycletouring by myself doesn't mean I don't like riding with people. I do. Ride with me and I'll talk your ear off. (Don't say I didn't warn you.)

The easiest way to find touring partners is not to have to look in the first place. You may already have a group of friends with whom you've ridden many miles, and you're so compatible that putting packs on your bikes and going out for a few weeks wouldn't be that big of a deal. Or your spouse, family or significant other is as crazy about cycling as you are. And they can't wait to get started on this touring business.

The second easiest way to find touring partners is to join an organized ride like the Greater Arizona Bicycling Association's ride from the Grand Canyon to Mexico, the Florida Bicycle Safari, or one of the many hundreds of similar events that take place each year. You'll be riding with a whole lot of people you've never known before, and you'll be surprised at how quickly you make friends. You can find these events listed in national cycling magazines such as *Bicycling*, regional newspapers such as *Spokes* (in the Mid-Atlantic states) and *The Bicycle Paper* (in the Pacific Northwest), and membership publications such as the League of American Wheelmen's *BICYCLE USA*.

BICYCLE USA even goes so far as to devote an entire issue to rides offered by bicycle touring companies. It's called the TourFinder and it comes out in the early spring. TourFinder lists general interest rides, self-guided rides, mountain bike rides and youth rides in the U.S. and other countries. (LAW's address is listed on page 39.)

If none of these ideas fits the bill and you still don't want to ride alone, you might want to advertise for touring partners. *BICYCLE USA* will publish free of charge listings for LAW members seeking touring companions, wanting to organize rides, or wishing to exchange information. Bikecentennial, the Women's

Cycling Network and the Women's Cycling Coalition also offer similar services to their members.

My one attempt at finding a touring partner through a LAW ad didn't pan out, so here is what I've gleaned from the experiences of others. The most important thing to remember when you're writing your ad is what's really important to you. If you're a diehard camper who wants to avoid motels at all costs, say so. If you want to do 50 miles a day and take time to smell the roses, or if you're into 100-plus mile days at a pace that would make a Tour de France rider jealous, put that information in, too. The same advice applies to dietary preferences, religion, politics, whatever. Likewise, when you respond to an ad, let the person or people who placed the ad know what's important to you. Take time to hear them out as well.

Since you and your potential touring partners will be spending days, weeks, months, maybe years in close proximity to each other, you might want to meet before you hit the road. If you're not able to do so, so be it. That doesn't mean you'll have a bad tour. But being up-front about what's important to you and having the pre-tour meeting are two excellent ways to facilitate good relations and open communication among your group. And these things are the very things on which your shared touring experience will depend.

• 19 •

"We Just Watch
Too Much Television"

Kansas was my 41st state. What it lacked in spectacular scenery, it more than made up in friendly inhabitants. From Rolla's one grocery store I phoned the Pentecostal church pastor's residence hoping for nothing more than permission to camp in his churchyard. Granted without hesitation. Toward evening, the pastor came to my camp, invited me over for a shower, dinner with his family, then an evening of TV with them.

The next morning, I headed north toward the Arkansas River (pronounced "Ar-KAN-sas" in Kansas) and made my next friend on a farm south of Ulysses. A dog came dashing out to the road to bark at me. Rather than yelling and sprinting away, I decided to stop and speak softly to him. Just what he wanted. He leaped up and down, tail wagging vigorously. Eager to please me, he showed off his finely honed vehicle-chasing skills, reserving his most ferocious outbursts for passing oil tanker trucks.

Not wanting to witness this dog's demise, I quietly got back on my bike and pedaled north while he chased a southbound car. About half a mile into my escape, I heard the sound of toenails clattering on pavement. My buddy had caught up with me. Up ahead was a hill—I'd sprint away and lose him there. I shifted into high gear and got out of my saddle to climb faster, but he stayed right with me. Finally, a car coming from Ulysses stopped and a man got out, opened the passenger door, and the dog got in. The man drove away without saying a word to me.

After lunch break in Ulysses, I continued north and entered the last thing I ever expected to see in Kansas: a desert. There were sand dunes covered by thin tufts of grass that were just barely holding on. In an effort to control erosion, many rows of used tires had been "planted" on the dunes.

The desert gave way to greenery along the banks of the Arkansas River. With my whole body shaking, I crossed the river's narrow bridge into Deerfield. Was this the bridge on which Hugh Baird Reynolds had been killed six years before? I'd never asked his mother, Dot Reynolds, exactly where it happened, nor had I mentioned the incident to anyone in Deerfield.

With the same trepidation, I crossed the Arkansas twice more the next morning before finding the county road that would take me north to U.S. 83 and Scott City. The county road started just outside Holcomb, the town immortalized by Truman Capote's *In Cold Blood*. Before their 1959 execution-style slaying by two drifters, the Clutter family farmed somewhere outside of town. If I passed by the farm, I didn't know it. In Scott City, the book was in the public library, but I was told that the Clutter murder case and Truman Capote were topics the locals no longer cared to discuss.

While I was at Pitt, I worked four doors down the hall from a professor who'd once been a Scott County boy. Gene Gruver was a soft-spoken man who stayed out of the rough-and-tumble of economics department politics, preferring instead to close his door and do his work. Periodically, he'd emerge from his office to go teach one of his classes.

Shortly after I started at Pitt, Gene's parents, Tom and Neva Gruver took a cross-country bus to Pittsburgh to visit Gene and his family. Gene took them around the department to introduce them to everyone, and they invited me to come stay with them if I was ever cycling across Kansas. A year later, on Thursday, April 30, I was bouncing up the dirt road to their wheat farm outside the semi-ghost town of Manning.

My arrival had been eargerly awaited by much of this part of the county—Neva even had the mailman on the lookout for me. The Gruvers had also held up lunch until I got there. Tom and Neva, their other son, Royce, his wife, Sue, their two-year-old son, Brad, and I joined hands around the table for grace, which in Tom's rendition was more an extended chat with God than a formal prayer. Brad was more interested in showing off his extensive collection of toys than in eating. He ultimately won the war of wills with his mother and began plowing the living room floor with his model John Deere tractor.

"My son drives a better tractor than I do," Royce joked.

The next morning, Royce took his parents and me over to a field he was preparing for planting. Royce started the used John Deere he'd bought at auction, then invited me to ride in the cab with him. After he plowed a few rows, he turned the controls over to me. I had to steer constantly to keep the tractor from veering off course. I also had to be on the lookout for Russian thistles—Westerners call them tumbleweeds—and badger holes. The former could lock up the plow and the latter could bounce the tractor and get a wheel stuck. The plow also could turn up rocks big enough to flip the tractor, an accident we probably wouldn't survive.

In addition to its physical risks, farming was also a huge financial gamble. "Around here, it's more profitable to grow oil than wheat," Royce told me. The Gruvers' property was surrounded by farms that had oil wells set out amidst the wheat and alfalfa fields. Unfortunately for the Gruvers, the oil company geologists found nothing that would warrant drilling beneath their land. In spring 1987, the price of wheat was slightly more than $2.00 per bushel. "Even the most frugal farmer has a cost per bushel of about $2.50 to $3.00," Royce explained. "None of us would be in this business if it weren't for the government subsidies."

I pictured Gene using this scenario to explain some bit of economic theory to his Pitt students. Out here, the stuff to which Gene had devoted his life was as comprehensible to his family as the native language of the local Chinese agricultural exchange student. "I've tried reading some of Gene's papers, but they're too dry for me," Royce said.

Royce gave a "pretty good" rating to my first-ever stint at the helm of a tractor, then he finished the day's plowing.

Afterward, we drove over to the grain elevator in nearby Grigston, where the manager offered me a tour. He handed me a hard hat, then opened the door to the man-lift, a cage about the size of a phone booth. He told me to push the "up" button, then wait for him at the top. I pushed the button, and the cage leaped upward. A few seconds later, I lifted my finger, and the cage came to a bone-jarring stop.

"You're not there yet!" someone hollered from below.

I was only about one third of the way into my ascent. Throughout the rest of the long ride, I began to comprehend why grain elevators were called the skyscrapers of the prairie.

Up on top, the wind nearly blew my hard hat off. I could see ten, 20, 30 miles across flatlands filled with green rectangles of wheat, alfalfa and pasture, interrupted by an occasional building. The nearest large city, Wichita, was more than 200 miles away. It was a place my hosts loved to visit, but as Neva aptly put it, "I can't wait to get back to these plains and stretch my eyes."

The elevator was criss-crossed by pipelines through which grain was circulated constantly. Pockets of stagnant grain can develop "hot spots," which can cause deadly explosions. Much of the manager's time was spent making sure this elaborate circulatory system worked. Before I left, the manager gave me a Grigston elevator baseball cap, telling me to "wear it, so people'll know you've been *here*."

Saturday evening was centennial celebration time in Healy, a place whose population wasn't much larger than its age. Just about every man, woman and child played a part in the patriotic pageant at the local school. The pageant was done to the accompaniment of taped music because there weren't enough people left over for a band.

The storm that had been brewing for the better part of Friday and Saturday let loose just before midnight. It didn't stop for three days. My farming hosts were grateful for the rain after a long dry spell. They teased me about bringing it with me. For them, it was "sit around and drink coffee" time. The talk was all about farming, a topic as foreign to me as Gene's work was to them. I'd never grown any food in my life.

The longer and harder it rained, the more confined I felt. The Gruvers treated their increasingly irritable houseguest with unfailing courtesy. More than anything else, I wanted to get back into my own private road-space. I was finally able to do so on Thursday, May 7, with a strong wind at my back.

Tom Gruver's Uncle Jesse had once been the Methodist minister in Grainfield, 50 miles north. I made that town my first overnight stop after Manning. I asked his present-day counterpart if I could pitch my tent in his churchyard.

"I don't care," he said.

Neither did the rest of the town, which was busy preparing for its annual carnival at the park across from my camp. I was completely ignored by everyone except the local farm implement dealer, who was setting up his carnival display. He invited me to climb a long, tall ladder and sit in the cockpit of a brand new combine. Its tires were taller than me. Compared to this 747, Royce Gruver's tractor seemed like a Piper Cub.

My next stop on the Gruvers' Kansas grapevine was with their longtime friend Gertrude Railsback, a retired teacher in Oberlin. As soon as I'd been properly fed and showered, we embarked on a whirlwind tour of the town. First there was the town museum, a grandma's attic sort of a place which included displays of arrowheads from all over the United States, an old post office, a general store, a sod house, a gown worn by a local resident at Theodore Roosevelt's inauguration, and a stuffed bald eagle.

Then there were the sidewalks downtown, many paved with bricks that read, "Do not spit on sidewalk." Gertrude said those warnings were part of a turn-of-the-century doctor's efforts to halt the spread of tuberculosis.

Onward to the town's newest addition, a manufacturing company that made boats with trailers molded to fit. Why a boat factory amidst these arid high plains? "The farm economy," the company president told me. His was a refrain I would continue to hear all the way up to Canada: the price of wheat was a dollar per bushel less than its production cost—and still falling. Farmers all over were going bankrupt, even the ones who adhered to Tom Gruver's "spend slightly less than what you take in" credo. The solution was to diversify the economy, he asserted.

"We want to make sure we're not wiped off the map," Gertrude added.

The next day, May 9, I entered Nebraska. Outside McCook, I spotted several snakes that had emerged from the marshes to sun themselves on the warm pavement. I saw hundreds more on my way up to North Platte—a few of them were rattlers, most just non-poisonous look-alikes. Many of them had been killed by motorists who'd deliberately run over them as they were crawling onto the roadway.

As I was registering and paying my overnight fee at a state recreation area in North Platte, the campground manager peppered me with questions about where I'd been, where I was going, and wasn't I just terrified to be traveling such a long way by myself.

"No, I've done this three times before," I said nonchalantly.

That pretty well ended the conversation for me, one to which I'd contributed little more than terse replies. I had grown quite weary of having to explain myself to everyone I met. What I did say made quite an impression on the manager, because he and a couple who came in to register after I left discussed it extensively.

Then this couple took it upon themselves to park near the secluded place I'd found for myself, and insisted upon driving me through the Nebraska Sandhills to their home in Alliance. The Sandhills were much too dangerous for me to traverse alone, they said. I'd heard the same warning about many other areas of the country—and I had never had serious trouble in any of them. Besides, I had wanted to see the Sandhills ever since I read about them in *National Geographic* when I was a kid, and no one was going to talk me out of riding through them now. Not even the woman, a Burlington Northern railroad mechanic, who said that one of the track crews had recently rescued a woman who'd been attacked on the highway near where they'd been working. Her husband nodded and murmured his agreement as he stood next to her, chain-smoking. Since I'm allergic to cigarette smoke, I couldn't imagine spending three hours inside a vehicle with this guy. Nor could I demand that he not smoke when he and his wife were the ones doing me the favor. So, I told them I accepted whatever risk was involved in being in the Sandhills by myself, and that I'd much rather pedal the 180 miles to Alliance.

I also informed them that my next day's route would take me up to Mullen, 79 miles away from North Platte. It just so happened that the woman had a niece there, and she and her family would be delighted to let me camp in their yard.

"Would you mind calling her to let her know I'm coming?"

"Sure."

The couple gave me the niece's phone number and also theirs in Alliance. They made me promise to call them when I got to Alliance, then they went back to their site and left me to my solitude.

Just outside North Platte, the Sandhills began in earnest. They were huge hills covered with yellow grass and nothing else. This was cattle ranching country, but I saw very few cattle and even fewer people. After finishing a particularly long climb, I got off the bike, leaned it against the highway guardrail, then sat down on a guardrail post. I strained to hear any kind of sound, but there was nothing. I'd never heard absolute silence before—it went "whoom" in my ears. They were working overtime, trying to pick up something, anything, and they hurt. Then, relief, the hiss of a westbound transcontinental jet passing high overhead. Nine months before, I'd flown to Seattle on a jet just like that one, wondering how I could ever get to that tantalizing, barren country below.

When I got to Mullen, I called my hosts-to-be, who knew nothing about my impending arrival. The lady and her husband and son had been out late the night before, and they must have missed her aunt's call. The family took me in anyway.

On Monday, May 11, I caught a tailwind and flew westward toward Alliance. The Sandhills flattened out and gave way to high plains. This was a big, silent stretch of country, one that induced me to just keep riding, riding, riding. I made few stops and said very little to the people I met along the way.

My minimalist conversation at one country store left another customer wanting more. Five miles up the road, his car overtook me, and he motioned for me to pull over. I did.

"I just couldn't help thinking that you wanted to talk back at that store," he said. I wasn't sure if joining him in conversation meant that he'd tell me why I should repent and come to Jesus, that he'd ask what I was planning to do in bed that night, or that he was just a lonely guy looking for someone to talk to for a few minutes. I didn't care to find out. I pulled my bike computer off its mounting bracket and punched its buttons at random, pretending that it was some sort of timer. (It wasn't.) Then I announced that "I, um, had to get going, because, uh,

I'm late." We exchanged awkward looks, mumbled hasty fare-thee-wells, then he got back into his car and drove west toward Alliance. I never saw him again.

When I crossed the Alliance city limits, I let out a victory yell. I'd just made 101 miles in eight hours—pretty respectable for a loaded-down cycletourist! I found a pay phone and called my guardian angel from two days before. She'd just gotten off the day shift at the railroad, and was very glad to hear from me. She urged me to come over to her place, which I did. She and her husband lived in a run-down trailer on the edge of town. Her husband was away, but the trailer reeked of his cigarette smoke. She was sharing coffee with a friend from work when I showed up, and both women marveled at how I made it through the Sandhills without any trouble. I didn't mention my encounter with the man who wanted to talk.

"I guess we just watch too much television," the friend said. I agreed.

My hosts for the night were the local Episcopal priest and his family, who served as Alliance's League of American Wheelmen hospitality home. They phoned a member of their congregation, a pharmacist up in Chadron, near the South Dakota border, who agreed to put me up the following night.

I tackled the steep grades of the Black Hills for no other reason than to say I'd bagged South Dakota. I was also growing weary of the grind-out-the-big-miles-in-big-gears pace I'd kept since leaving the Gruvers. My sore knees and backside were screaming for a rest. On Friday, May 15, I pulled into Devil's Tower National Monument in northeast Wyoming, feeling pretty smug about having ridden nearly 640 wind-assisted miles and looking forward to taking a break. What I didn't know was that my luck was about to change dramatically.

OF CONCERN TO WOMEN

I began touring solo in July 1980. It wasn't in my plans—I tried to find a partner before I left home, but none materialized.

Do I get scared out there? You bet. I've been shouted at, threatened at times, and have also received lots of sexual harrassment. Despite these negatives, I still enjoy touring solo. I enjoy the freedom of setting my own pace and keeping my own schedule. There's also a temperament factor at work here: I was an only child who grew up having plenty of solitude. Solitude remains one of the greatest treasures of my adult life.

The drawbacks? When you ride by yourself, you have only yourself for company. There's no one else to boost your spirits when you're down, no one to urge you onward when you feel like quitting, no one to share your triumphs over the mountain passes and the headwinds. In short, it can get pretty lonely out there. And you have to be careful that your loneliness doesn't lead you to let your guard down and trust the wrong people.

I do a lot of sizing up of the people I meet during my travels; they also do the same of me. They have a lot of questions, and most of these inquiries are motivated by nothing more than simple curiosity. Still, I'm not too forthcoming with specific details about my travels, especially my itinerary. When asked where I was going in 1987, I'd simply reply, "Canada," which was just as true in New Mexico as it was in South Dakota. As was the case with my other two long journeys, I didn't have my route planned out in advance, I just made it up as I went along. When I needed advice on specific roads, I tended to stick with "safe" sources of information like a local police department or a cycletourist hospitality home host.

While I'm on the road, I try not to make it look too obvious that I'm female. I keep my hair short—it's easier to keep clean that way—and tucked under a bicycle helmet. I also have the anatomical advantage of being a small-breasted woman and when I'm wearing an oversized tee shirt, you can't tell which gender I am! Lust-filled motorists occasionally discern that I fill a pair of black stretchy bike shorts differently than a man does, but I've also noticed that they tend to express whatever verbal reaction they have, then move along. I report the more persistent harrassers to the police or their employers, if they're driving some sort of company vehicle.

I also don't travel at night. The old highway patrolmen say it best when they note that there's a lot of alcohol on the road after dark. Drunk drivers and bicyclists don't mix.

As for weaponry, I've never carried a gun, can of mace or any other self-defense hardware. In the deep South, people warned me that my policy meant that I was taking a big chance on my personal safety. In New England and on the West Coast, it was rarely an issue among the people I met. As for guns, I'm not against them, but don't carry one because it's another heavy thing I'd have to carry uphill and into the wind. I also want people to trust me and be open, and I don't think they would be as willing to do so if I carried a gun.

•20•

Aladdin, Aladdin

Arriving at Devil's Tower was like the culmination of a pilgrimage to me. Six years before, Ann Arbor's cable movie channel offered a whole month of "Close Encounters of the Third Kind." I found its message of intergalactic peace and understanding to be quite compelling, and I watched it six times. It's still my all-time favorite movie.

Just outside the entrance to Devil's Tower National Monument was a little store where all the "Close Encounters" stars liked to hang out when they weren't on the set, the proprietors told me. They had the autographed pictures to prove it. Much of the filming took place across the road in what had since become a KOA Kampground.

But this pilgrim was on too tight of a budget to stay at the KOA shrine. I opted instead for the national monument's primitive campground, becoming the lone cycletourist in a place full of retirees in RVs and young, hotshot rock climbers who'd made the Devil's Tower pilgrimage for a very different reason than my own. I quickly noticed that neither group seemed to want much to do with the other. Once I set up my tent and found a nice tree to lean my bike against, I wandered around camp and chatted with the RV-ers and the climbers. Such practical politicking was prompted by nothing more than my need to share the road with members of both groups.

Saturday morning, May 16, was hot and dry, a good day for a climber's climb and Martha's hike on the trail around the base of Devil's Tower. The rock was covered with climbers who looked like colorfully dressed ants as they worked their way up the steep sides. I admired their effort, but feared high, open spaces too much to try rock climbing myself. The trail was all the challenge I cared to handle that day, and I ambled along, whistling the five-note theme from "Close Encounters."

Late Saturday afternoon, a quartet of women climbers from Minneapolis asked me if I'd like to split the cost of their campsite for a night and join their Devil's Tower victory party. Sure! I promptly moved tent and bike over to a new home. The women assigned me the task of augmenting the beer supply, so I pedaled over to the little store of the stars and made what turned out to be a politically incorrect choice: Coors.

"They give money to the contras," one of them told me when I returned. I was tempted to reply, "So do your taxes," but held my tongue.

And I had to really exert myself to keep quiet when they began running down all those RV-ers who "just sit on their butts in camp." I wanted to point out that our experiencing nature under our own power didn't make us any better than they were, nor did it give us any special connection to heightened environmental awareness. I thought back to that couple who adopted me in Rocky Mountain National Park in September 1981. They were traveling with another RV-er who was such an avid bird and wildlife watcher that she'd built a special bookshelf just for her field guides. We couldn't sit around her dinette table for more than a few minutes before she'd jump up, grab one of those guides, then regale us with stories of all her previous encounters with whatever it was that just went walking, crawling or flying across her site. As for me—the one who spent the better part of each day out in nature—I had no idea what those creatures were.

Oh, and as for the Coors? Once the festivities were well underway, the contents of those sinful silver cans were consumed along with the rest of the beer. So much for political correctness.

We finished our party in a light rain, then retreated to our tents. A violent thunderstorm followed, my tent got flooded, and I ended up hauling my sleeping bag and bike into the women's restroom for the night. I even got some sleep on that cement floor.

Sunday morning was foggy and drizzly, perfect weather for sleeping in late, then spending the rest of the day reading the paper. How I wished I could.

But I had to move on and my reason was very simple: I was running out of money. I needed to get to a town large enough to have a Western Union and a bank. The place most likely to offer such services was Belle Fourche, South Dakota, 50 miles away. If I could make it there today, I'd be able to accomplish this task first thing Monday morning.

So went my optimistic thinking as I stuffed my soggy tent into its sack and headed out to the highway. Yesterday, it was sunny, temps were in the 90s, and I watched those puffy storm clouds build up all day. Today, low 50s. But hey, that fog that obscured Devil's Tower would break soon, the rain would stop, and this headwind would get out of my face. My wishful thinking changed nothing.

I left camp without donning my cycling tights and was wearing nothing but a short-sleeved Lycra jersey underneath my rain jacket. But I pressed 10 miles onward through Hulett, which had a motel with a "vacancy" sign that flickered in the pouring rain. My feet were numb from the cold by the time I got to that handful of houses called Alva, another 10 miles up the road. Then came that long climb into the heart of the Bear Lodge Mountains. My body no longer shivered, it trembled all over. The climb was followed by a screaming downhill that had me gripping the handlebars for dear life and praying that the brakes would hold. I kept up a running commentary with myself to make sure I stayed coherent. I was edging ever closer to hypothermia.

Then came the answer to my wish for warmth, a town called Aladdin, population 15. Aladdin had a motel/cafe—just what I needed! I got off my bike and pushed it over to the front of the cafe, which was closed. But a middle-aged couple was inside, doing their cleanup from the night before. The lady saw me, and rushed over to the door to let me in. They abandoned their cleanup and turned their attention to the half frozen cycle-tourist who really needed help. The man brought me towels and a blanket to wrap around my trembling self, then he pushed mug after mug of hot tea at me. The lady made me breakfast while her husband prepared a room in the motel. They apologized for the sulphurous-smelling water in my room's shower, but I didn't care. That shower was hot and I stayed in for a long time. For all of this, my rescuers only charged ten dollars.

•21•

A Fan Letter To A Bank

Monday, May 18, was another cold, rainy day. But I'd learned my lesson and didn't forget to don the tights and the long- sleeved turtleneck under the jacket. They made a big difference.

Twenty soggy miles later, I was in Belle Fourche's big truck stop, which had a Western Union station. During my previous journeys, I'd become quite proficient at getting money sent to me via Western Union. All I had to do was call my credit union in Ann Arbor, ask Patty in cash transfer to wire the amount I needed to the Western Union office where I was, then take the Western Union check to a local bank and turn it into traveler's checks.

Thinking that things would be just as easy this time, I got lots of quarters in change, and marched over to the pay phone to call Dollar Bank in Pittsburgh. They told me that I had to have a bank account in Belle Fourche before they could wire me anything. "But I'm on the road," I pleaded. "I'm biking up to Canada from Mexico and I'm running out of money."

They still wouldn't budge. I had visions of going broke and being stranded in Belle Fourche, South Dakota. I'd had an account with Dollar for three years and wished I could have closed it that morning. But I needed to keep some money back there until I got settled in Tucson. I also needed $1,000 ASAP.

Having struck out with my bank, I went across the street to the Tri-State Bank, a financial institution that didn't know me from Adam. I explained my monetary crisis to a teller, who promptly summoned her manager. He invited me to come over to his desk and repeat my story. After I did so, he advised me to call my bank again and tell them "Federal Reserve Code 12," along with his bank's name and transit number. I went outside, pumped another handful of quarters into the bank's pay phone, and called Dollar Bank. The Tri-State strategy worked beautifully—victorious Martha strutted back inside and found out that her money would be in Belle Fourche "in about an hour." I mumbled something about riding down to the library, and was sure nobody had heard what I said.

I'd barely delved into the current periodicals section of the Belle Fourche public library when a librarian came over to me and asked, "Are you Martha?"

"Mmm-hmm."

"That was the bank calling. Your money's ready."

Indeed it was. And that's my fan letter to a bank.

•22•

Running Back
To Saskatoon

After completing a traveler's check autographing session at the Tri-State Bank, I booked myself and my mud-encrusted bike into a nearby motel. It was early in the afternoon, the rain had stopped, but the sun stayed hidden behind the clouds. So I set about the task of cleaning the bike. The motel's owner asked me if I needed anything to help me with this project. "WD-40," I replied, and he loaned me a big can of the stuff.

Unfortunately, the bike stayed clean for just a few hours inside my motel room. More rain and fog moved in during the night, and when I walked outside to check conditions the next morning, I could only see as far as the end of the parking lot. I decided to leave anyway, a decision I questioned by the time I got to the edge of Belle Fourche. It would have been so easy to turn around and go back to that motel, but the same optimistic/wishful thinking that had driven me to keep going through the Bear Lodge range on Sunday was driving me once again.

So I pressed onward through the fog tunnel, catching only the briefest glimpses of grassland dotted with rock outcroppings. An oil tanker roared by me, then I passed it a few miles up the road. The driver had pulled off the road and was putting his cowboy hat over his face in preparation for a nap. I kept going.

My computer stopped functioning at mile 11.3, and that got me off my bike for a frantic attempt to revive it with lots of tapping, shaking and pressing its buttons. Nothing worked. Day after day, it had been my positive feedback mechanism. I'd hardly noticed how much I'd come to depend on it—until now. It was supposed to be waterproof, as all bike computers were, but it had taken quite a drenching in the last three days.

So I returned to measuring my progress the way I had during my two previous long journeys: I counted mileposts. I counted mileposts as I slogged past the monument marking the geographic center of the United States, I counted mileposts past who-knows-how-many herds of cattle, I counted mileposts all the way into a tumbledown collection of houses and a store/post office called Redig, which was 50 mileposts north of Belle Fourche.

In Redig, the human inhabitants were far outnumbered by junked cars and farm implements rusting in every yard. The cheerful postmistress welcomed me inside her premises, which doubled as the community store and looked like grandma's attic gone out of control. The unkempt appearance of her store/post office and the town appeared to bother none of the locals who came in. In Buffalo, 20 mileposts to the north, they considered Redig to be the joke of Harding County, and they pronounced the name of the town like the first two syllables in "ridiculous."

I spent four days in Buffalo waiting out a rainstorm that I took personally and resented very much, but the South Dakotans welcomed the rain. This was ranching country and rain meant good forage for the cattle. I stayed with a retired rancher named Min Patenode, a 79-year-old who looked not a day older than 60. We met each other at the town's grocery store shortly after I rolled into town. She invited me to come stay with her in the senior citizens' apartment complex on the eastern edge of Buffalo. Shortly after I got myself and the bike over there, she organized an impromptu audience of fellow residents to hear me talk about my travels. Martha the reluctant celebrity made a brief speech, then took a few questions from the very polite, attentive audience of retired ranchers, most of them widows like Min. My feelings about being in the spotlight had changed since I'd been cycletouring five years ago. Back then, I welcomed, even sought out the attention. After my book came out in 1985, I found that even minor celebrity status could become a major irritation. It really made me appreciate the blessings of obscurity. Now I just wanted to ride.

But Min didn't see things that way. The day after my speech, she called a reporter for the local paper, who also taught at the local high school. He came out to Min's apartment to interview me, and I hoped that this would be all he'd do. I really wasn't up for a speech to his students. Fortunately, he extended no such invitation. He did ask if I'd like a copy of the paper in which my story would appear and I said, "No thanks." He seemed quite hurt, but I already had quite a collection of news stories that had been done on me over the years. Now I just wanted to ride—if the weather would only let me.

However, my body really needed the rain delay. I needed the time off the bike to rest the sore left knee I'd developed from pushing too hard back in Wyoming's Bear Lodge Mountains, and the numb right hand that had resulted from clutching the handlebars so tightly that same day. Min fed me well. I caught up on lost sleep and gave the bike yet another cleaning. The owner of the town's hardware store figured out the trouble with the bike computer—too much water in the battery compartment. He blew the water out of that compartment, wiped off the battery, put the whole thing back together, and everything worked just fine.

On Friday, the daughter of one of Min's longtime friends drove ten miles into town for the sole purpose of taking me on the Harding County tour. With Min acting as tour guide, we drove past her family's old ranch, then ate a huge lunch at another ranch nearby. Min and the family that owned this ranch had known each other for decades, and they savored the opportunity to update each other on all the latest gossip. I, on the other hand, was bored to tears and did my usual lousy job of hiding my boredom.

After lunch, it was on to what Min and our driver promised was a real Western town: Camp Crook, South Dakota. Indeed it was. I felt like we'd stopped to visit a movie set, but the high front buildings on the wide, muddy main street were quite real. So were the mud-spattered pickup trucks and the hand-lettered billboard that explained the history of "the biggest little town west of the Little Missouri River in South Dakota—and the only town!" Camp Crook was named for General William Crook, who commanded a U.S. Army contingent that had been sent there to protect railroad workers during the late 1800s. The town's population peaked at 300 around the turn of the century, and "many businesses flourished," according to the sign. I doubted if one-tenth that number lived there in 1987. Camp Crook seemed well on the way to becoming a ghost town.

We moved on to the young woman's house, where her mother showed me the family's vast collection of arrowheads neatly arranged in rows atop white planks. They didn't have to venture too far from home to find any of them, Mother told me. This area was a collector's paradise—full of artifacts!

Then it was back into town over an unpaved road Min wasn't sure we could drive because "the gumbo's still too wet." The "gumbo" to which she was referring was the local soil, which got very sticky after heavy rains. Every adult resident of Harding County could tell at least one good "stuck truck in the muck" story, and the gumbo was the villain in them all. We made it through without incident, unless you want to count our reaching the top of a particularly steep hill with Min shouting, "Watch it!" The car skidded to a stop. I looked all around, wondering what in the world was going on, and that was precisely the point. They'd driven me up this hill to show off their favorite vista. They chuckled at their clever joke, and all three of us admired the huge, grassy valley surrounded by gumbo buttes. Way off in the east was Buffalo, a little speck in the big grassy sea. Best of all, the sun was back again.

I left Buffalo the following day, Saturday, May 23. Min had been a superb hostess, but I was very tired of sitting around and eating too much. She gave me the names of relatives to look up in Washington State, and promised to let them know I might be coming through. She fed me a hearty breakfast. I thanked her for her hospitality, then I was back on the road again. My ride through the southwest corner of North Dakota was just long enough to get a flat rear tire and catch a ride to the Bowman truck stop, where I fixed the flat and filled the tire with an air compressor. Then it was on to Montana, where I turned north toward Canada.

My plan was to ride as far as Saskatoon, Saskatchewan, the town immortalized in the song "Running Back To Saskatoon" by the early 1970s rock band The Guess Who. The song clearly expressed the band's fondness for that place "where nothing much ever happens," and it became my motivational mind music during the final 400 miles of northward riding. I planned to rest for a few days in Saskatoon, then catch the VIA Rail train to Prince Rupert, British Columbia, where I'd board the ferry for Juneau, Alaska. After bagging Alaska, I'd return to Tucson.

Eastern Montana looked just like the Dakotas—gently rolling grasslands, more cattle, few people. This was big, silent country, well suited for solitary riding and deep introspection. On previous trips through similar territory, I'd ride along and express my thoughts out loud, with only the bike to hear. I'd hardly done any bike-talking on this trip, not because I was afraid someone might overhear what I was saying, but because I'd grown much more private with my thoughts and feelings during my five years in Pittsburgh.

Pittsburgh. Was there ever such a place? In the two months since I'd left, I'd alternated between hardly thinking about it and thinking about it constantly. My "constant thought" phases included a lot of rehashing of various parts of my life there and mentally beating myself up for doing such things as getting involved with George, becoming progressively more miserable in my jobs at the co-op and Pitt but failing to leave those situations until they became intolerable, and being so difficult and moody to my friends.

I missed those friends terribly—especially Jane's and Mafalda's insistence on staying in an upbeat mood regardless of what went down in their lives; the quiet, caring concern of the Naesers, Heinrichses and Staleys; and the fun-loving, "be yourself, always" spirit of the co-op members. Through all the gloomy weather for which Pittsburgh is famous, my friends kept my spirits up. They kept encouraging me onward through my unemployment and underemployment, which they knew would only be temporary phases.

When things fell apart at Pitt in January, they understood that I'd had enough of things going wrong in Pittsburgh and that it was time to make a fresh start elsewhere. My friends also understood the real purpose of this journey, that it wasn't so much a border-to-border state quest as it was an interlude in which I could sort out the roles that circumstance and my own actions played in my Pittsburgh misfortunes. They foresaw the mental boxing matches I'd have with myself when I confronted my own role in my misfortunes, but they assured me that this phase would be followed by what Jane called "an outbreak of inner peace." Yes, I did leave them insisting I'd never come back to that bad luck town, but my friends didn't believe me. Jane coaxed me back for a visit in late 1990, and I enjoyed it so much that I've made at least one Pittsburgh visit a year since then.

In Glendive, Montana, the rain came back, and I sat out the Monday of Memorial Day weekend with a fundamentalist minister and his family. We met as they were walking their Doberman through the town campground on Sunday afternoon, and their offer of hospitality saved me from two very wet nights in the tent. Although they were very devout in their beliefs, they didn't preach to me. I was grateful for that, because fundamentalists also tend to be ardent evangelists. During my stay in Pittsburgh, I'd been involved in an Episcopal church that had gone charismatic, and we church members were constantly being urged to share our faith with others and bring them to the church. I could never bring myself to do those things because I've always felt faith was something others should decide for themselves. I also had a lot of questions about my own faith, and didn't want to be preached at if I brought them up. So I drifted away from the church instead.

I bade my Glendive hosts farewell on Tuesday, May 26, a raw, cloudy day. Rain threatened, but never materialized. The following afternoon, the skies cleared and I caught a terrific tailwind that pushed me all the way to the Canadian border.

The Canadian customs agent looked me up and down, then gruffly asked me where I was going, how long I'd be staying, did I have any weapons, and where was my tent? After I replied, "To catch the train, then the B.C. Ferry to Alaska; two weeks; no; and it's strapped to the rack behind the seat," he let me go. I sheepishly rode over to the "Welcome to Saskatchewan" sign and snapped a photo, then went inside the customs house to pick up some Tourism Saskatchewan literature and a provincial map. The customs house people offered brusque answers to my questions, and I felt distinctly unwelcome. The thunderstorm that had generated the big tailwind was closing in, the next town was 10 kilometers away, and I really didn't have time to waste on translating that figure into mileage. I got back on the bike and sprinted into Minton.

The storm allowed me to enter Minton, convert some U.S. traveler's checks into that beautiful, multicolored Canadian currency at the community credit union, then go across the street to rent a room at the motor hotel. No luck, the place was booked. Then I tried the Friendship Centre, more out of curiosity than anything else. It was the senior citizens' gathering place, and I'd walked in on a hot rummy game played by two men and two women. I explained my predicament—no room at the inn and that storm starting to make big thunder along with all that wind outside. One of the men escorted me over to his Elks Club and offered me the place for the night. I accepted. This Elk-for-a-night had that club all to herself—and stayed warm and dry while the storm raged for the better part of the evening. This was only the first of many times that I would be done a low-key but heartfelt favor—such quiet kindness is the very essence of Canadian hospitality.

The following morning, I realized my running toward Saskatoon strategy just wasn't going to work out. My knee hurt too much, and my slather-on-the-heat-balm remedy hadn't helped. Nor had gearing down, spinning instead of pushing and telling myself that "this too shall pass." Even after I was hurt, I was still knocking down 70, 80, even 90 miles a day. That would have to stop.

I forced myself to quit at 50, check into the Ogema motor hotel and rest through the afternoon. I learned that afternoon TV in Canada is about as stultifying as American TV. That evening, I learned that a small town motor hotel's public room was the community social center, especially during the Stanley Cup finals. The local farmers and I were united in our distaste for the Edmonton Oilers, who were playing my old high school sports radio heroes, the Philadelphia Flyers. They were doubly impressed that a Pennsylvanian had bicycled all the way from Minton to join them, and this feat was good for a couple of beers on them. I re-learned an old college lesson, that Canadian beer is a lot stronger than American beer.

However, these men didn't take advantage of my inebriated state to proposition me. When the game was over, we wished each other well, then went our separate ways. Had this been an American small town, I wouldn't have entered the bar in the first place, because I'd probably be perceived as "asking for it," regardless of my intentions.

I got more proof that Canadian men were different the next day when I encountered a road under construction going north and a muddy unpaved road going west. I was standing outside the Kayville community store, pondering my next move, when a friendly wheat farmer named Sam Farmer volunteered to "save me a lot of trouble, eh?" and take me and the bike ten miles to Ormiston, where the paved road resumed and would lead into another highway heading north to Moose Jaw. I accepted his offer, he stowed the bike in the back of his mud-encrusted pickup, and over to Ormiston we drove at breakneck speed. He was quite pleased to be doing me the favor of "saving me a lot of trouble, eh?" and so was I.

Several hours later in Moose Jaw's city campground, a young man spotted my bike parked outside my tent and took an extended break from his evening ride to ask me about my travels. Although it was close to sunset, he seemed to have no intention of leaving the park. But I didn't feel nervous about talking to him—he just didn't seem like the type who would do me any harm. In fact, I relished this spontaneous meeting because it was the first fellowship I'd had with another cyclist since I stayed in that hospitality home in Alliance, Nebraska. What most concerned me about this fellow was that he had no headlight to illuminate his ride home. Finally, he realized that it was getting too dark to tarry any further, so he wished me bon voyage, and left.

My resolve to cut my mileage and rest my knee was overruled by my desire to get to Saskatoon and take a real rest. My numb right hand hadn't gotten any better, and a doctor in Davidson suggested that I have a neurologist look at it when I got back to Tucson. (I never did—the problem eventually went away on its own.)

Sunday, May 31, dawned overcast and drizzly. Seventy miles from Davidson was my goal, Saskatoon. Neither crummy weather nor achy body would deter me—I was going to keep going. And, no, the vicious sidewind that kicked up when I was still 20 miles out didn't slow me down either. I was on Saskatchewan's main provincial highway, Route 11, riding the shoulder as truckers went by with a giant whoosh of spray that left me cussing and grumbling. But I finally crossed the magic city limits, whooped it up while continuing to pedal, slogged over to the youth hostel at the YWCA, and at long last it was breakt-i-i-ime! Yeah!

• 23 •

Another Rocky Mountain Breakdown

My Saskatoon break lasted three days. After 2,900 miles of mostly country riding, being in a big city seemed strange. I felt out of place as I walked among all the harried-looking people hurrying along the sidewalks. They seemed so busy and important, and me? I was just idling until my train came on Wednesday, June 3.

I spent Tuesday morning in the public library, enjoying the opportunity to just sit and read some magazines. The other people in the periodical room kept giving me nervous glances and no one seemed to want to sit very close to me. I couldn't figure out why. After all, I'd taken a shower the night before, so that couldn't have been the problem. My clothes? I'd washed everything right after I'd gotten into town. I was wearing the same off-the-bike outfit I'd worn for months: venerable old walking shoes, warmup pants and a mud-stained yellow rain jacket over a stretched-out turtleneck. Perfectly acceptable garb to me and everyone I'd met on the way up here, but these people had apparently taken me for a homeless person.

They were right. I had no idea when I'd get down to Tucson or go back to Pittsburgh. In early June, the strongest ties I had to Pittsburgh were the mail I'd asked the post office to hold until I sent for it and the boxes of my things that were stored in a friend's house. Those ties would be severed once I acquired an address in Tucson. There was a part of me that found my homelessness exhilarating, but it was overruled by another part that found the reaction of the others in the periodical room so intimidating that I finally got up and left.

Outside the library, a poster taped to a light pole advertised a community meeting about the pending free trade agreement between Canada and the U.S. A line drawing above the text showed an American eagle with razor-sharp talons swooping down on hapless Canada. I felt like some *Innocents Abroad* character who'd accidently wandered into an anti-American demonstration. That was *my* country being portrayed by that menacing eagle and I felt very defensive. I certainly wasn't a great fan of the American government, but the American people had been exceedingly generous to me throughout my travels. So had the Canadians. I wanted to pen some sort of response on that poster, but I didn't want to make my nationality too obvious. Besides, confrontation was not what my travels were all about.

The train to the British Columbia coast was a delightful old-timer that rarely went fast and frequently stopped. It was more than an hour behind schedule when I got on in Saskatoon and it fell further behind as the day went on. No one seemed terribly disturbed by this. After all, there were more important things to be concerned about—getting a good seat in the vista dome car, wondering what those chefs were cooking up for the dining car and joining the other passengers in conversations that went on for hours.

It was my good fortune to find a seat next to Louise, a young woman from Ontario with a passion for travel. She didn't care where she was going, just as long as it was somewhere else. She'd already been to Australia and New Zealand and was taking this train to the Rocky Mountain resort town of Jasper, Alberta, where she hoped to find a lucrative summer job to finance her autumn trip to Iceland. Louise had been all over Canada, and proudly stated that the experience had made her feel truly Canadian. I told her that my travels in my own country had done the same for me.

Louise spent much of the ride into the Rockies greeting her favorite peaks like old friends. She'd worked in Jasper before, so this was like a homecoming for her. It was a spellbinding experience for me. I'd seen pictures of those mountains since I was a kid and they looked a little too picture-perfect to be real. Now I was in them and yes, they really did look like the pictures.

Louise kept talking up the Icefields Parkway, 180 miles of the world's most beautiful bicycling, starting just outside Jasper. I'd read all sorts of cycling magazine articles that said the same thing and I'd been toying with the idea of getting off in Jasper, riding a few miles down the parkway, then continuing with my railway journey. Louise's sales pitch sealed my decision. After all, Prince Rupert, British Columbia, and the Alaska ferry could wait a few days. Louise invited me to crash on the floor of the apartment where she'd be staying, and I accepted. After I reclaimed my bike, we walked over to her summer home and I, too, enjoyed a spirited reunion with her Jasper buddies. We carried it over to a local pub for a boisterous round of beer and deep-dish pizza. Once again, I was reminded of that old college lesson about the greater strength of Canadian beer. Just one mug did me in. On our way home, I noticed that it was close to 11:00 p.m. and only beginning to get dark. My newfound Jasper friends told me that summertime in the Canadian Rockies meant very long days—19 hours of sunlight up here. They didn't worry about running short of sleep— they'd make it up on those lo-o-ong winter nights.

The sun rose much too early the following morning. I dragged my party-weary self out of my sleeping bag, put everything back on the bike and announced my plan: I'd ride out to one of those terrific hostels along the parkway, spend a night, then come back to town. I pedaled over to a supermarket to stock up on provisions, as I'd be traveling along a wilderness road that didn't offer such things. Afterward, I visited the Parks Canada Information Centre to pick up the official road map for the Icefields Parkway, then rode out of town to find out if that road was as good as I'd heard.

It really was. The Icefields Parkway had a paved shoulder as big as a traffic lane and traveled through country so beautiful it was unreal. I frequently stopped for no other reason than to admire the glacier-topped peaks reflected in the Athabasca and Sunwapta Rivers. No way was I going back to Jasper. Alaska? Where was that? I was going to ride the 180 miles down to Banff! My home for the night was the Beauty Creek Hostel, a rustic little group of cabins that surrounded a campfire ring. There was no running water, not even a hand pump. If you were thirsty, you helped yourself to some snowmelt from the creek. Cooking, clothes washing or bathing involved dipping a pot into the creek and chopping enough wood for a fire to heat the water. Too much work for me, so I nibbled on my food supply and stayed dirty inside my sweaty cycling togs.

I was the only hosteller that evening. The hostel manager, a fur trapper from Quebec, said that the crowds wouldn't come until July and she was enjoying the final three weeks of quiet. Her sole companion in this wilderness was a large black dog that only understood French. The dog slept outside her cabin at night, usually along the path that led to the outhouse. She told me about the night she noticed a big black something nosing around near that path. She ordered it to "Couchez!" but it didn't lie down. It wasn't until the next morning that she realized that she'd given that command to a bear.

She'd made her point as clearly as those bilingual Parks Canada signs and pamphlets that warned that this was bear country and don't dare provoke them. I'd seen a cub along the roadside that afternoon. Instead of stopping to take a picture, I got the hell out of there. I didn't want to fend off an attack from mama bear, who was well hidden but no doubt close by.

Friday morning marked the beginning of some serious climbing over Sunwapta Pass. The Sunwapta River valley portion of the parkway ended a couple miles south of the hostel. Then came a stiff climb that had me off the bike and walking for two more miles. When the grade finally eased, I was surrounded by snowfields and glaciers. This was the Columbia Icefield, the largest icecap south of the Arctic. The cold wind swirling all around made it feel like the Arctic.

I ducked into a Parks Canada interpretive center to leave my Beauty Creek Hostel fee with a friend of the manager, who didn't have enough change for my $20 last night. I emerged to find two other cycletourists taking a break from their ride. They were a college-aged couple from Germany who smiled a lot and spoke only broken English. They were riding old-fashioned three-speeds with coaster brakes, the very antithesis of my high-tech 18-speed. How did they get up and down all these steep mountains? "We walk a lot," the girl said. She didn't appear to be at all bothered by that fact.

As for me, I was still feeling the sting of defeat from having to walk part of the way up here. Not to mention the ache of that cranky left knee that still hadn't healed from that rainy morning back in Wyoming's Bear Lodge Mountains. To save the knee from further damage, I was having to spin low gears and keep my daily mileage low. This wimped-out sissy cycling was getting me down. How I missed that high-gear, high-mileage blast through northern New Mexico and the plains states. I'd been in the best cycling shape of my life. My self-confidence had surged to an all-time high as well.

Before I came into Canada, I had written to Roger Humphrey in Washington State, requesting that he save me a place on this year's To Hel'en Back ride around Mt. St. Helen's in case I was able to fit the event into my itinerary. Knowing Roger, he probably had everything squared away for me, but I wasn't sure my knee would hold up long enough to get me back out of Canada. I was pretty sure I could make it to Banff. From there I could take a train to Vancouver, then get on a bus to Seattle and connect with someone or something going down to Tucson. It wasn't a plan I looked forward to following, but I knew I'd have to if my knee got any worse.

But I threw all of those depressing thoughts overboard as I crested Sunwapta Pass, then went barreling downhill into the North Saskatchewan River valley. I pretty well coasted all the way to my next hostel stop at Rampart Creek. I'd traveled 91 miles from Jasper, half the distance to Banff. The old confidence was coming back and, hey, I could make it the rest of the way!

Unfortunately, a nasty cold stopped me in my tracks. Friday night, I was feeling fine—dashing around the hostel grounds taking pictures of wildflowers, hiking along the banks of the glacial stream behind the place, and watching thunderstorms batter the mountaintops. Saturday morning, I could hardly move. Sunday wasn't much better. Monday morning the hostel manager had to drive to work in Banff and offered to take me there. I accepted.

Somehow, I found enough energy to cruise around Banff, take my sleeping bag to the dry cleaner and buy groceries at the Safeway. When I walked out of the store, I spotted another cycletourist and, of course, we had to pause and compare notes.

This man had been on the road for years. He supported himself by re-plastering and painting Victorian ceilings and biked to all of his jobs. I told him I'd read about him several years earlier in *Bicycling,* which prompted him to recap all the other publicity he'd had, including a write-up in *The New York Times.*

His recap seemed a little boastful to me, but I also felt quite envious and wanted some of that national publicity for myself. However, I also needed to balance that desire against the very real need to look after my safety and privacy. What a reporter might consider most newsworthy about me—the fact that I was a woman traveling alone—was the one thing I least wanted to broadcast to the world at large. So, while he gravitated toward the news media to gain free advertising for his unique trade and method of travel, I stayed away from them in order to protect myself.

(Two years later, he came to Tucson to repaint the lobby of the Hotel Congress. *The Arizona Daily Star* did a big writeup on him, and once again he recapped all his other publicity, as well as his ongoing efforts to keep it coming. As for me, I was too bashful to pedal downtown and say hello.)

I spent the night in the Banff youth hostel, which had more than 150 beds and felt like a small city. But for the very congenial group of Calgary alternative school students that had stayed at Rampart Creek on Sunday night, I'd had the wilderness hostels to myself. And I really enjoyed the solitude, especially after I got sick and needed to rest. In Banff, I shared a room with seven other women and kept the whole place awake with my coughing. Although they all were very polite to me the next morning, I'm sure they were glad that I wasn't planning to stay another night.

That afternoon, I put myself and the bike on the overnight train to Vancouver. It was a slow twilight ride through the rest of the Canadian Rockies, followed by an all-night roll down the Fraser River valley into Vancouver, a huge city on the sea that I was way too sick to enjoy.

Vancouver's hostel was an old Canadian Armed Forces dispensary, and the place was still run with military efficiency. Of course I disrupted the decorum of the women's dorm by coughing most of the night. At one point I was shaken awake. A weary Australian-accented voice told me to "try one of these," and a big cough drop was popped into my mouth. It worked—for a while.

Thursday, June 11, was homecoming day for me. Back to the U.S.A., land of green money and weak beer. I squelched my cough long enough to appear healthy for the U.S. Customs inspector at Blaine, Washington, then made a beeline for the town pharmacy. I needed to get some industrial-strength liniment for my knee and something, anything, for the cough. The pharmacist sold me some Icy/Hot for the knee and suggested that I see a doctor. "There's pneumonia going around," he warned.

The Blaine hostel manager insisted that rest would do more for me than an expensive trip to the doctor and that sounded like a better idea to me. He gave me an empty suite and I slept straight through until the following afternoon. I awoke to find that my 45-mile ride from Vancouver had taken on legendary status among the other hostellers. The lounge was abuzz with talk about how "she's so sick but she rode all that way and gawd, she's tough." How could I possibly spoil their fun by announcing that superwoman had just slept for almost 24 hours straight? Saturday was a strong 27-miler to the Bellingham LAW hospitality home, followed by an even better 47-mile ride and ferry trip to the San Juan Islands on Sunday. The San Juans were said to have some of the best cycling in the Northwest and I'd finally come to enjoy them. Since I'd turned the corner on this cold, I wouldn't have to end this journey in Seattle. From the Friday Harbor hostel, I phoned Roger Humphrey, M.D., informed him that I was feeling *great* and that I hoped to see him on To Hel'en Back in a couple weeks. And Roger had come through in fine form. Not only would he and his friends be expecting me, they'd found a sponsor for me. What a way to finish this long ride!

Monday morning, my plan was to bike the perimeter of San Juan Island, a 20-mile loop. But pedaling up the gentle slope to the edge of town left me coughing and gasping for breath. More than anything else, I wanted to make a nest in that nice grass by the side of the road and sleep, sleep, sleep. Instead, I turned around and headed back to Friday Harbor. My first stop was the holistic health center—closed on Mondays, the door sign said. Oh, well. I was really hoping I wouldn't have to go to that other place across the street, but c'mon bike, let's go over to the medical center—this shouldn't take too long.

It took the doctor less than five minutes to examine me and tell me I had bronchitis. He advised me to stay put and rest for a while, then wrote out a prescription for antibiotics. I spent the rest of the week recovering from the side effects of the antibiotics. It was several months before I regained all of my lung capacity.

I spent the rest of the week on my cot in the hostel, having intense discussions with three other women who'd also decided that this town was *the* place to hang out. We traded stories about our lives as a cycletourist all over the place, a University of Washington student in Seattle, an intensive care nurse in Germany and an electronic synthesizer musician in San Francisco. Once a day, we'd emerge for a Friday Harbor cafe crawl, then went back to the hostel to resume our hanging out. Except for my antibiotic-prompted need to make frequent dashes to the bathroom, this resting business was terrific. We even dubbed ourselves the "Friday Harbor Four."

We left together on Friday, taking the ferry over to Lopez Island to pick up Jill the "U-Dub" student's venerable old Datsun; packing our backpacks, bikes and ourselves into said car at the ferry terminal in Anacortes; leaving Ute the nurse at the bus station in Mount Vernon; then embarking on a mad dash down to Seattle to the accompaniment of a very Brian Eno-esque tape that was actually Caitlin's latest composition. Jill let Caitlin and me off at the Vashon Island ferry slip south of Seattle, and the Friday Harbor Four were now two.

Caitlin was totally immersed in her own little art world and dressed very much like the bohemian that she was. Her outfit—pretty much unchanged since she'd checked into the Friday Harbor hostel earlier in the week—consisted of several skirts, leggings and a long-sleeved blouse, all purchased from second-hand stores. She'd acquired a second-hand bike from the shop across the street from the hostel and was going to use it to "get around." Where? She wasn't sure. She was headed south to California—if someplace in between didn't catch her fancy first. At the moment, Seattle looked interesting, so she'd try it out in a few days. First, she wanted to check out that Vashon Island hostel that had that funky teepee.

Indeed it did, but I was more interested in staying indoors to safeguard my still-fragile health. Caitlin and I checked in together, then chose bunks at opposite ends of the hostel. No animosity had formed between us. There was just an unspoken, mutual understanding that the "Friday Harbor Four" week was over and now it was time to move on.

Saturday morning, June 20, offered profuse amounts of that liquid sunshine for which the Northwest is famous. It also marked the start of one of the biggest organized bicycle events in North America, the 200-mile Seattle to Portland ride that attracts nearly 10,000 cyclists. As I slogged through Tacoma and its southern suburbs, I wondered if I could possibly catch up with, then crash, this rolling party. Well, rain-induced chills put a stop to that quest and I opted instead for a motel just outside the Fort Lewis military reservation.

Sunday morning, more liquid sunshine, which was later followed by real sunshine. That afternoon, it was back to John Kelley's Centralia hospitality home for some merciless ribbing about how I'd *never* quit my job to go biking. Even his dog, Sugar Bear, seemed to be laughing at me. John had arranged my accommodations with a lady friend in Castle Rock for the following night, and of course the Humphreys were expecting me in Vancouver, Washington, on Tuesday.

Indeed they were. So was Gator, the pit bull, who barked ferociously until a very-pregnant-and-about-to-deliver Pat Humphrey came out of the house and called him away from the gate so I could come in. Pat told me that the dog had gotten quite protective of her during the past nine months, to the point of pulling her curling iron plug out of the wall socket. "He decided that it was too dangerous for me to use that thing," she said.

Once Gator figured out that I was okay with Pat, he wouldn't leave me alone. He all but knocked me out of the lounge chair on the back porch trying to get me to play with him. I had no choice but to stop reading and give him some attention.

I told Roger Humphrey about my bout with bronchitis, which prompted the Texas good ole boy-turned surgeon to ask,

"How're you fixed for drugs?" I still had some antibiotics that I was finishing off slowly, but he wasn't finished with me yet. "Why the hell didn't you get yourself on a bus and come down here? We would've taken care of you." Actually, I'd considered doing that, but rejected the idea, thinking it would be too big of an imposition on them. Not to Roger, who made it quite clear that my decision to keep on riding was the most dumb-fool thing I could have done.

The Humphreys put me up for one night, then traded me to the Vancouver apartment of another female To Hel'en Back rider, who drove me up to the start on Friday. The ride itself turned out to be a lot longer and tougher than my illness-weakened body could handle. At one point on the first day, I pushed my bike up a very long grade that John Kelley had mischievously dubbed "Angel Ridge." Very funny, Kelley. While I was walking to save my delicate knee and lungs, the others were still pedaling, which prompted me to start bawling my head off.

The end of that 111-mile ride found me moving into a bunkhouse at the Cispus outdoor education center in the Gifford Pinchot National Forest. I moped on my bunk, sure that I'd been the last to come in until two smiling women burst in and expressed relief that they'd *finally* made it. The older of the two, most likely the grandmother, greeted me warmly, then remarked on how the kids wanted to see everything, so they stopped a lot. Those kids had ridden day one's 70-mile option in baby seats on the adults' bikes. Happy to be off the bikes, they were now tearing around outside. This group had finished last, but it didn't matter to them. So I stopped feeling like such a failure, temporarily, at least.

Saturday was an off-the-bike day reserved for a bus and hiking tour of the devastated area around Mt. St. Helens. The first order of Sunday morning was a 15-mile ride to the top of a ridge east of the volcano. I still didn't have the lungs to attempt such a climb, so I caught a ride to the top. Then I coasted slowly downhill as the others zoomed by. By the time I reached the end 70 miles later, I was in such a deep blue funk that no other To Hel'en Backer could pull me out of it.

I was traded to yet another rider's condo before I caught a plane out of Portland on Tuesday morning. Despite my blue moods, all of my To Hel'en Back hosts had treated me with unfailing kindness. They truly were the best. My deepest regret is that I've never been able to repay them for what they did for me.

The plane rides to San Francisco, then Tucson, weren't filled with my reminiscing about the past three months' adventures. The other passengers, mostly men in business suits, didn't appear too interested in such things, so I kept quiet. Instead, I busied myself with mental lists of things I'd need to do in my new life—finding places to live and work, opening a bank account, registering to vote and getting my stuff shipped out from Pittsburgh.

Before the plane landed in Tucson, the pilot announced that it was 105 degrees outside, typical late June weather for southern Arizona. I'd never ridden in weather that hot, but I was about to do so. Ten miles stood between the airport and the headquarters of the Perimeter Bicycling Association of America (PBAA), the organization that put on the April Tour of the Tucson Mountains. The PBAA people had offered to help me find a temporary crash until I found a place to live. By the time I got to PBAA, I'd learned exactly what dehydration felt like, but even that didn't diminish the pride I felt in my 3,601-mile, border-to-border-and-then-some accomplishment.

•24•

What I Did On
My Vacation

The PBAA office was in the midst of serving as the headquarters of the 1987 bicycle Race Across AMerica headquarters, so their help in finding me temporary housing
was limited to PBAA director Richard DeBernardis driving me
downtown to the hostel at the Hotel Congress. Turned out I
didn't need any more help than that, as I found a room to rent
the following day.

The room was in the midtown Tucson home of a University
of Arizona graduate student who also worked as a per diem
nurse at two nearby hospitals. The arrangement was that I
could stay until her regular housemate came back from
Montana in mid-August.

From the very beginning of my life in Tucson, I was determined not to repeat the difficulties I'd had in Pittsburgh. Yes,
I'd moved to a city to which I had no previous ties other than
knowing another Pittsburgher who'd moved there. And no,
there wasn't a job waiting for me in Tucson. But this time
around, I wasn't going to let the fact that I didn't have a job
become a negative statement about me as a person. All it meant
was that I didn't have a job—yet. Since that prolonged jobhunt
I'd endured in late 1982, I had picked up many of what fellow
Pittsburgher-turned-Tucsonan Susan had called "skills that lead
to jobs," skills that could help me in my 1987 search.

As for Susan, we got together a few times after I returned to
Tucson, then went our separate ways. Since she'd moved west,
she'd developed quite a busy life and didn't have much extra

time to spend on me. Had this happened back in Pittsburgh, I would have developed a major case of hurt feelings because I would have been depending on her to make my necessary local introductions. In Tucson, I'd have to take that initiative myself, so I made that my first priority. I joined some rides offered by the local chapter of the Greater Arizona Bicycling Association (GABA), and volunteered for numerous stints of envelope stuffing at PBAA and produce stocking at the Food Conspiracy Co-op. Before long, I found that I'd developed a nice little circle of friends.

For most of that summer, I lived out of my bicycle packs. My old Pittsburgh bike shop buddy had moved and had turned my Cannondale racing bike and boxes of stuff over to a friend. That friend didn't ship the bike and the boxes until after I'd left the grad student's place and took another room on the west side of town.

Money also was slow in coming from back east. The unlikely hero in this saga was Dollar Bank, which didn't require another Federal Reserve Code 12 to close my account and send the balance to the credit union I'd joined in Tucson. A simple letter was all it took. Unfortunately, it took several letters and long-winded long distance calls to get the two credit unions back there to do what Dollar had done so easily.

My lack of possessions and money meant I was once again living a life of mandatory simplicity. I wasn't terribly bothered by this fact, it just was. To be sure, there were two very significant shortages that needed to be remedied, and I went about the tasks of making the phone calls and writing the letters to the keepers of my money and my possessions with a calmness I'd never had before. Where was it coming from? I wasn't quite sure, but it sure felt like that "peace which passes all understanding" I used to hear about in church.

Several of my new friends insisted that this serenity was the result of God working in my life. It felt awkward for me to say so, but I found myself agreeing with them. After all, it hadn't been but a few months before that I had expressed the belief that God would lead me to a place where I'd come down on my feet. In Tucson, I had landed, and this also would be the place where my spirituality would finally take root and grow.

Since I didn't have one, these friends heard a lot about my efforts to try to find a job. One day, one of them told me that I'd find exactly the job I needed, in a way I least expected. Her words turned out to be quite prophetic. In mid-September, I was finishing a volunteer stint at PBAA when a tremendous thunderstorm rolled in and delayed my 10-mile ride back to the west side. While I waited for the skies to clear, I picked up the afternoon paper, the one that was widely ridiculed for being so-o-o conservative. Of course I went right for the "help wanted" ads and, what's this? A writer's job over on the university campus? Should I go for it? Hey, why not? I went for it—and got it.

Right before I started my new job, I moved back to the center of town, not into another room, but into a little house. The rent was reasonable, it was a short walk to campus, and the property included two very friendly retrievers. They belonged to the landlords, who lived in the house in front of mine. The dogs made it quite clear that I was there to be their ball-throwing and belly-scratching pal. Not that I minded.

As a cyclist, I found myself in good and plentiful company in Tucson. The city's sublime weather and level terrain made for a cycling paradise and I was delighted to find there was no shortage of things for cyclists to do. In fact, one month of the GABA calendar offered more activities than the Pittsburgh or Ann Arbor bike clubs did in an entire summer. Every month, there was at least one overnight excursion as good as Sonoita-Bisbee, and I joined as many of them as I could.

The highlight of GABA-Tucson's calendar was—and still is—the October ride from the Grand Canyon to Mexico, 500 miles filled with plenty of climbing, descending and just plain cruising along. Each year, the cross-state attracts about 200 cyclists from all over the world. The cross-state is organized by a committee of GABA volunteers, all of whom earn free admission to the ride itself. The catch is that you work like a dog for eight months in order to receive that freebie. I speak from my own experience as a member of the 1988 committee, but the payoff comes in spending a week with some of the friendliest folks on two wheels.

The year 1988 was also *Bicycling* magazine's "Year of the Reader," an effort to involve its readers in the editorial process.

As part of this effort, the magazine sponsored a road test guest editor contest that invited readers to submit a 250-word essay on why they were qualified to be a bike tester. Up to five winners would be chosen and brought to the magazine's Emmaus, Pennsylvania headquarters to help the road test editor "ride and review a stable of hot new bikes."

Ah, *Bicycling*. My beloved bible of cycletouring had changed quite a bit since my housemate Paul had loaned me a stack of them during the summer of '79. Those magazines were full of beautifully written essays about cycletouring, the likes of which had largely disappeared from *Bicycling* by the mid-1980s. Those articles had been replaced by a plethora of advice on how to ride faster! harder! longer! On hot new bikes, of course.

Although cycletouring had fallen out of fashion with *Bicycling's* editors, I decided to enter the contest anyway. I stated that my testing specialty would be something that scarcely existed back in '79, the bicycle designed specifically for the small adult rider. My qualifications? Nine years of experience as a club cyclist, long-distance tourist and around-town commuter. Turned out I was one of three readers selected to spend the first four days of August in Emmaus.

Emmaus wasn't too far away from my parents' place in Westtown, so I flew into Philadelphia and visited them first. We hadn't seen each other in almost two years and there was some fence-mending to be done. After our weekend reunion, my mom drove me up to the magazine's headquarters. *Bicycling* is part of the Rodale Press empire, and it took us a good half hour of driving around Emmaus before we finally found the *Bicycling* building. Even so, we arrived before my appointed time. The road test editor took both of us on a tour of the renovated factory that now houses *Bicycling* and several other Rodale publications. The tour ended with a limousine pulling up outside the front door—for me. It belonged to the hotel that would be hosting me and the other two bike testers, and Mom took several pictures of me next to that long black car.

The other testers got the limo treatment at the Allentown airport, but without the mom taking pictures bit. They were a couple of fellows from Washington State and Nevada, and their dream bikes were a high-tech Italian racer and a recumbent. Both of them had apparently taken *Bicycling's* training tips to heart, as they rode at a much brisker pace than I did. The magazine's chief mechanic stayed back with me to make sure I didn't get lost on some country road. Meanwhile, the very athletic road test editor sprinted off with the other guys.

The bike I was assigned to test was a model manufactured by a cyclist I knew from my Pittsburgh days. Georgena Terry's specialty was building bikes to fit petite women and her specialty had grown into a thriving business. The bike was intended for fast recreational riders or competitors—just like my Cannondale. With me on board, the Terry was a very capable cruiser.

Although our riding speeds varied widely, all three of us were fast writers. Then came picture time. *Bicycling's* photo crew took us and our dream machines to a nearby park for an excruciatingly long photo session. The photos were followed by a big feast at the hotel and a limousine ride back to the Allentown airport the next morning. After all of this VIP treatment, I found the February 1989 publication of our reviews to be quite anticlimactic.

Just as Washington and Oregon had been in 1986, my final five states—Alaska, Florida, Hawaii, Maine and Nevada— would be vacation projects. Getting the bike into each of them would require a good bit more planning than I did for my three long tours. There were airline and lodging reservations to be made, routes to research and map out, and of course, requests for time off from work. Would spontaneity become a casualty of all of this additional planning? I certainly hoped not.

Hawaii was the first state on my checklist, mainly because I really got a good deal on the plane fare for late October 1989. My primary information sources were another GABA/Tucson member who'd ridden the entire perimeter of the Big Island of Hawaii, a *Southwest Cycling* article by a couple who'd sampled that island's north side, the League of American Wheelmen's annual *Bicycle USA Almanac* and the book *Hidden Hawaii*, by Ray Riegert.

The LAW Almanac listed the state's ride information director, Chuck Fisher, who turned me on to *Hidden Hawaii*. The book's emphasis is on getting away from the tourist spots in what has to be America's most over-touristed state. It can be done. In my own explorations of the Big Island, I came upon a town where the locals don't lock their doors. As for its name and location, that's a secret.

I'd never done any previous tours in which I planted myself in one place and really got to know the locale. For Hawaii, my base of operations would be the Kona Lodge and Hostel, located 16 miles away from the airport on the island's western coast. The hostel was a cheerful, grubby room full of backpacking students and local construction workers. Had I been ten years younger and on an indefinite road trip, I would have taken it. But I'd grown into quite a solitude lover and wanted more privacy, so I took a $150-a-week room in the lodge.

KLH was a very sociable place, and anyone was welcome to join whatever was going on, whether it was that perpetual bull session on the hostel porch—called a "lanai" in Hawaiian—or a hike down into the jungle below the property. Of course it would be a very brief hike, for without a machete, you wouldn't get very far. The place was seductive. It was hard to motivate myself to get out onto the road and do that 20 mile-a-day minimum to which I'd committed myself. When I shared that commitment with another KLH-er, he looked me straight in the eye and asked, "Why?"

Why, indeed. I spent my first couple days in Hawaii doing as little as possible. Then I got bored and called the local "ride the cruiser bike down the mountain" company. I found out that late October was their off-season, but took their suggestion to do an overnighter to Hawi on the northern tip of the island.

It was 65 miles one way, through jungles on the lower slopes of Mauna Loa volcano, lava fields below Mauna Kea, and windswept grasslands just like the ones in southern Arizona. In the last ten miles, I entered into an ultra-green land-scape that looked like something straight out of England or Wales. The trade winds beat me up and drove sharp needles of rain into my face, and was I ever glad to see Hawi, which looked like a coastal town from the Pacific Northwest.

I spent the night in an old plantation house-turned bed and breakfast that was run by a former Tucsonan. She told me that she'd decided to get out when Tucson's population hit 700,000—too big-city for her. So she moved her family to Hawaii, and proudly noted that her sons went surfing every day. She gave me a stack of surfing magazines to read with my breakfast, and I found that they had a lot more to say about the environment than some surfer-dude's search for the perfect wave or the latest neon clothing styles. How I wished that the major cycling magazines would adopt a similar theme.

On the way back to KLH, I retraced my route of the day before, which also was the Ironman Triathlon course. The race's 1989 edition had taken place right before I'd come to Hawaii, and I spotted a few competitive types heading north on foot and on bikes. Were they out training for next year or reliving the glories of this year? I could only wonder. As a cycletourist, my victories and glories were much different than theirs. For October 25, my victory came in making it back to my room at the lodge just ahead of a downpour that sounded as if it could have pounded right through the roof. I took myself out to dinner that night.

July 4, 1990 began with a predawn phone call from the coworker who'd drive me and the venerable old Nobilette to the airport. A few minutes later, Diana's twice-as-venerable old VW bus pulled into the driveway. We loaded up, then embarked on the first leg of my trip to Alaska. At the airport check-in, Diana pulled out a camera and snapped a few shots for the most avid Martha picture collector on the planet, my mom.

Although I wished I could have brought my bike on board the airplane to gaze fondly at it throughout the flight, Delta Air Lines considered it baggage that needed to be boxed. Like other airlines, they charged a hefty fee for this "privilege," but Delta was one of the two domestic carriers that accepted free bike boarding passes from an organization called USAmateur. The membership was $50 a year for League of American Wheelmen members, and I saved that amount and then some on this trip. (For more on USAmateur, see "Getting Yourself and Your Bike to the Start of Your Tour," page 54.)

Getting a bike into an airline box takes some doing. First of all, the box itself is huge and unwieldly and usually wants to fall over when it's time to put the bike inside. Then there's the bike itself—the pedals need to come off and the handlebars need to be turned sideways. I like to accomplish these two mechanical tasks the night before I leave on a trip, and at the same time make sure I pack the tools I'll need to redo the process when it's time to stop riding and come home.

My Alaska plan was to base myself at the youth hostel on the outskirts of Fairbanks, then pedal to nearby places of interest like Denali National Park and the Chena Hot Springs. I'd gotten information on cycling in this part of Alaska from David and Carol DeVoe, the state ride information directors listed in the *Bicycle USA Almanac*. They'd issued a prompt and detailed reply to my letter of inquiry, and extended an invitation to get together when I came to Fairbanks.

We met on July 5, a 90-degree day that felt delightful to my Arizona-conditioned self, but reminded the locals of hell itself. "It can get up to 100 here, too," Carol told me as we cruised around town.

David and Carol had toured extensively in Alaska and "outside," the term they and other Alaskans used when discussing Canada and the Lower 48. They also had provided touring information to several other 50-state riders and a few adventurous souls who intended to bike from Alaska to the southern tip of South America. I would have given anything to meet those people, just to compare notes!

Carol invited me to come out and stay with them at their house, 15 miles south of town and definitely out in the wilderness. They were a very quiet, subdued couple and would have been delightful company, but I declined their offer. The hostel was close to the roads that led to Denali and Chena, and it was only six miles away from the airport. But I would quickly come to regret my decision to stay there.

The hostel was a quonset hut on the edge of a campground run by a guy who called himself "Bull Moose." He had a bone-crushing handshake that he used to introduce himself to everyone—toddlers, senior citizens, it didn't matter. Bull Moose didn't manage the hostel, but he let the hostellers use the bathrooms and laundromat in his campground and made it very clear that we were not to abuse this privilege.

The hostel attracted an international cast of characters, including a German bus driver on indefinite holiday, a Harvard University student writing for the *Let's Go: USA* guidebook, a South African who built his own canoe and paddled several hundred miles of the Yukon River, and a Frenchman who parked his mountain bike next my to Nobilette and in very broken English told me that he was headed up to the Arctic Circle. There also was a sizable cadre of people who the hostel manager said were there "until they got back on their feet again." Her statement carried more than the financial connotation she intended. Those people were some of the hardest drinkers I'd ever seen. Once they'd passed out on a bunk, many long hours would pass before they'd even attempt to get back on their feet again.

Every other hostel I'd stayed in during my travels had banned alcohol from the premises, and this was in keeping with American Youth Hostels customs. When I asked the manager why this hostel permitted alcohol, she told me that it was an AYH supplemental accommodation and as long as everybody was cool about it, the beer stayed in the fridge.

I wasn't cool about it. In fact, it disturbed me greatly. During my three years in Tucson, I'd seen several lives ruined by alcoholism. Witnessing this destruction had caused me to lose my own taste for alcohol, and there was nothing I saw in the hostel that made me want to start drinking again.

I slipped out of the hostel early on Friday morning, July 6. Wouldn't be back for at least a couple days—this was my Chena Hot Springs ride. It involved riding 60-plus miles out of Fairbanks, most of that distance on a paved road that dead-ended at the resort that had grown up around the springs. I was hoping for some real Alaska wilderness, but the country looked—and sounded—like Michigan's Upper Peninsula. The pine forests hummed with the sound of mosquitoes, and those little pests just had to make my acquaintance whenever I stopped. I became very adept at slapping mosquitoes while shooting photos or taking a sip from my water bottle.

The road made numerous crossings of tributaries of the Chena River. Just before one crossing, an RV load of German tourists had their cameras trained on something in the water. It was a female moose eating an algae lunch—the green strands looked like a beard when she raised her head to glare at us. I feared that she'd get annoyed by our voyeurism, charge us, and I'd be left alone to fight her off after the Germans fled in their RV. Fortunately, she didn't move from her algae patch.

The hot springs resort was a rustic place that lacked any kind of entertainment other than eating in the restaurant, soaking in the springs or sleeping. The springs were very hot and sulphuric—just like the water coming out of the taps—and I suppose you'd get used to it after a while. The soak in the hot springs jacuzzi did wonders for my left knee, which had finally begun to recover from its 1987 injury.

By Saturday morning, I'd had enough of the restaurant, the hot springs and sleeping, so I decided to ride back to Fairbanks. Chena Hot Springs had turned out to be a big bore, but I vowed that Denali would make up for it. As I headed back toward civilization, I made plans to take the train down to Denali on Monday, take a good look around on Tuesday, then bike the 120 miles back to Fairbanks on Wednesday. Given my tortoise-like touring pace, I'd probably need all 23 hours of daylight to accomplish this feat, but I was up for the challenge.

The hostel was exactly the same as I'd left it—the international adventurers were still coming and going and the lushes still hadn't gotten back on their feet. On Saturday night, the rain started, and except for a brief respite on Sunday, that was the weather report for the rest of my stay in Alaska.

The hostel quickly became a showcase for all of the negative behaviors associated with cabin fever. Minor disagreements quickly turned into major word battles. The heat from the woodstove roasted some, but was totally inadequate for others. Several of the international adventurers got tired of just sitting around, so they joined the lushes in their beer bashes, which became twice as loud as they'd been before the rain.

As for me, I alternated between complaining loudly about the weather and huddling in my sleeping bag. I'd staked out a bunk that was in an alcove apart from the rest, perfect for a grouchy privacy hound like me. Occasionally, I'd emerge from my lair and slog over to the pay phone outside the campground restrooms and search for other accommodations by calling the local motels. I didn't lose too many quarters in the process—most of the innkeepers just weren't answering their phones. The ones who did told me that Fairbanks was booked solid. So, this bummed-out outdoor adventurer passed the time by reading the *Alaska Bicycle Touring Guide* and planning that next trip to Alaska—which would take place during a drought!

I also took a bus tour up to the Arctic Circle, which was just 200 miles north of Fairbanks, and spent my last full day in Alaska with the DeVoes, who challenged me to stay up all night and see that midnight sun for myself. It never broke through the rainclouds, but I can vouch for the fact that night never comes to Fairbanks, Alaska in the summertime.

During the wee hours of Thursday, July 12, I slogged six miles back to the Fairbanks airport. I hadn't done it with an excess of style or grace, but I'd bagged Alaska. State Number 47: check. Three more to go.

The year 1991 was a double-stater. In June, I signed out for a couple of much-needed weeks of vacation and used the Delta Air Lines/USAmateur combination to get myself and my bike to Burlington, Vermont. This time I'd revisit Vermont and New Hampshire, then ride the American Lung Association's Trek Across Maine, which ended on the Atlantic coast. The Trek was included in the *Bicycle USA Almanac's* list of annual cycling events in Maine.

My aunt, Jean Retallick Gouert, met me at the airport, then took me to her place in Stowe, 30 miles away. Jean is my father's younger sister, and she is as flamboyant and talkative as my dad is reserved and taciturn. But for the strong family resemblance, it would be hard to believe that they're at all related. Our drive back from the airport was filled with Jean's descriptions—or in her case, dramatic renditions—of life in the tourist town to which she'd moved right before I had left Pittsburgh. I couldn't wait to see it.

Stowe was indeed the quintessential New England town, lots of clapboard houses and the big white church right in the middle of things. Jean's church was the small Episcopal chapel on the way out to the ski resorts and she invited me to go with her the following morning. My first thought was: Jean? *Church?* For years, she'd been as uninterested in church as I'd been. Now she had a whole section of books on religion and spirituality in her extensive personal library. And not only did she go to this church, she also served on the vestry and the altar guild.

I declined her invitation, as I had nothing to wear except cycling and hiking shorts and some tee shirts. No problem, she said, people wore that kind of thing all the time. I still said no, opting instead to spend Sunday morning on Stowe's recreational trail, which was way too narrow and too crowded for bicycling. I even passed by the church, and was strongly tempted to park the bike and go inside. But I kept on riding.

However, Jean's involvement in her church had planted a seed in my mind. For many years, I'd been praying to a higher power I'd called "God." The ethical code I believed in and tried to practice came straight out of the Bible. I'd always found much to admire in the lives and teachings of religious people like St. Francis and Mother Teresa, not to mention the "liberation theology" espoused by Martin Luther King. And, of course, there was what I'd experienced throughout my travels—the good works that had been "done unto me" by people who said that their Christian beliefs had motivated their actions. Those actions spoke to me in ways that formalized worship services and glory-filled youth groups never did. My "Good Samaritans of the road" showed me what Christianity was really all about.

Although I'd spent much of my life being down on organized religion, I'd begun to feel the need to give my spiritual leanings a name. I figured that if my Aunt Jean could declare herself a Christian, so could I. In late 1992, I did just that. A few months later, I joined one of Tucson's Episcopal Churches.

This isn't meant to imply that I've become a saint. I haven't. Jean hasn't either. Get the two of us together, and anything's bound to happen. After she came home from church, we drove over to the nearby home of her son Tom, the older brother of the Steve I'd visited in California. We took one of Jean's favorite road-less-traveled routes out of Stowe, a rutted dirt track that led to a paved road that climbed an unbelievably steep hill. She said this hill was a favorite with the inn-to-inn bicycle touring companies. "What are they trying to do to their customers, kill them?" was my reaction. Well, we saw a touring contingent pushing their bikes up the hill as we were descending. Okay, I got it—they were cross-training!

A few miles later, we passed by an old dead tree with a broken-off limb "that looks just like it's giving us the finger!" Jean said. Indeed it did.

Unlike Steve Gouert, whose brief marriage had ended in a bitter divorce and child custody battle, Tom was very happily married. He and wife Lynn had one child, a very independent toddler named Christopher. Chris tolerated the necessary introduction to Cousin Martha, then retreated back into his own private world in the sandbox.

Chris' independence was offset by the most-eager-to-please-us behavior of Bucko, the family dog. He was what Jean termed a "size extra large" golden retriever, and he took it upon himself to regale me with gifts, starting with a soggy softball from the playing field next door. Profuse praise from Jean. (Thanks, Bucko, now I've got to throw it for you until my arm falls off. And that was just what he wanted!) After he tired of playing fetch (thank God!) Bucko went back into the bushes behind the house and emerged with...a fence rail! Much admiration from Jean, consternation from Lynn. I pulled out my camera and took a picture. But I'd had enough of this when he brought me my next present: a dead muskrat. We distracted the dog with the ball and Tom threw the muskrat back into the bushes.

After supper, it was time for more of Jean and Martha's excellent auto adventures. We found another one of those dirt tracks and sneaked up on the unsuspecting Von Trappe Family Lodge, which had made them a lot more money than "The Sound of Music." Then it was onward and really upward to Smuggler's Notch, once the choice route of colonial-era smugglers. In more recent times, it had been the scene of the local death-wish bicycle race, a race that was no longer run because too many wrecks occurred on the steep 11-mile descent back into Stowe. Jean and I stayed up and talked well into the wee hours of Monday morning, then crashed out for a few hours. Monday was a road day for me, and Jean marked the occasion by fixing me a breakfast that would last all the way until the home hostel in St. Johnsbury, almost 50 miles away. Then came the pictures of Martha in wild tie-dyed tee shirt holding bicycle outside Jean's apartment, a big hug, and I was off.

My route was mapped out by Jean, who advised me to take her favorite roads into Maine: Vermont's State Routes 100 and 15 to U.S. 2, and stay on 2 until Bethel, Maine, where the Trek started. Turned out to be a hilly 130 miles, but the climbs weren't any tougher than what I'd experienced elsewhere.

Although I was on a schedule, I felt the same exhilaration I remembered from my open-ended, come-what-may journeys of a decade ago. I hadn't trained for the this tour or practiced handling the loaded bike, but it all came back to me within five miles.

Northern Vermont isn't full of the knock-your-socks off scenery the state tourism board so avidly promotes. Yes, there are the dairy farms—lots of them—and numerous little towns prettified way beyond their working class origins. Both the farms and the towns became scarce after I crossed the Connecticut River and entered New Hampshire.

In New Hampshire, U.S. 2 wound its way through a thickly forested valley between two ridges of the White Mountains. This was logging country, and I found myself sharing a road with logging trucks for the first time in years. I was terrified. One year before I did the Arizona cross-state, a rider was killed by a logging truck outside Payson. Both the truck driver and the cyclist were highly skilled in what they were doing—they just happened to be in the wrong place at the wrong time.

Since those trucks and I were on the same U.S. 2, I decided to make sure their drivers would recognize my presence in time to avoid any trouble. I started waving to them. And they waved back. I figured that if they perceived me as a friendly, likable sort, they'd be less likely to run me over. Practical politicking rides again. But it worked. We shared the road without incident.

My home for the night was the Bowman Base Camp hostel, a popular accommodation for climbers wishing to experience the crummy weather capital of the East: Mount Washington. The place was wide open when I got there in the middle of the afternoon, so I unloaded the bike, went inside and made myself comfortable in what I described in my journal as "a real dump."

The hostel manager was supposed to come by at 5:00 p.m. to collect overnight fees, but the only one who showed up at the appointed hour was a teenaged boy with a rifle. I was too petrified to even plead for my life, but he put the gun down as soon as he saw me.

"I've been out hunting squirrels," he said. "I *hate* squirrels. They're out all over the place and I'm *sick* of them."

His hunt had been unsuccessful. I remembered from childhood hunts with my dad that a squirrel was a hard thing to hit, and he wouldn't even let me take a shot until I was sure I knew it was a squirrel.

The boy took my $10.80 hostel fee, we got to talking about life in a small New Hampshire town versus a large Southwestern city, then in a very hopeful tone, he asked me, "Do you shoot?" I've never turned down an invitation like that, so we got some .22 rounds and went up to the abandoned railroad tracks behind the hostel for some target practice. Our target was an old milk jug, and I could see why he wasn't getting any squirrels. His aim was terrible! I was grateful for all of that "hold steady and squeeze the trigger" coaching my dad had given me when I was that boy's age. On the way back to the hostel, he told me that he really wanted to get an Uzi. "Oh, good," I thought, "Now he'll never have to aim carefully at the squirrels again. He'll just vaporize them."

The next day, Wednesday, June 12, I entered Maine, feeling victorious about bagging State Number 48, but also regretting that my little solo jaunt ended so quickly. During my three days and 130 miles between Stowe and the Sunday River ski resort outside Bethel, I'd hardly thought about Tucson at all.

I had an entire Sunday River ski dorm to myself until the other Trekkers began arriving Thursday afternoon. They were an achievement-oriented bunch. To hear them describe it, the Trek would be a three-day, 200-mile time trial to the coast. After one man announced that his plan to average 17 mph on this thing, I asked him if he also planned on seeing anything. He didn't get it.

I wasn't sure I wanted to be a part of this event, but I'd paid the $300 minimum pledge. It was too late to back out now. My claim to fame among this group was that I'd come the farthest distance to do the ride, and I figured I might as well enjoy it.

The starting gun sounded shortly after 10 a.m. on Friday morning, and I was quickly passed by about 600 other people. Up hills and down hills, the brisk pace never let up, even when it started raining the following morning. The rain didn't let up, the race went on, and I hated it.

Well, most of me did. There was a tiny part, deep down, that enjoyed this pedaling madly along slippery roads, urging myself onward because everyone else was, too. This crazy little ride was so different from my predictable, workaday life, which often bored me. But not only was this ride crazy, it also was dangerous. My only contact with the earth consisted of two constantly moving, one-inch square patches of wet rubber tire that could hit a slick patch of pavement at any time. My brakes? Nothing more than four skinny rubber rectangles squeezed against wet metal rims. I was terrified to the point of wanting to go up to one of the Trek volunteers and beg to ride in a warm, dry van for the rest of the way, but I couldn't get up the nerve to tell anybody that I wanted to quit.

Instead, I continued in my long-standing tradition of taking the weather personally and let everyone know what I thought of it. At the Saturday night awards ceremony, the Trek leader invited me up to the front of the Colby College chapel so I could be recognized for coming the farthest distance. He really should have given me the Bad Attitude Award.

Sunday morning, overcast, but hey, aren't those a few rays of sun peeking through those clouds over by the coast? Su-u-ure, just like today's course is going to be all flat.

Shortly before the rain started again, I rode a few miles with an older woman who must have been the only Trekker who was carrying her gear with her. I certainly wasn't being that much of a purist—I'd put some of my gear in one of the rental trucks that was carrying Trekker luggage—but I kept the panniers and front handlebar bag on the bike. My older riding companion said she just didn't want to trust the gear-hauling to others, and she didn't mind being slowed down by the extra weight. She'd been cycletouring for about as long as I'd been alive, and she wasn't about to take up the Greg LeMond wannabee act that so many others were performing on this Trek. "What those people are doing is a ride," she said. Pointing at her own bike, she added, "*This* is a tour."

The Trek Across Maine in the Rain came to an end at the Samoset Resort, along the fog-enshrouded Atlantic coast. A Trek volunteer draped a medal around my neck at the finish line, then I went off to the all-you-can-eat lunch. I sat down at a table full of New Englanders, and finally remembered that the one who kept trying to engage me in conversation was the guy who'd said he planned to average 17 mph all the way to the coast. We both agreed that it had been a *hard* ride. I didn't ask him about anything statistical.

To bag Florida, I went on a safari. It was a fund raiser for the Orlando public radio station, WMFE-FM, and it was as laid back as the Trek was competitive. Like most Florida Bicycle Safari participants, I'd learned about the event from another cyclist who'd done it, and she also said that she'd definitely do it again. So would I.

On Friday, November 8, I was one of the few people flying into Orlando without intentions of going to Disney World. But that resort's ambience had permeated the Orlando International Airport, which was staffed with cheerful, well-mannered people and featured a monorail between the gates and the main terminal. I dubbed it "Airport World."

The Safari bus took me and about a dozen other out-of-staters to the starting and ending point, a Baptist church camp outside of Eustis. The people at the check-in table advised me not to pitch my tent too close to the lake, because a cold front would be moving in that night. Oh, good. I've already arrived in Alaska in the middle of a heat wave and here comes a cold wave to welcome me to Florida.

The cold wave brought rain, too. I spent a sleepless night in my tent, wondering if I'd brought some kind of a rain-curse like that guy in the "Li'l Abner" comic strip. And as the bottom part of my sleeping bag began to get damp, I also remembered that I had forgotten to waterproof my tent before I left Tucson. I finally dragged my sleeping bag into the women's bunkhouse and crashed out on a lumpy cot. A sweetly Southern-accented voice outside woke me up just before daybreak. "Ah've got good news and bad news," the lady said to a friend. "The good news is that it stopped raining. The bad news is that it's co-o-old."

Cold enough that the orange growers were worried about losing their crops and had put heating devices and fans in the groves. Cold enough that the boiled peanut vendor who'd set up next to a rest stop was treated like a hero. And cold enough that when the sun finally reappeared, it was greeted like a long lost friend.

The Safari certainly wasn't a race. It attracted a lot of the 40-plus crowd, and included many retirees. The organizers told me that they encouraged people to stop and enjoy the scenery, and the riders were only too happy to comply. A bunch of us also stopped at a yard sale, and one of the guys bought a boat anchor, which he hauled with him for a few miles before he stowed it in one of the Safari baggage trucks.

Our route took us through rural Florida, which was every bit as Southern as the South I remembered from a decade before. Remembering my earlier journey across the South, I stopped at as many gas and groceries as were available, and received the same "Y'all come back now" farewell in nearly all of them. (The ones who didn't give me that farewell were transplanted Yankees who hadn't learned the lingo yet.)

Our first day ended in Ocala, the unofficial capital of Florida's horse country. Camp was at the Central Florida Community College, but I opted for a nearby hotel for a camping gear-drying and much-needed sleep session. Next morning, November 10, I woke up too late for the optional 100-mile century ride, but since it was my 34th birthday, I decided to take the day off. I rode myself and my gear back over to camp to find that the day-off idea appealed to many other people as well. So we just sat around and talked the day away.

Next morning, it was back to the church camp for me and everyone else on the three-day Safari. My work schedule didn't leave enough time for the six-day version, but the full Safari is definitely on my to-do list for the future.

•25•

Not With A Bang,
But A Whimper

Well, Nevada—the state where tawdriness gets down to business—ended up being Number 50. Was I going to mark this occasion with another long, solo journey? Absolutely not! I wanted to celebrate the end of this quest with as many other cyclists as possible.

Late in 1991, I received the 1992 *Bicycle USA Almanac* and found it had little to say about cycling in Nevada. Was it because Nevada was a very sparsely populated place or because cycling was some sort of subversive activity that the state's gambling, er, gaming industry wanted to keep a lid on? I could only wonder. But Nevada did have a LAW ride information contact, Suzy Truax in Reno. I wrote her a note explaining what I'd been up to for the last decade and asked about big Nevada events that would provide a fitting end to my 50-state quest.

Weeks went by, no reply. I chalked it up to the Christmas mail deluge. Then those weeks turned into months. Still no reply. Finally, in late spring 1992, that long lost self-addressed, stamped envelope came back to me. Suzy confessed that she'd been doing a lot of asking around, as cyclists and events organized for them weren't too plentiful in Nevada. But she had located "America's Most Beautiful Ride," a June circuit around Lake Tahoe.

Lake Tahoe? In June? That's the height of the tourist season! I had visions of being pushed into the lake by road-hogging RVs. Uh-uh.

On a Saturday afternoon in May, I called Suzy at the toll-free number listed on her business stationery. We lamented the dearth of organized rides in her state, especially ones that catered to those of us who weren't Greg LeMond wannabees, noted that cycling was a whole lot more fun before the yuppies discovered it and turned it into something trendy, and found that we agreed on a whole lot of other things, too. Suzy fully understood my reluctance to orbit Lake Tahoe when every RV-owning Californian would be doing the same. She told me that the Lake Tahoe ride organizer was planning another event for the fall, a ride across the state on U.S. 50—the loneliest road in America, as *Life* magazine once described it. I found that ride much more appealing. Suzy was planning to go, so we made tentative plans to putz across Nevada together. But I heard nothing further from her, so I guess "America's Loneliest Ride" never happened.

In mid-September, I realized that 1992 was running out and I still hadn't bagged a state right next door to mine. As far as big events for non-racers were concerned, I had two choices left: a Greater Arizona Bicycling Association 100-mile day ride that started out of the casino resort in Laughlin, Nevada, and took in Arizona and California before returning to Laughlin; and the Southern Nevada Multiple Sclerosis Society's 150-mile weekend fund-raiser, which I assumed still met up with the Phoenix chapter's well-publicized "Best Dam Bike Ride" to the Parker Dam on the Colorado River.

The Laughlin ride had been on GABA's 1991 events calendar but had been cancelled after its main sponsor backed out. It was back on the 1992 calendar for December, but when I called the Mohave County chapter for details, they told me it had been cancelled again. So I called the Phoenix chapter of the MS Society and found out that the Las Vegans no longer met them for a post 150-mile barbecue at the Parker Dam. The Nevadans had instead set up their own "Las Vegas to London" ride, which went south from the Las Vegas suburb of Henderson to the London Bridge in Lake Havasu City, Arizona.

I made another call to the Southern Nevada MS Society and learned that their event would be held on the weekend of October 24-25, so I'd better sign up quick. I did. Then I sketched out the design of the bike jersey I'd wear for this auspicious occasion, and faxed it off to a bicycle clothing company owned by one of my old Pittsburgh cycling buddies. Schnaubelt Shorts translated my crummy drawing of a bike surrounded by the slogan, "The Best Way To See The Whole U.S.A.," into three really sharp yellow jerseys—enough to last through the big event.

Friday, October 23, was another one of those "box the Nobilette and hope the airlines treat it kindly" days. I was even more worried about the weather forecast, which said that the entire Southwest was about to get walloped by a huge Pacific storm front. But you'd never know it from the cloudless sky above Las Vegas that afternoon. Full of confidence, I strode off the plane with a big grin and carry-on luggage like no one else's: two bike panniers and a sleeping bag.

I strode onward past rows of slot machines busily separating people from their money. The endless stream of electronic bleeps and blips from the machines made me laugh, but I quickly realized I was the only one who found it funny. Gambling, Las Vegas-style, was a deadly earnest business.

In the ground transportation area, I encountered Las Vegas' legendary rudeness as I went from booth to booth, trying to find a shuttle service that went out to Henderson. At all but one booth, the answer was an emphatic NO!!! The lone affirmative answer came with a price of $118. Uh-uh. I stomped over to the baggage claim, retrieved my bike, put it back together and rode out to Henderson, an 18-mile trip.

My home for the night was the Railroad Pass Hotel and Casino, one of the MS-150 sponsors. It was at the top of a long, steady climb that went on forever. I was rewarded with a view of a wide desert valley that must have stretched all the way to California. The next morning, I'd find out just how far it went, and share the discovery with 500 other riders.

I wasn't the only MS-150 rider staying at Railroad Pass that night. There were a half dozen more from Lake Havasu City, and we went to dinner together. They certainly didn't rattle off endless statistics like the speed demons I'd met back in Maine, and what the heck, we'd probably cruise together tomorrow. After dinner, they went into the smoke-filled casino to get rid of some excess quarters. I went back to my room and turned in early.

A tremendous thunderstorm woke me up at midnight. I watched it rain nonstop for the next five and a half hours, and debated over whether or not I should venture outside at dawn. No, I'd stay here, wait out the storm, then go into Vegas on Sunday. But what if the ride went off, rain or shine? And I'd already coughed up the $20 registration fee and the $150 minimum donation to the MS Society, not to mention airfare and the cost of the hotel room.

At 6:00 a.m. I was in the hotel lobby talking things over with the Lake Havasu contingent. They were going to ride regardless of the weather, and they were driving over to the starting point in just a few minutes. I'd accomplished everything I'd come here to do, I said. I wasn't going outside in that storm.

Then I found out that I couldn't stay another night at Railroad Pass—the place was booked. I went back upstairs to don my black tights and yellow jersey, then took another look out the window, and hey! No rain!!! Now I was really rarin' to go. Since it was still cold and dark out there, I put on a jacket and reflective vest. After making sure that everything inside the bike panniers was well protected by plastic bags, I left the hotel and rode out into the darkest night I'd seen in a long time.

From the top of Railroad Pass, it was a five-mile downhill to the start of the ride. Far off in the distance, I could see the casino lights on the Las Vegas Strip. Up in these hills, I saw forks of lightning striking way too close to me. Then the rain started, violently at first, becoming even more so. I got off my bike and started pushing it downhill. I was trembling cold, trembling scared. I thought about trying to hitch a ride, but that strategy seemed about as smart as trying to ride in a predawn thunderstorm without the headlight I'd left attached to my mountain bike back in Tucson.

I got back on and coasted and braked for a couple more miles until I came upon a flooded intersection. I had to get off and push the bike through calf-deep water. On the other side of this lake, the road would take me that one last mile to the start. Someone in a van headed the other way rolled down his window and shouted to get my attention.

"The ride's cancelled!" he said. He was wearing a cycling jersey and I spotted a racing bike in the back of the van. The lady sitting next to him was dressed in street clothes—I surmised that she was intending to drive the MS-150 course and act as his support crew.

Wanting nothing more than to get out of the cold and wet, I asked them where they were going.

"Home!"

"Where's home?"

"Las Vegas!"

"Would you mind giving me a lift into town?"

"No problem!"

The couple rearranged the back of their van to make room for me and my bike. As for not getting to do the ride, that disappointment wouldn't set in for a couple of days. I was just happy to be out of the storm. I asked them to take me to the Las Vegas International Hostel and they did. There I stayed until it was time to fly home on Monday.

Sunday morning was sunny and cool, the perfect kind of weather for observing Las Vegas in action. I pedaled the one mile between the hostel and the Strip, then got off and walked the bike along the extra wide sidewalks past CircusCircus, Westward Ho and the Riviera. I took some pictures and watched people hurrying in and out of the casinos, but declined to join them in playing the only game in town. I'd gambled enough already.

APPENDIX 1
LIST OF STATES AND PROVINCES
•••

(Listed in the order in which they were pedaled.)

June-October 1980: 2,500 miles
(Began in Windsor, Ontario, June 1980.)
Ontario
New York
Ontario*
Michigan
Wisconsin
Minnesota
Wisconsin*
Michigan*
(Ended in Ann Arbor, Michigan, October 1980.)

May 1981-June 1982: 8,300 miles
(Began in Ann Arbor, Michigan, May 1981.)
Michigan*
Ohio
Indiana
Illinois
Missouri
Arkansas
Mississippi
Louisiana
Mississippi*
Alabama
Georgia
South Carolina
North Carolina
Virginia
Maryland
Pennsylvania
Delaware
New Jersey
New York

Connecticut
Rhode Island
Massachusetts
New Hampshire
Vermont
Massachusetts*
New York*
Pennsylvania*
West Virginia
Ohio*
Indiana*
Illinois*
Iowa
Nebraska
Colorado
Utah
Idaho
California
Arizona
New Mexico
Texas
Oklahoma
Arkansas*
Mississippi*
Tennessee
Kentucky
Illinois*
Indiana*
Ohio*
Michigan*
(Returned to Ann Arbor, Michigan, June 1982.)

August 1986: 160 miles
Washington
Oregon

March-June 1987: 3,601 miles
(Began in Phoenix, Arizona, March 1987.)
Arizona*
State of Sonora, Mexico

Arizona*
New Mexico*
Oklahoma*
Kansas
Nebraska*
South Dakota
Wyoming
South Dakota*
North Dakota
Montana
Saskatchewan
Alberta
British Columbia
Washington*
Oregon*
Arizona*
(Ended in Tucson, Arizona, June 1987.)

October 1989: 183 miles
Hawaii

July 1990: 152 miles
Alaska

June 1991: 336 miles
Vermont*
New Hampshire*
Maine

November 1991: 128 miles
Florida

October 1992: 25 miles
Nevada

*Traveled through this state or province more than once.

APPENDIX 2
SPECIFICATIONS:
NOBILETTE TOURING BIKE

Frame
    Materials: Reynolds 531 double-butted tubing, Prugnat lugs
    Braze-on fittings for: fenders and rear rack, water bottle
    Size: 48 cm (measured from bottom bracket center to top
        tube center)
    Completed June 1980, Ann Arbor, Michigan

Wheels
    Hubs: Campagnolo Nuovo Record 36-hole low flange
    Spokes: Wheelsmith, laced in 3-cross pattern
    Rims: Mavic MA40 27 x 1¼
    Tires: Specialized Touring or Continental Super Sport most
        commonly used

Drive Train
    Pedals: Initially, Campagnolo Nuovo Record quill type with
        Christophe toeclips, then Look clipless
    Crankset: Avocet triple, 165 mm crankarms; 26-42-46
        teeth
    Bottom Bracket: Phil Wood
    Freewheel: Shimano 13-15-18-21-24-28
    Chain: Shimano Uniglide narrow
    Front Derailleur: SunTour Mountech
    Rear Derailleur: Shimano Deore
    Shifters: Shimano handlebar-end mounted

Steering
    Stem: TTT 65mm
    Handlebars: Cinelli 38cm
    Handlebar tape: Black cloth
    Headset: Campagnolo Nuovo Record

Stopping
    Brakes: Royal Gran Compe 400 sidepulls
    Brake levers: Shimano 600 aero

Seating
    Saddle: Vetta Turbo Triathlon
    Seatpost: Shimano Dura-Ace

Luggage Carrying
    Blackburn rear rack, braze-on mounting type

Mileage Measurement
    Ciclomaster fork-mounted computer

APPENDIX 3
TRIP LIST

● ●

This list represents what I included—and what I recommend for use—on long cycling journeys. My own traveling load weighed between 20 and 25 pounds, a light load by cycletouring standards, but I'm a firm believer in the "less is more" philosophy in cycletouring and in life.

One big hint: no bicycle touring luggage is 100% waterproof, so line your packs with big plastic bags and put items used in conjunction with each other inside smaller bags—Ziploc brand sandwich and freezer bags are good for this purpose.

On-the-bike wear
Helmet (always)
Prescription sunglasses
Fingerless cycling gloves (warm weather)
Winter riding gloves (cold weather)
Black cycling shorts (always)
Tights (worn over shorts when temperature is below 60° F)
Tee shirt (warm weather)
Turtleneck shirt (if temperature is below 60° F)
Rain jacket/windbreaker (doubles as another layer of insulation
    during cold weather)
Mid-calf length cotton or light wool socks
Cleated cycling shoes

Off-the-bike wear
Prescription glasses (hint: carry your prescription with you in
    case you break your regular glasses or your suns!)
Walking shoes
Change of socks
Underwear (I usually pack two sets)
Mid-thigh length walking shorts (warm weather tours)
Long pants (cool weather tours)
Long johns
Tee or turtleneck shirt

Personal hygiene
Bath towel

All-purpose liquid soap/shampoo such as Dr. Bronner's

Dental floss (can also be used to clean screw threads on small bike parts and to repair cycling gloves)

Dental floss holder (for teeth only—keep out of the bike cleaning projects, okay?)

Toothpaste

Toothbrush (old ones can be recycled for use as bike part cleaning tools)

Comb

Petroleum or non-petroleum jelly (use as lip balm or as an aid in removing bike chain grease from legs)

Heat balm (for sore muscles)

Sunscreen (minimum sun protection factor: 15)

Vitamin and mineral supplements (whatever you usually take—if you take them)

Women's sanitary protection: I have found o.b. tampons to be the most comfortable for cycletouring use

Prescription medication: carry in original container(s) and take your doctor's prescription along too

Toilet Paper

Sleeping bag
In a heavy duty plastic bag that goes inside a stuff sack

Tent, tent poles and stakes
Packed in same manner as the sleeping bag

Therm-A-Rest sleeping pad
Packed in same manner as the tent and sleeping bag

Camera, film and film processing mailers

First aid kit
Bike shops and outdoor stores sell good, lightweight models

Wallet with necessary identification
On your person or easily accessible at all times

"Field Office"

(I like to carry this material inside one of those zippered plastic
envelopes that are commonly used for storing pencils inside
a loose-leaf notebook)

Notebook

Address book

Pen

Maps

Travel tickets

Traveler's checks (Store the check number slips in another
location—either inside the wallet on your person or
elsewhere in your packs. You might also want to have
a backup copy of the check numbers with you or in the
care of a trusted person back home.)

List of what you have along

Other important documents (passport, letters of introduction,
etc.)

Bike lock

Cable lock is sufficient if you'll be traveling through rural
areas and small towns. Take a U-lock if your route is
more urbanized.

Bike repair

Two extra tire tubes

Tire tube patch kit

Tire levers

Tire pump

Tire boot (duct tape, strapping tape, or 2 to 3 inch section of an
old inner tube)

Extra brake and derailleur cables

35mm film can with extra screws, bolts, a couple chain links
and other small parts (which can loom large if you need
extras, but don't have any)

Rags (old socks work very well)

Small container of lubricant (be sure the container is leakproof)

6-inch crescent wrench

2-6 mm allen wrenches

Flat blade screwdriver

Phillips screwdriver

8-9-10 mm "Y" wrench

Spoke wrench
Chain rivet extractor
Hub cone wrenches
Vise-grip pliers
Swiss Army knife (also useful in many ways other than
    bike repair)

Meal preparation

I've heard too many leaky fuel tank and exploding stove
    stories to want to carry these items along with me. I'd rather
    dispense with the cooking and dishwashing chores and
    forage in grocery stores instead. Useful tools for such
    nutritional quests? Money, for sure. Also, my Swiss Army
    knife, which has several different size blades, a can opener
    and a corkscrew. I also like to have a heavy-duty plastic
    fork and spoon handy—these aren't at all difficult to find in
    late 20th century America. In addition, I tend to save plastic
    yogurt cups for later use as bowls and drinking cups.

For Further Reading

Most of these books are still in print and can be ordered through your local bookstore. As for the others, they are indicated with an asterisk (*). Check for them at your public library.

The best introduction to cycling:

Forester, John. *Effective Cycling, Sixth Edition.* Cambridge, Mass., and London: MIT Press, 1993. In addition to being the most comprehensive reference guide on the market, this book teaches the principles of vehicular cycling. Knowing and practicing these principles can save your life out there.

Cycletouring 101:

Van Der Plas, Rob. *The Bicycle Touring Manual: Using the bicycle for touring and camping, [Second Edition.]* Mill Valley, Calif.: Bicycle Books, 1993. Contains everything you'd ever want to know on how to be a cycletourist: finding your way, taking the kids along, keeping a record of your tour, touring abroad, mountain bikes and tandems on tour—it's all in there.

Cycletouring history:

Leonard, Irving A. *When Bikehood Was In Flower: Sketches of Early Cycling.* Tucson: Seven Palms Press, 1983. Reprint of the original hardcover edition published in 1969 by Bearcamp Press. Includes stories of America's first cross-country rider, Thomas Stevens, who made the journey in 1884, and Margaret Valentine LeLong, who ignored the dire predictions of friends and relatives and rode solo from San Francisco to Chicago in 1896. She made it—and had a wonderful time doing so.

Stevens, Thomas. *Around the World on a Bicycle*. Tucson: Seven Palms Press, 1984. He took on America, then he took on the world. Condensation of Stevens' two-volume account of his global ride during the 1880s.

Women's cycling issues:

Mariolle, Elaine and Shermer, Michael. *The Woman Cyclist*. Chicago: Contemporary Books, 1988. Intro book that also includes topics of interest to women such as finding bikes that fit us properly, cycling during pregnancy, and dealing with sexual harrassment on the road. What really steals the show is this book's discussion of how the mass media cover—and don't cover—women in sports.

Cycletouring accounts:

*Madden, Virginia Mudd. *Across America on the Yellow Brick Road*. Alamo, Calif.: Crow Canyon Press, 1980. Describes the author's 1978 cross-country journey with a friend. Personal growth story interspersed with a narrative of the ride. "It was not a 'fun' trip. It was not a vacation. It only changed my life." (p. 182).

*Miller, Christian. *Daisy, Daisy: A Grandmother's Journey Across America on a Bicycle*. New York: Doubleday, 1981. An Englishwoman's trek by folding bicycle, Greyhound bus and her thumb.

Murphy, Dervla. *Full Tilt: Ireland to India with a Bicycle*. New York: Overlook Press, 1987. Reprint of the 1965 work published in the U.S. by E.P. Dutton. Murphy rode a three-speed clunker from Ireland to India in the early sixties. She narrowly missed being attacked by a wolf in central Europe and later fell and broke her ribs in the Middle East, but survived to tell the tale.

Savage, Barbara. *Miles from Nowhere: A round-the-world bicycle adventure*. Seattle: Mountaineers, 1985. Author's account of her global ride with her husband. Offers good humor even in the gloomiest of circumstances. Savage was killed on a bike ride near her California home as this book was going to press.

Schnell, Jane. *Changing Gears: Bicycling America's Perimeter*. Atlanta: Milner Press, 1990. Schnell took early retirement from the U.S. Central Intelligence Agency, then embarked on a ride around the edge of America. She started out with a partner, but ended up covering more than half the of the 12,000 miles alone. In addition to logging mega-miles, Schnell also indulged her passion for bird-watching, compiling an impressive bird list in the process.

*Sumner, Lloyd. *The Long Ride*. Harrisburg, Pa.: Stackpole Books, 1978. Lloyd leaves his home in rural Virginia and really sees the world. One of my all-time favorite adventure stories.

Index

Lone Rider Productions
Post Office Box 43161-F
Tucson, Arizona USA 85733-3161
Telephone (602) 690-1888

Share the adventure!

Give **Discovering America** to your friends and family.

Price $15.95

_____ copies @ $15.95 per copy = $ _____

Arizona residents add 5% tax $ _____

Shipping: $2.00 for first book,
75 cents for each additional book $ _____

TOTAL $ _____

Please enclose check or money order in U.S. funds.
Send to:

Name: _____

Street: _____

City: _____ State: _____ ZIP: _____

Would you like to be on our mailing list? ____ Yes ____ No

(Note: All Lone Rider Productions mailing lists are proprietary.
We do not rent or loan them out, or trade them with any other
business or organization. They are used solely for the purpose
of announcing Lone Rider events and products.)